An Honorable Wish

A Lady's Wish Series

AN UNEXPECTED WISH

AN HONORABLE WISH

An Honorable Wish

Eileen Richards

LYRICAL PRESS
Kensington Publishing Corp.
www.kensingtonbooks.com

LYRICAL PRESS BOOKS are published by

Kensington Publishing Corp.
119 West 40th Street
New York, NY 10018

All Kensington titles, imprints, and distributed lines are available at special quantity discounts for bulk purchases for sales promotion, premiums, fund-raising, educational, or institutional use.

Special book excerpts or customized printings can also be created to fit specific needs. For details, write or phone the office of the Kensington Sales Manager: Kensington Publishing Corp., 119 West 40th Street, New York, NY 10018. Attn. Sales Department. Phone: 1-800-221-2647.

Lyrical and the L logo are trademarks of Kensington Publishing Corp.

First Electronic Edition: November 2015
eISBN-13: 978-1-60183-445-4
eISBN-10: 1-60183-445-4

First Print Edition: November 2015
ISBN-13: 978-1-60183-446-1
ISBN-10: 1-60183-446-2

Printed in the United States of America

For Darla and Erica, two of the best friends a writer could have. I couldn't have done it without you. Thank you for your patience and honesty.

ACKNOWLEDGMENTS

It's true what they say about your sophomore book: It is the most difficult to write. It didn't help that my characters just did not want to behave! I'm truly blessed to have such good friends around me to talk me off the ledge when needed.

To Delilah Marvelle: I needed some information on naughty picture books published in the 18th century in order to hide one on a dusty shelf in the library for Juliet to find. Delilah knows her naughty books. Thank you so much for taking a desperate e-mail from a fan. You provided some great information. I hope I did it justice.

To Ann, Adrienne, Jeni, Dawn, Wendy, and Penny: Thank you for letting me blow up your phones and vent. I love you guys. Group texts are fun!

To Martin, the best editor a girl like me can have: I'm still in awe of what you see in me. I hope I can live up to your expectations.

And to my husband, Rick, who basically ran my world while I wrote this book: I could not have done this without you. Love you more.

Chapter One

He had finally lived up to his brother Nathaniel's low expectations of him.

Tony Matthews stared through the veil of newly budded leaves to the village of Beetham below. The cold stone of the Fairy Steps seeped into his bones from his perch at the top. Spring fought against the winter chill in the air in the faint green of the grass and the blooms of early flowers. New life.

God, how he wanted a new life, a different direction.

What seemed like a good idea at the time, in hindsight, was now a nightmare.

Usually, the rolling hills of the southern portion of this part of the Lake District soothed Tony's soul unlike any other place. The restlessness inside him eased with each breath of the fresh clean air.

Not this time. This time he was trapped in his own stupid arrogance. This time he'd finally lived up to his father's legacy.

He'd taken a man's estate in a card game. A game he wasn't even planning to play except for alcohol-fueled bluster and a dare from a friend. He'd played and lost a fortune, then played again and won an estate.

The man, George Chelsworth, ended up being a neighbor of his brother's home, the Lodge.

Honor and pride wouldn't let Chelsworth back away from the bet. No, the man had signed away his estate and his livelihood to Tony. It was a matter of honor, even as Chelsworth's hand shook while he penned his name.

Tony hadn't wanted to take the estate. The alcoholic stupor had started to wear off with the realization that he'd stepped into his father's shoes. Only this time on the winning side. Tony had sunk to the lowest depths of vile.

Nathaniel was never going to forgive him. Hell, Tony would probably be thrown out of the family and left to his own devices. He had money. He had the reputation of a rake and a gambler, well-earned at this point.

But it wasn't who Tony really was. His entire life was an act. One he didn't want to maintain any longer, an act that was beginning to become a reality.

The fact that it had taken no effort to become this vile man scared the hell out of Tony. When he looked in the mirror, he didn't know who he saw anymore.

He wanted the house, but not this way. The estate must be in a bad way already, given the owner was willing to wager it in a card game. If it was making any living at all, Chelsworth would not have been at the tables.

Unless the man was sick with gambling. Tony knew that sickness existed. His sister-in-law's brother was addicted to gambling, always pushing for that next win.

Tony could walk away from the games without looking back. He was sure of it, at least on most days.

His problem was infinitely more difficult. He needed a way to repair the mistakes he had made without alerting Nathaniel. Tony could not disappoint him again.

Nathaniel was a man of high regard in Beetham and in Town. His business prowess was legendary. Nathaniel had a lovely wife, a child, a house, and the respect of his peers. He had everything Tony wanted but hadn't been able to achieve.

And now Tony had lived up to his brother's greatest fear: He'd become their father.

Hence the trip to Beetham. Tony needed to convince Chelsworth that he meant to tear up the vowels. He would not take a man's livelihood. He would not allow gambling to define him as a man.

Chelsworth had to be desperate. Tony could offer to buy the estate. He had wanted to invest in property. He wanted to do something with his life other than what he was doing: drinking and gambling.

He pulled in a breath of the clean fresh air of the country. He'd forgotten what clean air smelled like. He'd forgotten what the wild spaces of the Lake District felt like. Unconstrained. Open.

No more choking on the London air. No more buildings closing in on him as he walked narrow streets. No more gaming hells. No more lies. No more hiding.

Tony wanted what Nathaniel had: a life of honor and respect. Honor had been missing from his life for a very long time, if it had ever existed at all. The only respect Tony had gained had come from winning more than losing in the hells of London. He wanted more. He wanted Nathaniel's respect.

Leaves danced as a cold wind whirled around him. A woman cackled in the distance.

Tony frowned and looked around for the origin of the voice. No one was there. The cackling grew louder as the leaves spiraled up around him, pulling at his coat, knocking his hat to the ground. He moved to catch it before it blew down the steps.

"What the hell?"

A twig snapped behind him. Tony turned to find Juliet Townsend tiptoeing past him at the edge of the woods, carefully avoiding making any noise.

She was dressed as a boy.

"Miss Juliet, up to your hoyden ways again, I see." Tony crossed his arms.

Juliet huffed and kicked at the weeds beneath her feet in scuffed boots that seemed to flop about on her feet. She was covered in dirt. Her dark brown hair was tucked under an old hat that had been pulled down low over her face.

Tony raised one eyebrow. "Hiding from someone?"

Juliet turned and faced him, resigned at being discovered. "You weren't supposed to see me or recognize me."

"Why?" Tony moved closer. She was dressed in brown breeches that were a tad too tight around her hips. She had on a rough linen shirt and waistcoat. "From whom have you stolen that outfit? One of the grooms?"

No one was as stubborn as Juliet Townsend. She pushed her spectacles back on her face. "Aren't you supposed to be in London?"

"I asked you first."

She flounced toward him and plopped down at the edge of the steps. "If you must know, I'm helping a friend."

"Dressed as a boy? Have you lost your senses?"

Juliet was different from her sisters. She wasn't afraid to take up a cause and see it through. Tony sat next to her on the stone steps. "Who is this friend?"

She glowered at him. "You must swear not to tell a soul."

"If your sister disapproves, it must be bad."

She grinned. "What would be the point of it if it weren't?"

"One day, Miss Juliet, your wild ways are going to get you into trouble."

Juliet looked out across the trees. "You are probably right. My friend, Penelope Williams, and her family are tenants of the Horneswood estate nearby. Her father was in a terrible accident that left him disfigured. Anne would not approve of the friendship."

"She is not your social equal, Miss Juliet."

She glared at him. "I don't care about that. Penelope is a dear, and I have found that I enjoy the work."

"What do you know of farming?"

"A great deal more than you, I'd wager. I've read at least three books on the subject."

"You have me there. The last time I read a tome on agriculture, I was having trouble falling asleep."

"You are too wicked, Mr. Matthews. Horneswood's land steward is threatening to have them evicted. They have nowhere else to go. Penelope and her brother may end up working in a factory in Lancaster, or worse."

"There's nothing wrong with factory work, Miss Juliet. It puts a roof over one's head. It might be a better fate than the workhouse."

"I knew you wouldn't understand. I'd help them if I could, but Nathaniel won't let me give them money from my settlement." She stood and dusted off her pants, drawing Tony's attention to her nicely rounded bottom.

Tony had no idea that breeches would look this good on a woman. Perhaps they should become the fashion. He pulled himself up and started down the stairs. "In this instance, I'd have to agree. Help them with food or support, but you'll need your own funds for when you marry. Now, allow me to escort you home."

She stared at the horse tethered at the bottom of the steps. "Thank you, no. I prefer to walk."

"Don't be a ninny. If we ride, we'll be home in half the time."

"I'm inappropriately dressed. If my sister sees me thus, I'll not be allowed to call on Penelope again." Juliet skirted around Tony toward the path through the woods.

"How do you plan on avoiding her? Sneaking in through the kitchens?"

Juliet smiled widely. "A splendid idea."

"Miss Juliet, there is no way I'm allowing you to go through those woods unaccompanied."

"I walk through these woods daily. I'm safe enough."

"And if you're seen? Word would reach Anne before you could even reach the kitchen door. Enough nonsense. I'll see you home."

She looked at the horse and shook her head. "He's huge."

"You've been around horses all your life."

"If I must." She stomped down the narrow stairs. He followed her down, enjoying the view of her hips swinging.

"If we are seen together, I'll be in great peril of ruining my reputation."

"If we are seen, you'll be chastised for being so inappropriately attired and not because you are in my company. We are practically brother and sister."

Tony almost ran into her as Juliet turned suddenly.

"Your brother is married to my sister. That does not make us family."

Tony gripped Juliet's arms to keep her from falling backward down the stairs. Her eyes were pools of dark chocolate as she stared up at him through the magnified lenses of her glasses.

"Please, sir, release me."

"I wouldn't want to have you take a tumble down the stairs. How shall I explain it to your sister?" He cleared his throat and released her.

Juliet continued down the steps, her hands finding purchase in the stone walls. She stumbled to a stop at the bottom. "I shall not get on that horse."

"Why not?"

Juliet didn't answer but started walking down the lane toward the lodge. *Stubborn woman,* thought Tony. He grabbed the reins of the horse and rushed to catch up with her. "It's just about teatime; the horse can get us to the house faster."

"The house is barely a mile away. Hardly worth troubling the horse, if you ask me." She moved to the other side of the lane.

"You are afraid of the horse? I didn't think you were afraid of anything."

"Don't be silly; everyone has fears." Juliet walked faster, her loose boots making a clumping sound with each step. "We had no notice that you were coming home, Mr. Matthews."

"The Season was over. I thought it time."

"Beetham is a quiet village. Will you be able to bear being away from the gaming tables while you are here?" There was a sneer in her voice.

"You'd be surprised," he mumbled.

Juliet looked up at him, a questioning look on her face. "Excuse me?"

"It's of little matter."

"We heard about your exploits in Town, Mr. Matthews," Juliet continued.

"What have you heard?"

"That you prefer to spend more time in your clubs than you do at home."

He slowed and his horse butted him with his head. "Easy, boy." He rubbed the muzzle. "Juliet, you know better than to listen to gossip."

She started walking again. "Take care that you don't end up penniless like my brother."

Tony winced. If the truth were made known, he would probably lose Juliet's friendship as well.

Juliet's face grew solemn. "Do you think there will come a time, Mr. Matthews, when you'll grow tired of cards?"

"One never knows. It might be sooner than you think."

Juliet evaluated his words. Could it be he was finally tired of the gaming hells? Her brother never seemed to tire of them. "What do you mean?"

"It's of little consequence." He looked back at the horse, a strange expression on his face.

In the three years she'd known Tony Matthews, she'd sensed that all wasn't what it seemed with him. Certainly on the surface he was affable, fun, and carefree. But there were depths hinted at in quiet moments like these.

She was never able to crack the façade to see what really lay beneath. She suspected there was a great deal more to the man than the pieces he allowed others to see.

They rounded the bend and approached the park of the Lodge.

She touched his arm. "Mr. Matthews, the only expectations you need to live up to are your own. You do know that."

Tony glanced down at her hand on his arm. An odd kind of warmth radiated up Juliet's arm.

"Miss Juliet, thank you." His voice was gruff.

"I shall see you at tea."

Juliet sprinted around the house and snuck into the house through the kitchen door. She slipped off the too-large boots, leaving them by the door, and crept up the stairs in her stocking feet, avoiding the creaky stairs.

The clock in the hallway chimed the hour. Juliet moved more quickly down the darkened hallway to her room. She closed the door behind her and quickly changed into a suitable day dress, stashing the breeches and shirt in the bottom of her cupboard.

Juliet looked down at her hands, caked in dirt. Pouring water into a basin, she scrubbed, trying to remove most of the dirt from her fingernails.

There was a rap on her door. "Juliet? It's time for tea."

"Coming!" She scrubbed faster. Foolish of her not to wear gloves while digging in the dirt. She was going to have to get a proper pair if this kept up.

Juliet's sister Sophia stepped into the room and closed the door behind her. "Did you know that Tony is here? Good heavens, what have you been up to? You are in no state for company, covered in dirt as you are."

"Really, Sophia. It is not that bad."

"Very well, but do something with your hair—it is a mess. And come down as quickly as you can." Sophia closed the door behind her.

Juliet fussed with her hair. Tony Matthews never came home unless he had to, usually when he needed money from Nathaniel.

Juliet was well over her infatuation with Tony, though they remained friends. In the three years that Nathaniel and Anne had been married, she had worried for him. Gambling was a sickness that ruined greater men than Tony would ever be. It had ruined her brother. It had ruined his father. It was only a matter of time before it ruined Tony too.

Chapter Two

Juliet found a quiet corner in which to hide and observe. The others sipped their tea and talked idly. Lady Danford had her chair near the fire. Nathaniel and Tony sat near their grandmother and Sophia was slumped in one of the chairs by the window. Juliet opened her book on the latest farming techniques. Considering how far they were from Town, Nathaniel had a surprisingly well-stocked library.

"I miss London. I can't believe we had to come back early all because Juliet can't breathe the air and Anne is breeding. Again." Sophia spit out the words.

"Sorry to spoil your fun, Sophia. Just let me die next time." Juliet pushed her spectacles further up on her face and turned back to her book. She didn't regret having to come back from Town early. The place was loud, filthy, and smelly. London's only redeeming quality was the number of bookshops.

"I missed Lady Etherton's ball."

Juliet winced at the whine of Sophia's voice. It was like needles in her eyes. "Althea sent me the details, if you'd like to read them. You didn't miss much."

"Gossip from the wallflower wall? No, thanks." Sophia flounced back in her chair and proceeded to stare out at the garden. "The last thing I want to hear is what a laughingstock the family is. You are the only girl I know who allows her stuffing to pop out of her bodice."

Heat crept into Juliet's face. She glanced at Tony, who had spewed his tea. *Brilliant.* Now he was remembering their dance. Never again would she try to fix the cards she had been dealt. She buried her nose deeper into the book.

Tony set down his teacup. "Is that what that was? I thought all ladies kept their handkerchiefs in their bodice."

"Most ladies have something in their bodice with which to hold it in," Sophia cackled.

Juliet cringed, unable to believe that Sophia had actually uttered that statement aloud.

Juliet loved her sister; she really did. On most days. The rest of the time was up for discussion. This was one of those times. She wanted to hit Sophia with her book just to shut her up.

"Juliet, I've invited Simon Bartleby to tea today," Nathaniel said.

Please, dear God, not him. Juliet groaned behind the book. The man was an arrogant, puffed-up prig.

"Good Lord, why?" Sophia said with a frown. Juliet had to agree.

"He wants to borrow some of my agricultural journals. It seems Horneswood is changing hands. The new owner wants to make some changes." Nathaniel sipped his tea.

Horneswood was sold? Juliet sat up and closed her book. This might be just the thing the Williams family needed.

"Does he know who the new owner is?" Tony asked.

The funny tone in his voice caught Juliet's attention. She studied him as he avoided her eye.

Nathaniel shook his head. "I don't know the particulars, except Chelsworth lost it in a card game. Foolish man."

Sophia laughed. "That sounds like something you'd do, Tony."

A dark flush stole over Tony's cheeks. "I'd not stoop so low."

There was something different about Tony. His tone sounded almost vicious to Juliet. "No one believes that you would."

Anne came into the parlor and threw herself into an overstuffed chair. "Juliet, what are you reading that boy? He's had nightmares for two days and I can't get him to take a nap."

Juliet blushed. "Just some pirate stories."

"Please do not read him any more. I need him to sleep." Anne leaned back and closed her eyes.

Nathaniel got up and kissed his wife on the forehead. "Go up and take a nap if you're fatigued."

Anne got that look on her face. "Only if you'll join me."

Juliet wanted a man to put that look on her face. Simon Bartleby was not that man.

"Do you have to do that here?" Sophia complained. "It's positively obscene."

Anne laughed and pulled Nathaniel down for another kiss. "Your turn will come, dear Sophia."

"I won't be doing any of that in public," Sophia grumbled.

"Let them alone," Juliet whispered. "We should be so lucky to be so loved."

"You're tired because you're breeding again," Lady Danford said. "It's a good thing we left London. The air would be bad for the baby."

"The air is bad for most people," Tony grumbled.

Sophia turned back to the room. "The air never bothered me."

A footman stepped into the room and announced, "Mr. Simon Bartleby, sir."

"Look, Juliet, it's your beau," Sophia snickered.

Juliet peered over the edge of her book. She had to admit that Simon Bartleby was handsome. His dark hair and blue eyes were striking. He wasn't as tall as Tony, but he was slim and dressed well. If he wasn't so arrogant, she might be inclined to like him better.

"Lady Danford, Mrs. Matthews, Mr. Matthews. Thank you for inviting me," Mr. Bartleby said with a bow. He strolled over and kissed Juliet's hand. "My dear."

Juliet pulled her hand free and resisted the urge to wipe off his kiss. He had wet lips. *Disgusting.* "Mr. Bartleby, what brings you here this afternoon?"

"Mr. Matthews has agreed to let me go through his back issues of the *Agricultural Journal.*"

"Riveting reading, I'm sure," Tony said quietly. He winked at Juliet.

Juliet fought a smile. "Mr. Bartleby, allow me to present to you Mr. Tony Matthews. He is Mr. Matthews's younger brother."

"Mr. Matthews, what brings you to our little village?" asked Simon.

"This is home, Mr. Bartleby." Tony kept his voice cool. "I don't know why everyone is surprised that I'd want to come home."

"Perhaps because there are no gaming hells, dear," Lady Danford said. "Though I imagine you could join the games down at the pub if you decided you couldn't live without it."

The room was silent for a long moment. A flush of red flared on Tony's cheeks. Juliet almost felt sorry for him.

Anne cleared her throat. "Let's have tea, shall we?"

* * *

Tony sipped his tea as he studied Simon Bartleby. The man was clearly an aristocrat. Bartleby carried himself with an air only achieved in a titled household.

Tony could tell that Juliet didn't like Bartleby, and it was easy to see why. He arrogantly expected her to fall all over him. She was having none of it, and that pleased Tony for some odd reason.

Bartleby's attentions to Juliet bothered Tony.

Why? They were friends, nothing more.

But only because you won't pursue her yourself, Tony thought.

He had to admit it was his fault that Juliet had fallen out of love with him. Of course it had been a schoolgirl infatuation, not real love, so it hadn't much mattered.

He wondered what real love would feel like with Juliet.

"What do you think of the gentleman courting Juliet?" Sophia whispered over her teacup as she joined Tony in the corner of the room. "He was interested in me, but the man is a land steward."

"What a snob you are, Sophia," Tony said. "Nathaniel told me that Bartleby was the younger brother of the current Viscount Northam."

"The key point in that statement is *younger brother*."

Tony chuckled. Some things just didn't change. "It doesn't appear that Juliet likes him much."

"The man is so full of himself there's no room for anything else." Sophia sipped her tea. "Juliet could never stand such arrogance. I've been watching. Waiting for her to put him in his place."

"Now that would be something to see."

"Oh, we'll never see it," Sophia continued. "Juliet prefers to chastise in private."

"What's the fun in that?"

Sophia giggled. "Exactly my thought."

Nathaniel's voice boomed over their conversation. "Mr. Bartleby, have you heard from the new owner of Horneswood?"

Tony stilled.

"Just one letter from the man's solicitor, laying claim to the place and wanting an accounting of the state of the tenants." Simon puffed out his chest. "I have related the state of the tenants. It seems we'll have to evict one particular family."

Juliet gasped. "On what cause?"

"They've been unable to make their rent. It is a sad case. The father was injured some time ago and has had a very slow recovery. The family has been unable to cope with his serious injuries."

"Yet you'd evict them without giving them a chance?" Juliet exclaimed.

"My dear, you understand little of business," Bartleby said in a condescending tone.

"You understand little of Christian charity, sir," Juliet said. She stood. "If you'll excuse me."

Tony watched her stalk out of the room and close the door behind her. This must be the family she was attempting to help. "Surely the family will recover?" Tony asked Bartleby.

"It's doubtful. The son is but sixteen and too inexperienced to take on the responsibility." Bartleby lifted his nose further into the air.

"You can ask the new owner to give them more time, Mr. Bartleby," Lady Danford said gently. "The Williamses have been in Beetham for generations. It doesn't seem right to send them away."

"It has been almost two years. The new owner has made it very clear that any lands we can use for pasture should be converted. The Williams farm is prime land for grazing sheep, my lady."

"When do you expect the new owner to arrive at Horneswood?" Tony asked.

"That's not been determined, sir," Mr. Bartleby replied. "Mr. Chelsworth is still in residence."

"How is Mr. Chelsworth?" Anne asked. "This has to be very difficult for him."

"His honor as a gentleman is at stake, ma'am," Mr. Bartleby said. "He has yet to return from Town."

"What honor is there in taking a man's living away in a card game?" Nathaniel spat.

Tony ground his teeth together. "The man should not have wagered his living in the first place."

"Very true, Mr. Matthews, but many men find it difficult to push away from the gaming tables until it is too late," said Bartleby.

"It's a sickness," Anne agreed.

"Very much so, ma'am," Mr. Bartleby said. "Sir, might I view your agriculture journals now? If the ladies will excuse us, of course."

Nathaniel set his cup down. "Come to the library and you can go through the collection."

"If you do not mind, I think I'll join you," Tony said carefully. "There may be some issues I haven't seen yet either."

"I didn't know you were interested in agriculture," said Nathaniel.

"I've always been interested," protested Tony.

"Gentlemen, let's not bicker in front of our guest," Lady Danford said.

Lady Danford, who had essentially raised Tony and his brother, could make Tony feel as if he was twelve again with just a look. "Yes, ma'am."

Once they were settled in the library, Nathaniel poured three glasses of port and passed them around. He led Bartleby to a table. "I've laid out all the issues from the last year. I can dig up different ones if you don't see what you're looking for."

"Very kind of you, sir. Thank you. I'm certain these will suffice."

"I had some books, but they are missing at the moment," Nathaniel said.

Juliet. Tony had seen her with one of them right before Bartleby's arrival. "Is there anything specific you're looking for?"

"Sheep. The new owner wants to raise sheep for wool." Bartleby shuddered. "Filthy creatures."

"Raw materials can be very lucrative, Mr. Bartleby. I'm surprised the previous owner hadn't thought of it," Nathaniel said.

"It's definitely more cost effective to buy local than to import," Tony said, sipping his port.

Nathaniel stared at him.

"If you'll excuse me, I must get back to the estate," Mr. Bartleby said. "Thank you for the journals, Mr. Matthews."

Tony stood as Bartleby took his leave. He frowned as the door closed behind him.

"I had no idea you were interested in the business side of things," Nathaniel said with a chuckle. "I'm rather glad to hear it. I'd almost given up hope."

Tony sat quietly for a long moment after Bartleby left. There was something not quite right with the way Bartleby had described the estate. He'd assumed that Horneswood was in trouble, given how deep Chelsworth had been playing that night. It would bear further investigation.

Nathaniel refilled Tony's glass and handed it back to him. "Care to tell me what precipitated this trip to Beetham?"

Tony swirled the brandy in his glass, watching the light catch the amber liquid. "Why is everyone so surprised that I would want to come home?"

"I wasn't convinced you could tear yourself away from the tables."

"I doubt that I will stay very long. I wouldn't want to inconvenience you." Tony couldn't prevent the bitter tinge in his voice.

"What do you think of Simon Bartleby? I thought he'd make a good husband for Juliet," said Nathaniel.

"You cannot mean to match Jules with that nodcock?" Tony said.

"He's perfectly respectful. His brother is a viscount. I happen to like the man."

"It's clear that Juliet does not. She left in the middle of tea."

"She'll get over it. Sophia wouldn't have him."

Tony could understand why. "Have you met the previous owner of Horneswood?"

"No, I've never seen him. He is just another absentee landlord who has overextended his income."

"How do you feel about the new owner wanting to farm sheep?"

"I rather like the idea. Having good raw materials for the mills in Lancaster would be a great asset. The more we can locally source, the cheaper we can keep the product."

Tony could barely contain his grin. "I thought that might catch your eye, given the cost of importing raw materials."

"Ian McDonald should be here in the next day or so. Now that you're here, we can make some decisions on expansion." Nathaniel rose and went to his desk. "You will be needed in London afterward to work with the investors."

He had already discussed the matter with Ian McDonald before he had left London. McDonald had land in Scotland and was considering it as well. They both had benefited from Nathaniel's investments in textile mills. It was the perfect opportunity for Tony to tell Nathaniel his news. Yet he hesitated.

"It shouldn't be a terrible inconvenience, should it? You did specify you were staying for just a short time," added Nathaniel.

"The Season is pretty much over. There won't be many in London for the summer."

"True. I hadn't thought of that. Perhaps Bath or Brighton might prove more lucrative over the summer?"

Brighton was the other side of the world as far as Tony was concerned. "It's not my favorite."

"I thought you rather liked it."

Tony shook his head. "I've never even been there."

"Well, now you'll have the opportunity."

Tony glared at his brother. "Thank you, no." How could he explain without giving away the true reason he was in Beetham? "If you must know, I was considering the purchase of an estate. I thought perhaps somewhere near here."

"This is a sudden development."

"Not really. I've been considering it for a long while now."

"You are welcome to stay as long as you need while you conduct your search, Tony. We keep country hours here, so we'll have dinner earlier than you are used to."

"Thank you, Nathaniel."

Chapter Three

Juliet wanted nothing more than to hide. From everyone. She should never have let Mr. Bartleby get the better of her temper. She should have stiffened her spine instead of running off like a child. She glanced over at Tony, talking with Nathaniel by the fire.

Tony was still the most handsome man in the room. Tall and rugged, with the bluest eyes. She imagined the ocean would be that color, if she ever saw it.

"Still pining for Tony, I see," Sophia said, coming up behind her. "I thought you were over your infatuation with him."

"I am."

"Then you shouldn't sneak glances at him when he isn't looking." Sophia laughed softly.

"I've caught you looking as well," Juliet whispered back. "He's very handsome."

"Even in Town, few young ladies could resist looking at Tony." Sophia came around and took a seat beside her sister. "He is a beautiful man, isn't he? I love the new styles for men, don't you?"

"I hadn't really noticed."

"Liar."

"He does have beautiful eyes." Juliet couldn't keep the wistfulness from her voice.

"So you do still care for him."

"Mr. Matthews is family—we *have* to like him."

"Do you think I could win him again?"

"I don't understand why you must fling yourself at any eligible bachelor in the vicinity. If you must do so, please choose Mr. Bartleby."

"Mr. Bartleby is a poor steward," Sophia said with a sniff. "Besides, Nathaniel has selected him for you."

Juliet closed her eyes and wished for divine intervention. She didn't want Simon Bartleby. He was arrogant and pompous and very full of himself. Not to mention short. The man was barely taller than she.

"What are you two ladies discussing so secretly?" Tony said, coming over to their part of the room.

"We were discussing when Mr. Bartleby would propose to Juliet. I say it will be before the month's end. What do you think, Tony?"

Juliet felt her face flush. "Sophia, please."

"It's a good match, considering Mr. Bartleby has no funds but good connections," Sophia continued. "And Juliet has funds but no connections."

"We have the same connections, Sophia."

"Indeed we do not, sister dear. We barely move in the same circles."

"Still planning to marry a man with a title, Miss Townsend?" Tony said.

Juliet snorted. She covered her mouth with her hand and met Tony's laughing eyes. *Oh God. His eyes.* She looked away quickly. She had to stop allowing herself to be captivated by him.

"Well, that's better than marrying the younger brother of some impoverished viscount," Sophia spat.

"I will not be marrying Mr. Bartleby," Juliet mumbled.

"Why not, Miss Juliet? He seemed like a nice enough chap for a steward," Tony said.

"An impoverished steward," Sophia sneered.

"I'm not a snob, Sophia. If I had feelings for him, it would be different," insisted Juliet.

"And I am a snob?" Sophia said.

"If the slipper fits," Juliet responded.

Tony laughed loudly, drawing the attention of Lady Danford and Anne.

"What trouble are you three stirring up now?" Lady Danford said from across the room. "Please tell me you aren't teasing poor Juliet about that idiot Mr. Bartleby."

"Grandmother!" Anne gasped.

"He's a suitable gentleman, Grandmother," Nathaniel said. "It connects our family to a very old earldom."

Juliet stared down at her hands. *Please let the ground swallow me up now.*

"Never fear, Miss Juliet. Nathaniel always had a penchant for dynastic marriages," said Tony.

Juliet stared at Tony, pleading with him with her eyes not to say another word. The last thing she needed was for Tony and Nathaniel to start arguing again, especially over her.

"That's not it at all. Juliet likes him," Nathaniel said defensively. "Don't you?"

Juliet felt all eyes on her. She looked up at Nathaniel's hopeful face. "I don't know him well enough to like him."

"There you have it. We'll just have to have Mr. Bartleby to dinner more often."

Juliet fought the urge to groan. Simon Bartleby was an ass. If he treated her like she was stupid one more time, she was going to hit him with a book. Hard. It was probably the closest he'd ever come to the printed page.

"Aren't you lucky?" Sophia whispered in Juliet's ear.

"Do be quiet," Juliet said.

"You are eyeing those cushions as if they were weapons. Thank God we aren't in the library, where the dueling pistols are."

"Dueling pistols? That would work," Juliet said dryly.

Tony chuckled. "A bit too permanent, I think. Stick with the cushions."

"I wonder if I can convince Anne to play," Sophia said, apparently already bored with the topic of Mr. Bartleby. "Otherwise it will be dreadfully dull tonight. Tony, will you dance with me?"

"Perhaps. But given the way Anne is nodding off over there by the fire, I doubt it," Tony said.

"I'll go ask her." Sophia stood.

Tony took the now vacant seat next to Juliet, his body taking up most of the small settee. "Do you really hate the thought of Mr. Bartleby that much?" he asked.

"He is a horrid man. Do you remember when I told you about the family I was helping on the Horneswood estate? It is the Williams family Mr. Bartleby means to evict."

"Was there truth in what Bartleby said?"

"Unfortunately, yes. Mr. Williams was badly injured and hasn't been able to work the farm as he should. The younger Mr. Williams has done what he can, but he's only sixteen."

Juliet played with her gown, unsure how to get the rest of it out. How could she tell Tony the rest of the horrible things Mr. Bartleby had said? "I can't do anything to help them."

She jumped when Tony took her hand. She looked up and sank into those deep blue eyes. *Lord, his lashes are long.* His mouth was moving. He had nice lips. Why hadn't she noticed his mouth before? "Pardon?"

"We're old friends, Jules. You may tell me anything."

Just then Sophia flounced over and grabbed Tony's hands away from Juliet. "I convinced Anne to play us a jig. Shall we dance?"

"But we were talking—" Tony protested.

Juliet smiled, relieved that she didn't have to continue. "Go dance."

"Are you are sure?" asked Tony.

"Quite. It does no good to deny Sophia. She will have her way." Juliet watched as Sophia led him to where the footmen had cleared a spot for dancing. Anne was playing a jig, her fingers moving rapidly across the keys of the piano. Juliet settled back into her seat and watched, as she normally did.

It would be easy to allow herself to fall in love with Tony again. He smiled at Juliet as he danced. When he looked at her with those blue eyes, Juliet's heart lurched. Tony twirled Sophia, causing her to laugh. They were a perfect couple, her dark beauty the perfect foil for his light coloring.

Next to her sister, Juliet was bookish, pale, and thin. She sighed, realizing that the rest of the evening would pass with her watching Sophia and Tony dance. She made her way across the room.

"Juliet, dear, where are you going?" Lady Danford asked as she went past her chair.

"To read, my lady."

Juliet made her way to the library. Truth be told, she was exhausted. The work she was doing at the Williamses farm was harder than she was used to. Today she'd mucked out stalls, preparing the barn for lambing. She had blisters on her hands and she was bone weary.

She crept to a back shelf and moved a particular volume to get to

her secret stash of books. While rummaging through the library looking for books on agriculture to help the Williamses, she'd removed a
particularly heavy tome and found three small books hidden behind
it. Two of the books were written in French but had a wealth of pictures. The other was a novel.

Juliet's curiosity had gotten the better of her when she'd glanced
through the pictures in the French books. Never in her life had she
seen such pictures. She had no idea men and women did such things
together.

She wasn't totally ignorant. She knew the basics of how children
were begotten, but these books were much more than that. Anne
would lock her away in her room if she knew about the books.

The novel was one her friends had alluded to in London. She hadn't
been able to work up the courage to purchase such a scandalous book
from any of the booksellers in Town, so she had been pleased to find it
in Lady Danford's well-stocked library.

Juliet settled in a chair by the fire. She opened the book and
started reading.

Tony watched Jules leave the room and close the door behind her.
He had been hoping to share the next dance with her. The music
ended and he released Sophia with a bow.

"Shall we dance another?" Sophia asked.

"Please do not think me rude, but no. I'm a bit tired. I pushed hard
to get here before dark."

Sophia smiled. "How about cards, then?"

He grinned and shook his head.

She didn't give up. "I hate it here. It's so deadly dull."

Tony leaned against the fireplace. "You don't realize how noisy
London is until you come home. It's so peaceful here. Quiet."

"Dull. Thank you for playing, Anne," said Sophia.

"I enjoyed it. It's been a while." Anne sat down beside Nathaniel.
"I may go up, dear."

"Are you well, Anne?" asked Lady Danford.

"Quite well. Just tired. The first few months are the most difficult.
Nathaniel, do you mind if I say my good nights?"

Nathaniel kissed Anne's hand before whispering something into her ear. As she excused herself, Nathaniel watched his wife leave the room.

Tony was envious of his brother once again. While he was glad he hadn't married Sophia three years before, Tony knew he was meant to marry one of the Townsend girls. It sounded fanciful, but Tony couldn't shake the thought that Providence had predicted it. Tony just needed to settle on the right sister. That left Juliet. The bluestocking, with her round eyeglasses that magnified eyes so dark, he could barely make out her irises. The hoyden dressed in breeches outlining a shape that was clearly not girlish.

"If you'll excuse me, I think I'll follow Anne's example and retire. It was a long journey," Tony said to the group. He bent and pressed his lips to his grandmother's hand.

"What were you and Juliet talking about so seriously, Son?" Lady Danford said softly.

Tony gripped the hand of his grandmother, who had saved Nathaniel and him. Her skin was papery, dry, and cool; old. "Juliet only said that she has befriended the daughter of one of the tenants of Horneswood, nothing more."

"You know how she is," Lady Danford said. "The chit would be raising money in the village to save them if she could, or giving up her own funds."

"I admire that about her. She did the same in London."

"Your brother thinks to marry her off to Mr. Bartleby."

"Mr. Bartleby is a gentleman. It is an equitable match."

"My maid has a sister in the village. She's heard talk that he's not dealing with the tenants in an honest way."

"I never realized you were such a gossip."

She smacked his arm and he chuckled. "I've missed you, boy."

He leaned over and kissed her cheek. "Believe it or not, I've missed you too."

Tony left the parlor and then silently entered the dark library. A fire burned cheerfully, but no candles were lit. He had missed Juliet; she must have taken her book upstairs. But then he spotted her, curled up in a chair asleep, a book open on her lap. He picked up the book and looked at it, his eyebrows shooting up when he read the title: *Fanny Hill*.

Juliet apparently had very naughty reading tastes. Tony flipped through the pages, looking at some of the pictures. He then looked down at the woman asleep in the chair. She was full of surprises. He touched a finger to her hand. "Juliet?"

"What time is it?" she said sleepily.

"Just past nine. I thought you were reading agricultural books, not this. I'm surprised this put you to sleep," he said, gesturing with the book. "It's interesting reading."

She snatched the book from his hands. "If you tell Anne—"

"I won't tell Anne."

"I should go upstairs." Juliet gathered the books and clutched them to her chest.

"Don't leave. Please finish what you were going to tell me." Juliet looked puzzled. "About Mr. Bartleby?"

"He's a hateful man. I can't believe Nathaniel means for me to marry him."

"You can refuse him." Tony took a poker and stirred up the flames of the small fire. He needed more light to see her face.

Juliet stared into the fire. "I can't disappoint Nathaniel. Our family owes him so much."

Tony sank into the chair across from her. "Why do you dislike Bartleby so?"

Juliet gripped the book, her knuckles white. "He tried to compromise a friend of mine."

For a moment, Tony was speechless. "Who?"

"Miss Penelope Williams. As I told you, her family are tenants of the estate Bartleby manages."

"Are you sure she didn't misinterpret his meaning?"

Juliet glared at him. "He told her he'd waive the rent if she became his mistress. Penelope came to me in tears, begging me to help her. I tried to talk to him."

"My guess is that Mr. Bartleby did not take too kindly to your interference."

"He's despicable. He forbade me to see Penelope again."

"Is that why you were dressed as a boy? To avoid Bartleby?" Tony smiled. "Lady Danford knew you were up to something. Is Mr. Williams now an invalid?"

"Yes." She leaned back in the chair with her eyes closed. "It's so sad. If they'd only give Aaron Williams a chance, he could make a go of it."

Tony couldn't stop the pinch of jealousy at the affection in her voice. "Is he the son?"

"Penelope's younger brother. He's just sixteen."

Tony played at brushing lint off his trousers. "He's seen you in those breeches?"

Juliet glared at him. "Of course. He has me cleaning stalls to prepare for lambing."

Tony could just imagine watching Juliet cleaning stalls in those old breeches when he was sixteen. "I suggest you dress appropriately next time."

"You have no idea how much work there is to do."

"If you would like some help, I'm happy to oblige."

"Are you sure? It's very hard work."

"I shall overlook the insult that you think me too weak for hard labor but will tell you that Lady Danford has asked that I keep an eye on you."

"They could really use the help."

Her skin was almost translucent in the firelight. She really was lovely. In Town she was always with the other bookish young ladies gathered near the wall, waiting for a gentleman to notice and ask them to dance. He had not been able to help himself. He'd danced once with Juliet before making his way to the gaming tables.

"What time shall we leave in the morning?"

"Seven."

"Good God, are you serious?" He was never up that early. Not even to travel.

"I wouldn't want to disrupt your schedule, Tony. Perhaps it is just as well. All those years at the gaming tables might have weakened your muscles."

He couldn't stop himself from rising to the bait. "It's a very dangerous game to threaten a man's strength, Miss Matthews."

"Then you'll just have to prove yourself tomorrow at the Williamses farm." Juliet stood, clutching her books, and dipped a curtsy. "Good night. I'll see you in the morning."

"It will be worth it to see you in those breeches again."

Juliet gave him an impudent grin. "Too bad I intend to wear a dress."

Tony stared at the open door long after Juliet had exited. Finally he threw himself back into his chair and stared at the fire. Hard labor would do him good. Help him work off some of his guilt and keep him out of Nathaniel's way. He needed to see what Bartleby was up to. It wouldn't be a bad idea to get to know some of the tenants before he decided what to do with the estate. There wasn't much else he could do until Chelsworth was back in Beetham.

Chapter Four

Tony guided the horse cart down the lane. He was barely awake. Who got up so early in the morning?

Juliet had met him at the stables with a huge basket from the kitchens. He'd placed the basket behind them in the cart. She sat beside him, her hands folded demurely in her lap, quiet as a mouse.

Ordinarily, Juliet was *never* quiet.

The morning was beautiful. It had been a long time since Tony had seen a sunrise. He turned off the lane and followed the line of trees to a large stone house surrounded by several outbuildings. It was clear that at one time the Williams farm had been one of the larger ones in the area. Now he noticed the roof needed serious repair.

Tony jumped down from the cart and handed Juliet down before she could do it on her own. He'd play the gentleman whether she wanted it or not. When she went to pick up the basket, he brushed her hand away. "Allow me."

"Thank you, Mr. Matthews," she said and smiled softly.

They were so formal with each other this morning. He watched Juliet smile as a young lady approached them. The two ladies greeted each other and were joined by a gangly young man who couldn't keep from staring at Juliet.

"Miss Juliet, would you introduce me to your friends?" asked Tony.

"Of course," Juliet said. "Mr. Matthews, may I present Miss Williams and Mr. Aaron Williams. Mr. Matthews's brother is married to my sister."

Aaron Williams was lean and wiry, like most young men his age.

He had a shock of red hair and fair, freckled skin. "Welcome to the farm, sir," he said.

Miss Williams was a pretty girl with auburn hair and pale skin. She dipped a curtsy. "Welcome, sir."

"We brought something for your larder," Juliet said.

Tony passed the basket to Aaron, who took it into the house.

"Thank you, Juliet; that's very kind," Penelope Williams said softly. Her voice was melodious and sweet.

"So where do we start today?" Juliet said and smiled at her friend.

"Mr. Matthews could help Aaron in the fields today. Mother wants us to plant the kitchen garden," answered Penelope.

Aaron was back in a flash, pulling on his gloves. "If you're ready, sir, we can start out to the back pasture," he said to Tony.

Tony nodded, distracted as Juliet and Penelope spoke softly together. He turned and found Aaron also watching the young ladies. "Let's walk out to the back pasture and you can explain what we'll be doing," Tony said, breaking the spell.

Aaron hesitated and looked back at the house. "If you don't mind, sir, my father would like a word with you first."

"Certainly." Tony followed Aaron into the stone house. Inside, it was dark but spotlessly clean. Aaron led them to a room with a window that faced the back pasture. An older man sat in a chair with a blanket over his legs.

"I'm Henry Williams," he said, his deep voice booming from the gloom of the large sitting room.

Tony moved forward and shook the man's hand. "Tony Matthews."

"I know who you are," Mr. Williams said.

Tony's stomach twisted. "Pardon?"

"My son informed me that you've just returned from London. Do you by chance know of Mr. Chelsworth?"

"I'm not acquainted with the man." The lie fell all too easily from Tony's lips.

Mr. Williams's face fell. "I was hoping . . ."

Aaron knelt beside his father. "Don't worry, Father. We'll make this work."

"It's no use, Son, but I appreciate your trying."

Seeing Mr. Williams sitting in that chair, hopeless, tore at Tony's heart. "I'll speak with my brother. If we hear of anything, we will let you know."

"Thank you, sir," Mr. Williams said.

"Come, Mr. Matthews, we'd better get started." Aaron grasped his hat in his hand as he led Tony back outside.

Suddenly, the boy looked older than his years, making Tony realize how much time he himself had wasted when he was sixteen. This young man was carrying his family's problems on his shoulders. Tony had no concept of what it felt like to carry such burdens. Those always fell to his brother.

Shame edged in. He'd squandered so much time and money on gaming, without any thought to the future. Now, the future was uncertain. It wasn't something he was used to dealing with, and Tony wasn't sure he liked the feeling.

Juliet followed Penelope as she walked to the back of house, where the kitchen garden was located. She loved it here on the farm. Life was so much simpler, like it had been for her before Anne had married Nathaniel.

As much as Sophia hated those days, Juliet had loved them—the cottage, with its cozy hiding places, the smell of the apple cake Anne had learned to bake, long walks in the woods. These simple things had made her happy. Yet everyone else had wanted more.

Her first Season in London had been a disaster. Town was so noisy that Juliet hadn't been able to sleep. The rigorous schedule of calls, teas, and shopping filled the days. There wasn't time for reading. It took hours just to dress for a ball.

But there were things she had loved about Town. The smell of the books in the bookshops, the tart-sweet taste of ices from Gunter's on her tongue, the feel of Tony's arms as he waltzed her around a brilliantly lit ballroom.

"Mr. Matthews is very handsome," Penelope said softly. "Is he your beau?"

Juliet laughed. "No! Why do you ask?"

"He watches you."

"You must be mistaken, Pen."

But she knew that Tony *was* constantly studying her, even if she wouldn't admit it aloud. She'd noticed last night in the drawing room, then again in the library. Juliet looked up and found Penelope with that knowing look in her eye.

"Would it be so very bad?" Penelope asked.

Juliet shook her head to clear her thoughts. This was madness. And if she let herself go down that path again, she was only setting herself up for more hurt. "Perhaps we should start in the garden?" she said, changing the subject. "Or is there something else I can help with?"

Penelope looked uncomfortable. "The truth is, Miss Townsend, Mother found out what Aaron had you doing yesterday. Mucking the stalls for lambing."

Juliet closed her hands over the blisters that had formed. "It needed to be done."

"You're a proper young lady and shouldn't be doing that sort of work. Mother is right in that."

"I don't mind the work." In fact, she'd relished it. The Williams family were struggling, but they were bonded together in a way she'd never experienced. "Lead the way and we'll get started."

"Please don't be angry," Penelope begged.

"I'm not," Juliet said and gave her a reassuring smile.

It was all just another reminder that everyone considered her interest in Penelope and her family inappropriate. Juliet understood well how the world worked. In Town, the Townsends were lower on the social pecking order than many other young ladies. You didn't stray from the sphere in which you were born. But in Beetham, they were the highest-ranking family.

The sun grew warm as they worked in the loose soil, planting rows of cabbages, carrots, and other vegetables. Penelope had given Juliet a pair of old work gloves that were way too big for her and she finally ended up pulling them off. They chatted about novels and planted without really noticing that the sun was high in the sky.

The air had warmed, but the cool soil felt good between Juliet's fingers. She'd had no idea she'd like gardening, but now the miracle of taking a seed and watching it grow into something useful enthralled her.

Her mind spun through the journals she'd read on agriculture and increasing production. "I read in one of Nathaniel's journals that if you put just a bit of manure into the soil, it will help the seeds grow stronger."

Penelope laughed. "What do you think you've been digging in?"

Juliet quickly yanked her hands from the dirt. "Really?"

"Nothing goes to waste on the farm," Penelope said as she tossed a clean rag to Juliet to wipe her hands with. "I think we're done."

Juliet stood, dusting the dirt from her old dress. Neat rows of newly planted seeds lay before her. Small placards marked each row. "Thank you for allowing me to help. I enjoyed it. I may have to try gardening at the Lodge."

"I'm certain Mr. Matthews wouldn't allow his sister-in-law to get her hands dirty in the kitchen garden, Miss Juliet," a male voice said from the edge of the yard.

Juliet's heart lurched and Penelope went pale.

"Mr. Bartleby, good afternoon. I didn't know you were expected today," Juliet said stiffly.

"This is part of Horneswood, Miss Juliet. If you will excuse us, Miss Williams?"

"Are you sure, Miss Juliet?"

"Pen, it's quite all right."

Juliet watched as Penelope walked toward the house, giving Mr. Bartleby a wide berth. She hated seeing the fear in Penelope's eyes.

"You should remember your place, Miss Juliet," Bartleby said as he moved closer.

Juliet had done nothing wrong and she refused to let Bartleby take her joy from the day. "It's our Christian duty to help those less fortunate, Mr. Bartleby."

"While I admire your charity, I'm quite certain your brother, Sir John, would disapprove of Miss Williams as a friend for you."

Juliet could think of nothing to say in response. Her brother would not approve, but her sister Anne might.

Simon Bartleby moved even closer and took her hand. He rubbed the dirt from her fingers with a gentle caress.

His touch revolted her. She snatched her hand free and stepped away from him. "You forget yourself, Mr. Bartleby."

"We are practically engaged, Miss Townsend. Your brother-in-law has given me leave to call on you."

Juliet's stomach roiled. She was definitely going to have to deal with Nathaniel. "I know what you said to Miss Williams."

Mr. Bartleby laughed. "And you believe what she told you?"

"Of course I believe her." Juliet raised her chin defiantly.

"You think me capable of ruining a farmer's daughter?"

"I think you capable of a great many things, Mr. Bartleby."

He raised his hand as if he were going to slap her, his face florid. Juliet had always suspected Mr. Bartleby was the type of man who struck out in anger. She braced herself for the blow, knowing she'd pushed him too far. In the beginning she'd hoped her disdain would discourage his attentions. Now she actually feared him. She knew this man would hurt her.

Simon Bartleby lowered his hand and smiled that slick, oily smile of his. "Such spirit, my dear. You don't know how I'm looking forward to breaking you in."

Juliet gasped and stepped back, almost tripping over a rake on the ground. There was no way she'd marry this man. Nathaniel could crow all he wanted, lecture her for hours every single night. It would make no difference.

Bartleby reached out and grabbed Juliet's wrist. She tried to wrench free, but he wouldn't relent.

"Release me." She yanked hard on her arm, wincing at the pain. Fear curled inside her. They were very much alone. The only people within shouting distance were Mrs. Williams and Penelope, and even then it was doubtful they would hear her.

"Am I interrupting something?"

Juliet sagged with relief as Tony strolled into the garden. Bartleby released her and took a step back. She rubbed at the red marks on her wrist.

"Mr. Matthews, I had no idea you were here," said Bartleby.

"Obviously," Tony replied curtly.

Bartleby glared at both Tony and Juliet. "My business is done here. Good day, Miss Juliet. I look forward to seeing you again soon."

Tony watched as Simon Bartleby walked past him wearing a smug expression. He clinched his fists to hold back the urge to smash them into the bastard's face.

Juliet was pale. Shaken. She was still rubbing her wrist to ease the pain.

Tony's protective instincts were always strong around the Townsend sisters, but today was different. Juliet was different. In the years he'd known her, he'd never seen her this frightened. "Did he harm you?" he asked, reaching for her wrist.

"No."

Juliet's skin was smooth, almost translucent, with the red marks of the man's fingers imprinted on it. Tony fought back his anger. "What did he want?"

Juliet gently pulled her arm from his grasp. "To frighten me."

"Did he?" Tony already knew the answer, but he wanted to hear her say it aloud. Juliet was fearless. He'd seen her stare down more intimidating men than Bartleby.

"Yes."

"I'll speak to Nathaniel."

"No, please don't. Mr. Bartleby will only go so far."

Tony suddenly realized he was missing a huge piece of the puzzle. "Should you risk it, Juliet? Is he worth it?"

"The man is a toad, but he won't hurt me. I think he's stealing from the tenants."

"That's a very serious allegation."

"I don't have proof yet, but I will."

"I forbid you to pursue this, Juliet. And if Nathaniel wants a dynastic marriage for this family, he'd have better luck with Sophia."

"Sophia wouldn't have Bartleby," Juliet said in a tone that brooked no further discussion of the matter.

"If you've recovered, we should be on our way."

Juliet nodded and moved toward the house. As she passed, Tony caught a bit of her scent. She smelled of flowers, earth, and woman. There was a smudge of dirt on her cheek and he couldn't stop himself from taking his thumb and removing it. Her skin was soft, so soft. He savored the warmth of her cheek.

Juliet's lips parted in surprise. Tony could feel minute tremors running under her skin where he touched her. Her eyes were wide and as dark as midnight.

"I've readied the cart for you, Mr. Matthews."

Juliet jerked away as Aaron Williams spoke. A flush of pink colored her cheeks.

"Thank you, Aaron. Same time tomorrow?" Tony was surprised his voice was as calm as it was.

"If you'd like, sir." Aaron looked over at Juliet and smiled. "Will you be here tomorrow as well, Miss Juliet?"

"I've not decided yet." She glanced back at Tony, a puzzled look on her face. "I'll just go say good-bye to Pen and your mother."

"Sorry to interrupt," Aaron said to Tony after Juliet had left them.

Tony wasn't sorry for the interruption. One more moment and he would have been kissing her. And kissing Juliet Townsend was the last thing he needed to be thinking about. "You weren't interrupting anything." He began walking to the edge of the garden.

Aaron walked beside him, not taking his eyes off Juliet's retreating back. "She's quite pretty."

"Who?"

"Miss Townsend. Do you think you could make sure she comes along tomorrow?"

"We'll see."

Secretly, he wanted Juliet at the Lodge, along with plenty of witnesses, in case Mr. Bartleby came calling. There was something about the man that grated on his nerves. He had an air of entitlement that made Tony instantly hate him.

Tony had seen the same type of man in the gaming hells and at the card tables. Sharks come to feed on the unwary. He had played the games long enough to recognize them. Bartleby had that look.

He found Juliet already by the cart, talking softly to Miss Williams. Juliet was reassuring her, judging from the look on their faces. Tony understood Miss Williams's fear. Bartleby would take what he wanted and thumb his nose at any broken laws. Penelope Williams was a lovely young woman, and he'd already threatened her once.

Penelope had been terrified when she came looking for them in the fields earlier. He and Aaron had already started back to the house for a bit of lunch when she caught up with them and breathlessly explained the situation. Tony had suffered a panic that he'd not experienced before. According to Miss Williams, Juliet had been in danger.

He'd slowed before rounding the corner of the house. He hadn't wanted to alert Bartleby of his presence. He'd seen the way the man had treated Juliet before, seen her revulsion. She was definitely much safer at the Lodge. Tony would have a word with Nathaniel about him.

"I'll send a note about tomorrow," Tony heard Juliet say to Penelope.

"Don't, Miss Juliet. He might come back." Miss Williams's voice was just a whisper.

"Don't worry about him," Juliet said confidently.

The little fool was purposefully putting herself in Bartleby's way for some reason, perhaps to prove this crazy idea of hers that the man was a thief. Tony took Juliet's hand and helped her into the cart.

"Please give our thanks to your family for the ham," Mrs. Williams said, coming into the park from the house to bid them farewell.

"I will," Juliet said with a smile.

Tony climbed into the cart and placed the now empty basket between them. He took the reins and motioned the horses to start. As the cart pulled away, he said, "Perhaps you can tell me what you were discussing with Miss Williams?"

Juliet didn't look at him. Instead she folded her hands in her lap, the only sign of her nervousness her fingers working at the dirt on them. "There's nothing to say. Thank you for stepping in with Mr. Bartleby, though it wasn't necessary."

"So I noticed." He slowed the horses to a stop once they were out of sight of the Williams house.

"Why are we stopping? Won't we be late for tea?"

Tony jumped down and led the horse and cart farther off the road. He wanted a private conversation with Juliet Townsend. "It's time for a chat."

He held out his hand for her to take. Juliet's eyes widened as she took in where they were, off the main road, with no one nearby. "Surely you aren't going to pull the same tactics as Bartleby."

Tony winced. How could she believe that of him? "You know me better than that."

Juliet remained in the cart with a stubborn expression on her face, refusing to take his hand. "There's nothing for us to discuss."

He held out his hand, feigning a patience he did not feel. "I know a pond where you can wash the dirt from your hands."

Juliet finally relented, placing her hand in his and allowing him to help her from the cart. They followed an overgrown path to a small pond. Tony and Nathaniel had swum there as boys in the heat of summer. Fed by a spring, the water was always icy cold. Large boulders surrounded it, creating natural places to jump off and into the deep water.

Juliet walked to the edge of a large rock. "This is beautiful. How did I not know this place existed?"

"I came here when I was younger," Tony said as he removed his gloves and put his hands in the water. It was cold, just as he remembered. "Come, rinse your hands."

Her eyes widened, but she stepped to the edge of the pond and knelt down. She placed her hands in the water and shrieked. "It's so cold!"

He grinned as he knelt by her side, taking her hands in his. He washed the dirt from her hands. She had blisters on her palms from the work she'd done. "Where were your gloves?"

"I don't have work gloves and my regular gloves are too fine."

Her voice was breathless and he couldn't stop himself from looking into her deep brown eyes.

He tightened with desire. He'd been able to resist all the ladies of London, but he couldn't resist this wisp of a girl who was fiercer than a lion. He quickly looked down at her hands. "I think you have half the garden on your hands."

She tried to pull them from his. "I can do it myself."

"I want to." He pushed up the sleeves of her plain dark dress with his wet hands. He brushed his thumb against the red marks Bartleby had left on her wrist. "Why did Bartleby treat you that way?"

"I shouldn't have taunted him," she said quietly.

"That was still no excuse." He gently rubbed at the dirt around her nails.

"I think the fact that Horneswood has changed hands is causing him to worry," Juliet said. "He's the younger brother of a viscount. He has no choice but to either work or marry money. If he loses his position . . ."

There were many such men in England. Hell, he'd been one of them two years earlier, thought Tony. Only he'd found another, less honorable method to survive.

Having seen the state of the Williams farm, Tony could understand why Juliet wanted to help. Mr. Williams was a broken man. If Tony was going to own the land, he'd take care of the tenants. "You don't have to marry him, Juliet."

She pulled her hands from his and shook them dry. "I don't plan on marrying him, but I'm afraid he'll use my friendship with Miss Williams as leverage."

"I won't let that happen."

Tony helped her stand up. Her head came to just his shoulder. Her foot slipped on the rock and she grabbed his arm.

"Steady," Tony said with amusement.

Juliet looked up at him, her eyes sparkling. "We almost landed in the pond!"

"It'd be a cold swim this time of year."

"Tony, there is something I would ask of you."

"Certainly."

Color flared across Juliet's cheeks. Her eyes met his. "Would you kiss me?"

"Pardon?"

She looked away, staring out at the pond and beyond. "I don't want my first kiss to be from Mr. Bartleby. There is a meanness in him."

Women had always wanted Tony to kiss them, usually followed by wanting even more. But Tony had never been anyone's first kiss.

"I won't expect you to marry me or anything like that. It's just a kiss," said Juliet.

"I didn't think you would." Tony's hands enveloped her face, his fingers sliding underneath her bonnet and into her soft hair. "Are you sure?"

She nodded slightly and closed her eyes.

His mouth brushed against hers. Gentle, easy. He brushed a thumb across her pursed lips. "Relax your mouth, Jules."

Juliet's mouth softened and he kissed her again. She tasted of ginger biscuits. Of spring and home. Her jaw was fragile beneath his hand, her skin warm against his cold hands. He deepened the kiss slowly, letting her scent and taste fill his head with impossible temptations. Impossible dreams.

Juliet's hands released their tight grip on his arms to find their way around his shoulders. She stepped closer, brushing her body slightly against his.

He twisted his head to take the kiss further, his tongue brushing her bottom lip. His other hand found her waist and he pulled her flush against him.

Her foot slipped on the smooth stone, tipping them toward the cold pond. Juliet pulled her mouth away and gripped his arms, letting out a surprised shriek. He steadied himself on the rock, tightening his hold to keep them both from going into the water.

His heart was another matter. It thumped hard in his chest. He looked down at the woman in his arms. Her eyes were like liquid chocolate, warm and dark. Her mouth was red from his kisses.

He wanted to kiss her again. Keep kissing her as long as she would let him. Instead, Tony carefully stepped off the rock and helped her down. "We should return to the Lodge."

She nodded as she lowered her gaze, a blush staining her cheeks. The moment was lost.

How could one slip of a girl twist his heart around in so many different ways?

Chapter Five

The ride home was quiet, an uncomfortable, don't-know-what-to-say kind of quiet. Juliet hated those types of silences.

She never should have kissed Tony. What kind of ninny asks a man to kiss her?

But heavens, what a kiss! Not the peck of a family member but a lips-pressing, breathing-each-other-in lover's kiss. The kiss of a man who knew how to kiss a woman.

It was best not to dwell on it. It clearly meant little to Tony. He would leave for London and Juliet would be back to pity dances with him when she was in Town.

She was taking the stairs to her room to change when Sophia found her, breathless and panicked.

"Juliet, I really wish you'd stop disappearing for hours at a time."

Sophia's impatient tone was like being doused in cold water, waking her from her daydream. "What is it?"

"Mr. McDonald has arrived. You have to help me."

"It will be good to see him again. Why are you so upset? He's been here many times before."

"He's rude and impertinent!"

Juliet smiled. She liked Ian McDonald, even if he was one of the trustees of her settlement. He had a dry sense of humor and a way of seeing the world differently from the rest of them. He was intelligent, so he missed nothing, especially when it concerned Sophia. "You just don't like the fact that you can't manipulate him like most men. Or the fact that, as trustee, he's not easily swayed when you want access to funds."

"It's not like that," Sophia said mulishly. "I just can't stand the way he finds fault with everything."

"I hadn't noticed that he found fault with anything."

"Just don't let me be alone with the man, please." Sophia looked down at her sister's dress. "You are covered in dirt."

"I was on my way to my room to change."

"Did you just come in with Tony?" Sophia gave Juliet one of her measured looks.

Juliet squirmed, afraid Sophia would guess what had happened. God forbid, for if she found out about the kiss, Sophia would torment her for days with that bit of knowledge. "I'm going to be late if you don't let me go."

"I hope Mr. McDonald isn't staying here."

"I'm positive he will be," Juliet said and then rushed to her room, closing the door behind her. She flew to the mirror and looked at her lips. Did she look as if she had been kissed?

Juliet thought her heart would stop when Tony took her hands and cleaned them in the pond. No man had ever bathed her hands. His touch had been gentle as he brushed his fingers over the marks that Bartleby left behind.

She covered her face with her hands. She had asked for the kiss. It would have been ungentlemanly of him to refuse.

Juliet pulled a dress out of her cupboard and tossed it on the bed. She poured water into the basin and took a cloth to wash the rest of the dirt from her hands and face. When she was cleaned and changed, she made her way downstairs to the drawing room for tea.

Tony was already there. He stood as she entered, but her smile was for the tall Scotsman standing next to him. "Mr. McDonald, what brings you to Beetham?"

"Miss Juliet, how lovely to see you." He bent and kissed her hand. "When you and your sister left Town, it was as if all the light had gone out of the city."

Juliet laughed and looked around. "Where is my sister?"

"She made some excuse about helping our nephew," Tony said.

Juliet had to give Sophia her due; she had found a way to avoid Mr. McDonald.

"Sit down and have some tea, child," Lady Danford said.

"Yes, ma'am." Juliet took a seat next to the lady. "May I get you something?"

"Now that you're here, these young gentlemen will quit entertaining me. But that's as it should be. You'll keep them on their toes."

Juliet grinned and accepted a cup from Lady Danford. "I doubt that, ma'am."

"The country seems to agree with you, Miss Juliet. I've not seen you looking so pretty," Mr. McDonald said.

"Thank you, sir. I do love it here."

Mr. McDonald smiled widely as Tony frowned at both of them.

Anne breezed into the room. "I'm sorry I'm late. I wanted to see little Nash for his tea."

Juliet sipped her tea and let those around her talk. Every now and then, she'd look up to find Tony watching her before he'd quickly look away. It was puzzling. "How long are you staying with us, Mr. McDonald?" she asked.

"Just a few days. I'm on my way home. Now that the Season is over, I can take some time to work my own lands."

"We'll have to have some sort of assembly while you and Tony are both here," Anne said. "It's not often we have two single gentlemen in the neighborhood. The ladies in the village will be thrilled."

"We'll include Mr. Bartleby as well," Lady Danford said.

Juliet would be expected to spend the entire evening in the company of Mr. Bartleby. Her heart sank.

"Really, Anne, you don't have to go through the trouble," Tony said. "I'm sure we've both had enough of assemblies while we were in Town."

"Speak for yourself, Matthews," Mr. McDonald quipped. "I, for one, would love to be able to dance with the young ladies without having to trip over fifty other gentlemen. I vow to have at least two dances with you, Miss Juliet. That is, if you can stand me stepping on your toes."

"I'm sure you're a fine dancer, Mr. McDonald," Anne said as she passed him a plate with some cake.

"I assure you, I'm not. But Tony is a fine dancer."

"I'm a passable dancer," Tony mumbled.

Juliet met his eyes. "I think you dance very well."

"Until the embarrassing incident," Sophia said as she stepped into the room. She'd changed from her dull, old day dress into a prettier one. She took a seat next to Anne and accepted a cup of tea. "Mr. McDonald, I'm so sorry I wasn't here to greet you."

"I want to hear about this embarrassing incident," Mr. McDonald said.

"There is no need to bore everyone with that old story," Juliet said hurriedly. The last thing she needed was her handkerchief episode aired during tea. She shot Sophia an I'll-get-you-later look.

"Are you serious about an assembly, Anne?" Lady Danford said. "It's a great deal of work."

"I think it would be good fun. We can easily have it here. It's been an age since we've hosted a gathering," Anne replied.

"Perhaps you can announce your engagement to Mr. Bartleby, Juliet." Sophia's voice held a hint of malice.

Juliet felt her cheeks heat. "Perhaps not."

Lady Danford snorted into her teacup. Anne shot Juliet a quelling look.

"Who is this Mr. Bartleby?" Mr. McDonald asked. "Surely there's not another man vying for your affections, Miss Juliet."

"He's the land steward for the Horneswood estate," Tony said, setting his cup down with a pointed look at Mr. McDonald.

"Isn't that the estate you asked—"

Juliet looked over at Tony. "I didn't know you knew of Horneswood prior to coming to Beetham."

"I didn't—"

"I was mistaken," Mr. McDonald interrupted.

Juliet raised her eyebrow at them both. "What's going on?"

"Nothing," said Tony and he stood up from his chair. "McDonald, why don't we leave the ladies to their tea and go find Nathaniel?"

"I think Nathaniel is in the library," Anne said.

Ian McDonald also stood. "If you will excuse us, ladies." He bowed and followed Tony out of the room.

"That was strange," Anne said, pouring herself more tea.

Tony had been acting oddly since his arrival yesterday, thought Juliet. If Ian McDonald knew of Horneswood, then he and Tony had obviously discussed it before their arrival in Beetham.

But how was that possible?

Sophia sat down beside her. "We need to talk."

"I thought we already had."

Sophia glanced at the garden doors. "Outside," she whispered. Then, more loudly, "Anne, do you mind if Juliet and I take a stroll in the garden?"

"Please don't go out there and argue under the library window. You know how much Nathaniel hates that."

"We won't."

Juliet barely had time to gather her shawl before Sophia dragged her by the arm toward the door. "Sophia, slow down, please!"

"We have to hurry before they come back," Sophia said. She kept walking, a death grip on Juliet's arm, until they were at the edge of the garden and away from the house.

Juliet yanked her arm free. "What is this about?"

"Mr. McDonald is here to propose to me." Sophia looked more desperate than she had in a long time. Usually, Sophia could quash any overt interest a gentleman had in her in less time than it took to sip her tea.

Juliet wished her sister liked Mr. McDonald. He was charming and fun, but there were no sparks between them. "It's an equitable match."

"Not as far as I'm concerned. I want one more Season to—"

"To find a wealthy husband with a title, but consider, Sophia: Isn't it more important that you care about the man you marry?"

"Finding a wealthy husband means everything! It means I'd be accepted everywhere socially. Please help me."

Juliet freed herself from Sophia's desperate grasp. She felt like the stick for the dog today. "Help you with what?"

"Keeping Mr. McDonald from proposing."

Her sister had finally taken leave of her senses. "He's wealthy. He's a gentleman. He has a wonderful sense of humor."

"When we say that about a young lady, they tend to be plain," Sophia snapped. "I don't want him to propose."

"Then refuse him. It's not as if you haven't had practice."

Sophia put her hands on her hips. "Just because I receive marriage proposals and you do not isn't a reason to jump down my throat."

Juliet looked up to the heavens for patience. She could stand here and argue with her sister for hours. Or she could go along with whatever crazy scheme Sophia had concocted. Yes, definitely, the path of least resistance was preferable. "What's the plan?"

"I want you to pretend you are attracted to Ian McDonald," Sophia said with a smile.

"Mr. McDonald is going to know it's not real."

"If you don't help me, I'm going to Anne with those books you've been reading."

Juliet experienced a shiver of fear. "About the agriculture journals?"

Sophia smiled an evil smile. "Those naughty books, the ones you've been hiding in your room. Really, Juliet, they are obscene. No young lady should see those."

"Anne doesn't care what I read." *Oh God.* Juliet could feel the color drain from her face. How had Sophia found out? She had kept them hidden. "You've been going through my things."

"Anne will care about these books. They aren't fit for good society. Good Lord, if this got out, you could ruin us all," Sophia said.

"Did you remove them from my room?"

"I left them where they were, for now," Sophia said. "I've also decided to not tell Anne quite yet, but I want something in exchange for my silence."

Dash it all, thought Juliet. "What would you like me to do?"

"You must keep Mr. McDonald occupied. You cannot let him have the opportunity to propose. Am I clear?"

"Sophia, if he proposes, just tell him no."

A strange look crossed Sophia's face. "I can't."

"I don't understand. Do you have feelings for him?"

"Of course not," Sophia said a touch too quickly. "Just do as I ask or I'll give Anne the books, understood?"

Juliet hated the look of triumph on her sister's face. "Perfectly."

Tony walked past the library to the breakfast room. McDonald was such an idiot. He'd almost given away the entire game. Tony had seen the puzzled look in Jules's eyes. The woman was smart. Too smart.

"This doesn't look like the library," McDonald said, circling the large table.

Tony closed the door. "Keep your voice down. I don't want the servants to hear." He couldn't risk gossip getting out. "What in blazes were you thinking?"

"You haven't told anyone about your good fortune?" Ian crossed his arms, a smug look on his face. "I should have known you wouldn't have the bollocks to tell them."

"Once the situation is remedied, I'll tell them," Tony said.

"Chelsworth finally responded to your letter. Seems his stupid honor is worth more than the estate. He doesn't want to renegotiate the terms of the debt."

Tony cursed. "What am I going to do now?"

"Chelsworth should be at the estate by now."

Tony did not have much time before word reached Nathaniel's ears. "What are the rumors in Town?"

"Surprisingly, there aren't many. The man is known to play deeper than his pockets allow. No one was surprised when he finally gambled away his land."

"I'll have to call on him. Insist he deal with the issue. Will you be here to help me?"

"I was hoping you'd already had this discussion with Chelsworth, or at least mentioned it to Nathaniel. I should be in Scotland."

"Hard to do that when Chelsworth wasn't around." Tony should have been planning his move to the estate and buying the right sheep for the land; instead, he was trying to keep things quiet. The very last thing he needed was for Nathaniel to find out. Tony wanted to show his brother he was capable of cleaning up his own mess.

"What are your intentions toward Miss Juliet?" McDonald asked. "I noticed how you were looking at her. I hope they are honorable."

Tony glared at him. "I could call you out for that statement."

McDonald laughed. "You should have seen your face when she smiled at me."

"Perhaps I should ask you *your* intentions."

"Hold on; I'm just a friend. I just happened to catch the look in your eye when she walked in. She is not one you can trifle with."

"I have no intention of doing so. And if you'll be staying longer, you'll have the opportunity to spend some time with Miss Townsend yourself."

McDonald tensed but said nothing.

Tony chuckled. "We are a pair, you and I."

"All I want is to give Miss Townsend the opportunity to get to know me," McDonald said. "Unfortunately, she is avoiding me. Perhaps you could help?"

"Of course."

It would give Tony the opportunity to keep Juliet from guessing why he was in Beetham, as well as the chance to better understand his own feelings.

Chapter Six

Juliet tried to focus on the book in her hand, but anger still simmered.

Tony had told her to stay home. Stay home instead of going to help Penelope. Stay home like a good little girl. Penelope was *her* friend, not Tony's.

Worse than just sitting at home was waiting for Simon Bartleby to call. Nathaniel had announced with an overabundance of happiness that she could expect a special call from him.

She prayed he'd catch some sort of disease that would keep him quarantined for ten years. She didn't care if his brother was the Prince of Wales—she wasn't marrying him.

"When is your suitor calling?" Sophia said as she flounced into the room. "I think he might propose."

"He will have to learn to live with disappointment," Juliet grumbled.

"Your first proposal and you're saying no. I'm surprised."

Juliet frowned at her. "My feelings prevent it. You've turned down proposals for much less."

"Yes, but they were all beneath me. This is likely the only proposal you'll get."

"I'm waiting for a gentleman who appreciates a woman with a brain."

"I glanced at those naughty books of yours, Juliet."

Juliet looked up to find Sophia had her most superior smile on her face. "You've been in my room? Again?"

"Yes. I'm puzzled as to why you'd bother with them at all. Really, the one with the pictures is disgusting."

"Really, Sophia, have you no respect?"

"Tony looked positively crushed that you'd only talk to Ian Mc-Donald," Sophia said, ignoring her sister's indignation.

Juliet refused to discuss Tony with her sister. She didn't have a clue why he was acting the way he was. "Ian McDonald wanted to talk to you. I don't know why you dislike him so. He's a nice man."

Sophia refused to look at her. Instead, she played with the sleeves on her dress.

"You like him," Juliet said with a smile.

"*No. I. Don't.* The man is insufferable."

"The lady doth protest . . ."

"I'm not marrying some Scotsman from the edge of nowhere. I'm marrying someone wealthy and titled."

Juliet reopened her book and searched for the last page she'd read. "Suit yourself." Mr. McDonald was a good man who was in love with her vain sister. "Let him see the real Sophia. He'll be over his infatuation."

"Oh, I don't know why I bother to discuss anything with you."

A footman entered and said, "Mr. Bartleby is here to see you, Miss Juliet."

Sophia stood. "Time to let you receive your first proposal."

"Stay, please," Juliet begged. "I don't want to be alone with him."

"Whyever not? He won't be able to propose if I'm here."

Juliet really wanted to avoid this. She closed the book, tossed it on the chair, and rose. Her dress was old and faded. She smoothed the creases left from sitting curled up in the chair. Her hair was its usual disaster, but she doubted that would scare him away.

Simon Bartleby came into the room and smiled at her. She curtsied. "Good afternoon, Mr. Bartleby."

"Miss Juliet, a pleasure." He pressed his too-wet lips to her hand.

"Please sit down." She took her seat in the chair, moving the book to the table.

"Reading?" He glanced at the book. "Agriculture. You surprise me."

"Helping the Williams family has gotten me interested in gardening," Juliet said.

Please let him get to the point so he can be gone.

"I stopped by to see Mr. Williams and noticed Mr. Matthews there. Do you know why he is taking an interest in the farm?"

Bartleby's tone belied his innocuous question. "Mr. Matthews is helping because I asked him to."

Juliet wasn't going to prolong the visit any longer than she had to.

"It's very fine weather," he said quietly.

"Indeed it is. Spring is my favorite time of year."

"I'm sure you know why I've come," he started hesitantly.

"Yes."

He knelt before her on one knee.

Juliet bit her lip. "Mr. Bartleby, please get up."

He took her hand. "Miss Juliet, would you please do me the honor of becoming my wife?"

She pulled her hand away. "Please stand, Mr. Bartleby."

He reluctantly got to his feet.

Juliet paused to sort out her words. There was no reason to be rude. "You do me a great honor, sir, but I feel I must decline."

"You must decline?" Mr. Bartleby said angrily. "I do not understand you. You have very few connections. You're nothing to your sister, and yet you refuse me."

"I'm surprised you issued an offer of marriage given that I'm so far beneath you."

"This is about the Williamses. The chit is a farmer's daughter, nothing more."

"No woman, regardless of her station, should be treated thus, Mr. Bartleby. That is what I cannot forgive."

He moved closer, threateningly closer. She fought the urge to cringe.

His hands grabbed her arms so tight she couldn't stop a wince of pain. "Release me."

"Think on this, Miss High and Mighty. I can ruin you. I can ruin your Mr. Matthews."

Her heart thudded in her chest. "You have no power over me or anyone else in this family." Juliet fought to keep the tremor from her voice.

His hands tightened, and she yelped with pain before she could stop herself. He grinned before shoving her away from him. Juliet backed away from him as quickly as she could, putting the chair between them. She rubbed at her arms and said, "Leave now and I will not mention your manner to my brother-in-law."

"How foolish you are, Miss Juliet. He's done nothing but encourage the match. I suggest you get used to the idea of becoming my wife. It will happen." Bartleby picked up his hat. "Good day, Miss Juliet."

Juliet collapsed against the chair, shaken.

Surely Nathaniel could see the evil in this man. She had to make him believe it. Or Tony. Tony would understand. He would help her.

Unfortunately, Sophia held those erotic books over her head.

If she singled out Tony, Sophia would go to Anne with the books she had been reading and all hell would break loose. Nathaniel would marry her off to Bartleby to keep her from ruin.

Juliet raced up the stairs to her room and closed the door. She dug the books from their hiding spot beneath the papers on her dressing table. Sagging with relief, she sank into her chair.

They were still there. She clutched the books close. She would hide them. She would make sure Sophia couldn't find them. No proof, and Anne would think Sophia was just making trouble again.

But where? The library was the logical choice, but she'd never get into the library without being discovered. She didn't relish explaining to anyone why she had the books in her possession. Sophia wouldn't hesitate to rifle through most of the rooms, except perhaps Tony's room.

His room was perfect. She'd hide them in the bottom of his closet. No one would know the books were there and she could retrieve them when he left.

She glanced at the clock. She still had time to sneak in and hide them before he returned from the Williams farm. She clutched the books and crept out of her room.

Tony guided the horse down the tree-lined path, going over what he'd learned. After the discussion with Mr. Williams the previous day, he'd suspected the estate was mismanaged. It explained why Mr. Chelsworth was losing money. It explained the condition of the farm. It didn't explain why Simon Bartleby was hounding the tenants for more money.

Lack of crop rotation, bad weather, and many other factors would explain the poor performance. But that wasn't what he'd heard from the other tenants. The tenants wanted to raise sheep and depend less on crops for cash. Bartleby had put a stop to it all.

"I don't know how you're going to make sense of it. Not without talking to Chelsworth or Bartleby," McDonald said as he rode beside him.

"I know," Tony said. "The only thing I can think of is that Bartleby wanted the land for himself. He's the younger son of an earldom. What is he doing as a land steward?"

"Perhaps the family has fallen on hard times," McDonald suggested.

"Perhaps, but why Juliet? Bartleby could find much wealthier young ladies in Town." Anne had sold her mother's jewels to provide dowries for the other two sisters. It wouldn't have been enough to purchase an estate like Horneswood, no matter how cheap the price was.

"Only Bartleby can confirm this story. It does seem odd that he's not in London shopping for an heiress. Then again, Juliet is very intelligent. Perhaps that drew Bartleby's attention."

"I'm not sure I understand your meaning."

"Juliet has spent a great deal of time studying your brother's business journals." McDonald chuckled. "She has a quick mind. I've been impressed with her ideas." His voice held a note of pride. "She's made some investment suggestions that I've taken advantage of."

"Juliet Townsend? Are we talking about the same woman?"

"The very same. I've used her advice and made a tidy sum, not to mention growing her own settlement. She's worth much more now," McDonald said. "You do realize that I am one of the trustees of her settlement, don't you?"

"I had forgotten. Do you have an example?"

"Railways. She swears that in ten years they will be the main mode of transportation in England," McDonald said. "I'm not sure, but I'm willing to take the chance. She isn't wrong often."

"That's highly speculative." Tony frowned. He knew Juliet was smart, but this was amazing. "I wonder if Bartleby has discovered this."

"It's possible that Nathaniel has told him as part of their discussions."

Juliet always read widely. Nathaniel was always missing his business journals. Tony smiled. Good for her.

"Does it change your opinion of her?"

"Not at all. I wish I had that talent."

"I'm not looking forward to another evening like the last. Every time I attempted to talk to Miss Townsend, Juliet was there to dissuade me. Do you have any idea what those two are playing at?"

Tony had been forced to dance only with Sophia. If he tried to dance with Juliet, or even talk to her, he'd had to go through Sophia. "You must have done something to insult the lady if she'd gone to these strides to avoid you."

"Not that I'm aware." McDonald looked serious. "I don't expect her to marry me. In fact, I'll not be asking her. But I expect her to be friendly to me at least."

"Perhaps you should tell her that. It would ease the tension."

"You don't just tell a woman you've no plans of offering for her. Not and survive to tell about it."

"It would end this game she is insisting on playing." Being in love with someone who didn't love you back, didn't even like you, was painful. "What are you going to do when she does marry?"

"Maybe when that happens I can move on. I'm getting tired of living alone in that big house." McDonald looked out into the surrounding grounds. "You could really make something of this property if you wanted to, Matthews."

"It has potential if managed correctly. It's getting the family past the fact that I won it in a card game that's the difficulty. Nathaniel is going to kill me. I've fulfilled all his fears of becoming our father."

"You can stop gambling, can't you?"

Tony was quiet a minute. "I have stopped. The only reason I played this particular game was because it gave me access to several investors for Nathaniel. He is a horrible card player." He nudged his horse a little faster. While he'd not found a game while in Beetham, he still felt the pull to play. He had resisted thus far.

"Just say you bought the place," McDonald said. "We'll keep it between us."

Tony mulled over the idea. It had merit. "That's a good plan. I want to wait before announcing it to the family, though. Juliet will expect me to immediately solve the problem of the Williamses and I'm not sure I can."

"That will not do," McDonald said with a chuckle. "Her temper can rival Sophia's."

Tony knew Juliet's temper only too well. He'd experienced it when he'd asked her to stay home today rather than go to the Williamses'. "If the Williamses prove not to be the injured parties here, I'd rather handle it without Juliet knowing."

"That won't happen."

"Something just doesn't feel right about the entire situation." Tony had to trust his instincts. They'd proven right too many times. "Don't say anything to anyone for now."

"Certainly," McDonald agreed.

They rode in silence for a long while. Tony's thoughts centered on how he'd deal with the fact that the Williamses' farm was not performing the way it needed to. He understood the challenges, especially given the severity of Mr. Williams's injuries, but could he let them stay without paying something? Juliet would expect him to give them charity once she found out about his ownership of the estate.

One thing he had learned from Nathaniel was that there could be no emotional decisions in business. If he planned on supporting a family with this estate, he'd have to follow similar rules. It was a tangle. He was glad he'd made the decision to keep things quiet for the moment.

They dismounted at the stable. Tony handed the reins to a groom. "We should have time to change before tea."

"I can't wait to see what Sophia is going to do next to avoid me," McDonald complained.

"I'll say something to Jules. She has to know what's going on." Juliet had looked even less happy about Sophia's machinations last night. If they could get back before tea, Tony might have time to get the information from her.

Tony wondered how much Simon Bartleby knew about Juliet's dowry. It was common knowledge that Nathaniel had settled money on the girls in the amount of five hundred pounds. It wasn't enough to buy an estate, but it was enough to get the man back to London. If he knew the true amount, it would be a further enticement.

This was one of those times he wished London wasn't so damn far away. He'd love to have someone dig into Bartleby's background. "Do you know anyone in York, McDonald?"

"I might. Why?"

"Can you send out some inquires about Bartleby? I want to know why the man is a land steward here of all places."

"I'll send a note this afternoon," McDonald said. "The man might have true feelings for Miss Juliet."

"Bartleby left marks on her yesterday, gripping her wrist so tight," Tony growled out. He'd hurt her. He'd do it again, Tony was sure of it.

"I'll let you know as soon as I have an answer." McDonald looked down at his stained buckskins. "I think I'll rinse off the farm before tea. Wouldn't want Miss Townsend to have another reason to avoid me."

Tony chuckled. He needed to do the same. He made his way to his room, anxious to get out of his filthy clothes. He smelled like the farm.

Sophia must be stopped. Ever since she had discovered the naughty books in Juliet's bedroom, Sophia had been lording it over her. Enough was enough.

Tony's room was the perfect hiding place. He was away with Mr. McDonald and would probably be gone until past teatime. It would be an easy thing for Juliet to sneak into the room and slip the books into the bottom of the cupboard without being discovered.

Juliet gathered the two small books and walked determinedly to the other side of the house, where Tony's room was. She opened the door and slipped inside, closing it behind her.

Oh. Dear. Lord.

"Tony!"

Juliet clutched the books to her chest. He was shirtless. She couldn't look away. Her mouth went dry.

"Juliet, what are you doing in here?"

"I—uh—eh." She gulped. "I thought you were out with Mr. Mc-Donald."

He was the most gorgeous man she'd ever seen. His chest was muscular and broad, sprinkled with hair. Hair that trailed down in a nice tidy line into his pants.

Tony moved closer, forcing her to back into the door. "What are you doing in my room?"

She closed her eyes, hoping that not seeing him would allow her brain to form words again. "I need you to hide these books."

"Books? Let me see."

Juliet opened her eyes and looked up at him. He was so tall. "I need to explain."

Tony laughed. "Nonsense." He pried the books from her hands.

"Tony, no!"

Tony took the books and stepped away from her as he flipped through the pages. He turned one of the books to look at the pictures. Then he looked at her with heat in his eyes. "These are worse than the one you were reading in the library. You naughty thing."

Heat crept into Juliet's cheeks. She made a grab for the books. "I told you I had them."

He dodged her. "I thought you were joking." He turned another page and tilted his head.

Juliet swiped at his arm. This was too much. She needed those books back. "Oh, come, Tony. I'm certain there is nothing in those books that would shock you."

He paused and gave her a long look. "You might be surprised. What were you planning to do with these?"

"Hide them on the floor of your cupboard where the maids wouldn't find them," Juliet grumbled.

"Why?"

She didn't want to tell him the truth, so she shrugged instead. Surely that was answer enough.

"Does this have to do with your behavior last night?"

"Was something amiss with my behavior last night?"

Tony shook his head. "You know better than to lie to me. Tell me what's going on."

Juliet crossed her arms. "Nothing is going on. Can I not enjoy the company of a gentleman without raising suspicion?"

"So you admit to liking Mr. McDonald?"

Juliet glared at him. "Mr. McDonald is a friend, nothing more."

"You seemed a great deal more interested in him than friendship would account for."

"That's not true! Give me those. I'll find another location to keep them." Juliet reached for the books, but he held them high in the air where she couldn't reach them. "Please return them."

"Not so fast. Why are you looking at these?"

She poked him in the chest. "Why is it that men are allowed to look at such things while we women aren't even allowed to ask questions?"

"Jules, don't get angry with me. I just asked a simple question."

"May I have my books back, please?"

"On one condition."

"What is it with this penchant for conditions? First Sophia and now you." Juliet stomped her foot.

He chuckled, clearly enjoying teasing her.

"What is the condition?" she asked.

"You learn to ride a horse."

Juliet could feel the color leave her face. "Not that. Tony, please, not that."

"Jules, it will be fine. There's nothing to be afraid of." He tucked a stray hair behind her ear.

"I can't do it." How was she going to get out of this?

"We'll take it slow. In fact, wear your breeches. It will be easier than riding sidesaddle." His voice was gentle.

"I will do anything, Tony. Anything but go near horses." She hated the pleading tone of her voice.

"Then tell me why you're so curious about these books," Tony said as he picked up the smaller of the two and flipped through it. "Especially this one." He opened the book and showed her a picture. "Explain."

"Anything but that." It was either die by horse or embarrassment. "I have several married friends and I was simply curious about what they were talking about."

Tony showed her another picture. "You were curious about this?"

"That one is odd to me." Juliet didn't think her face could get any redder. Maybe the horse wasn't so bad. "It looks like she's kissing him on his—uh, privates? Why would someone do that?"

Tony snapped the book shut and turned away from her.

"Do people really do the things in that book?" she couldn't stop herself from asking.

"Some do, yes."

"So that picture you showed me is something a wife would do?"

"I wouldn't know . . . but I doubt it."

"Please hide the books for me? I don't trust Sophia not to grab them and show them to Anne. I will never hear the end of it if Anne finds out."

"I'll hide them." He studied her for a long moment. "But you will get on a horse."

Juliet shook her head. She looked up into his face to tell him so but became lost in the warmth of his eyes. They were dark, almost a stormy blue gray. "Tony?"

He moved close again, and this time she refused to back up. He was trying to intimidate her.

His chest brushed her crossed arms. His skin was warm. She looked up at him and raised an eyebrow.

"It's quite dangerous to enter the bedroom of a man, Jules." His voice was gruff, rumbly and low.

"You weren't supposed to be here." Her pulse picked up its pace.

Tony cradled her face with his hand, rubbing his thumb on her skin. "I think I should kiss you again."

"Why?"

"I don't know." His lips brushed softly against her mouth.

Juliet's hands curled into the hair on his chest. His skin was so warm, the muscles hard beneath. She raised up on her toes to better fit her mouth to his, his hard body pressing into her softer one.

His tongue touched hers and she opened her mouth further and mimicked Tony's actions. Her heart pounded in her chest as he turned his head and deepened the kiss.

His hands captured her hips and pulled her closer, molding her to his hard body. She melted against him, soaking up his heat.

Who knew this could feel so good? None of Juliet's married friends had mentioned this tingly feeling, or the sheer warmth of it all.

"We have to stop, Jules. Make me stop," he said.

She reluctantly pulled away, her heart racing, her body screaming for more. Looking at the naughty pictures just made it worse. She could imagine doing those things with Tony.

"If you keep looking at me like that, we're going to be in a great deal of trouble." Tony's voice sounded rusty.

Juliet never wanted trouble more in her life, but this sort of trouble would end up breaking her heart. Again.

This time it would be a thousand times worse because now she knew Tony's touch, his kiss. She knew what she'd be missing. She stepped back from him, removing herself from temptation. "We need to stop this, Tony, before one of us gets hurt."

He opened his mouth to say something, but Juliet was afraid to hear it. She didn't want to know that he was playing with her. The consequences for her were too great. She bolted from the room as if the fires of hell were on her heels.

She had to protect herself from getting hurt. She had to find a way to avoid Tony Matthews.

Chapter Seven

Tony swirled the brandy in his glass. Juliet had asked him not to kiss her again. He wasn't convinced he would be able to comply with her request. He couldn't explain why, but he needed to kiss her, needed the feelings that flowed through him when he was with her. Feelings of home, of affection, of lust. He had no idea how to explain it, but he couldn't just stop.

"Bartleby came by today to call on Juliet. I thought he would propose to her," Nathaniel said from his seat at the dining room table.

The ladies had already left them to their brandy and smokes. Now that Tony thought about it, Juliet had been unusually quiet at dinner. She'd sat between him and McDonald. Now Tony could feel McDonald's eyes on him. "She said nothing to me."

"I'm sure if she accepted his proposal, we'd know," McDonald said. "Ladies like to be engaged."

Something inside Tony twisted. She wouldn't accept Bartleby, would she? Surely not after the way he had treated her yesterday. "I don't think it's such a good match. What made you think of it, Nathaniel?"

"He's the younger brother of the Viscount Northam, from a very old family," Nathaniel said defensively.

"Reading *Debrett's* again?" Tony quipped. Surely Juliet wasn't interested in this type of loveless pairing. "What do you know of the man?"

"Bartleby?" Nathaniel shrugged. "He's your typical gentleman. He's not wealthy, so I'm sure Juliet's dowry drew some interest. He seemed to genuinely care for her."

Tony exchanged a look with McDonald. "If she likes him well enough, I'm sure she'll say yes." He shot a look at Nathaniel. "She will have a choice, won't she?"

"Anne would have my hide if I didn't give her sisters a choice," Nathaniel said. "There just weren't that many men interested in Juliet. All they saw was Sophia. I think the only time Juliet danced was when she was with you."

Tony was grateful for that, for he didn't like the thought of any man touching her, especially now. He didn't want to put a name to the feelings churning inside him. It would be better for all if he simply didn't acknowledge them. Better if he never touched Juliet again. He just didn't know if he could stop himself.

"I'm sure Miss Juliet will find her own husband, in her own time," McDonald said. "She is far from being on the shelf."

"What were you doing at the Williamses' farm?" Nathaniel asked his brother. "Surely Juliet hasn't convinced you to help her with her latest charity."

"She did ask me to help," Tony replied. "I'm thinking of buying Horneswood. The owner has clearly not taken care of the tenants or the property."

"This is a new development," Nathaniel said with surprise.

"I've been thinking about it for a good while now," Tony said.

"I think it's a good idea," said Nathaniel. "It's good to see you taking an interest in something other than gaming hells."

Heat crept into Tony's face. "I do more than visit gaming hells."

"Of course. Now, shall we join the ladies?"

Tony downed his brandy in one swallow. His own brother thought the worst of him. He had to make sure the truth never got out. "Let's keep this our secret for right now, Nathaniel. I haven't made up my mind yet."

"Understood. I'm glad you're taking this seriously. I was beginning to fear you'd never grow up."

Tony refused to feel guilty for lying to Nathaniel. Better a lie than disappointment and disapproval.

Juliet stared sightlessly into the fire. Tony had kissed her again. She'd felt his skin beneath her hands. Even now she could remember the tickle of his chest hair against her palms. She could remember the pressure of his mouth on hers. She was starting to crave it, like sweets.

"Juliet, you're a little flushed. Perhaps you're sitting too close to the fire," Anne said gently.

"I'm fine, really." Juliet longed to confide in her sister, someone who would understand these mad feelings inside her, but she was too afraid.

Sophia moved closer to her. "How did your visit with Mr. Bartleby go? Did he propose, as we suspected he might?"

"That nodcock proposed? I hope you turned him down," Lady Danford said.

"He did propose and I refused," Juliet said, turning back to the fire.

"I saw him storming out of the drawing room," Sophia said. "You must have been harsh."

Harsh was a good word to describe Bartleby himself. Juliet swore the man took pleasure in causing her pain. "I was polite but honest," Juliet said. She looked over at Anne. "Please make Nathaniel understand. I'm so grateful for all he has done for us, but I cannot marry Mr. Bartleby."

"Dearest, you will marry who you love. If you don't love him, that's the end of it. Nathaniel means well."

"I think Nathaniel will be happy when both of us are married," Sophia said. "He was rather put out when I didn't accept any of the proposals I had in Town."

"You're entirely too picky, Sophia," said Juliet.

"You're a fine one to talk. You turned down your only proposal."

"I think a lady should refuse her first proposal. If you say yes to the first man, you might miss out on the right one," Lady Danford said. "In my day, it was much simpler. Your father made the arrangement for you."

Juliet shivered. "I wouldn't like that."

"Neither would I," Sophia chimed in.

"Be thankful, then, that you won't have to do that," Anne said. "Marry for love. I highly recommend it."

"Recommend what, love?" Nathaniel said, coming into the room. He kissed Anne's hand.

Juliet almost sighed. She wanted what Anne had—a man who loved her. "She recommends marrying for love."

"I heard Bartleby called today, Juliet," Nathaniel said. "Did he propose?"

"Yes, he proposed, but Juliet said no. Mr. Bartleby left here angry," Sophia said.

"That's too bad. He really cares for you, Juliet," Nathaniel said.

"I doubt he'll be too upset about it for long. I don't think his feelings run that deep," Juliet said curtly.

"Maybe he'll try again," Sophia said. "You could still change your mind."

"Doubtful."

"Are we playing music tonight, Mrs. Matthews?" Mr. McDonald asked.

"I'm not in the mood for dancing tonight," said Juliet.

"Cards?" Sophia said. "Perhaps a game of whist?"

Juliet continued to gaze at the fire. She wasn't in the mood for any of it.

"I, for one, am glad you turned that buffoon down. He thinks he is so much better than the rest of us," Lady Danford said with a sniff. "I cannot abide that sort of condescension."

Juliet turned and flashed a smile at Lady Danford. It was nice to know she had someone's support.

"I don't understand why you don't like him," Nathaniel said.

"Dear, you wouldn't. Juliet doesn't love him," said Anne.

"Don't worry, Nathaniel. I promise not to live with you forever," Juliet vowed.

"That's a relief," Nathaniel said.

Juliet jumped when Tony bent his head down to her and whispered. "Someone's been keeping secrets."

"I don't know what you're talking about."

What could he know? He knew about the books. He knew about Penelope. What else was there?

"Meet me in the library in fifteen minutes."

His voice was low, rumbling along her spine. Juliet fought the shiver of awareness. She nodded. She looked up and found Mr. McDonald watching her.

Juliet rose and went over to Mr. McDonald to ferret out what Tony was talking about. "How was your day today, sir?" she asked.

"You mean following Tony around on a horse all day?" Mr. McDonald quipped.

Juliet glanced around, uncertain of how to steer the conversation.

"You appear to have something on your mind," Ian said.

"Tony said something about me keeping secrets. Do you know what he meant?"

Mr. McDonald had the grace to blush. "I might have told him about your dowry and your talent for investments."

"What?" Juliet lowered her voice. "Why?"

"We were talking about Bartleby and his interest in you."

"You think the only kind of man I can get a proposal out of is one like Bartleby?"

"That is not what I meant."

"Perhaps you could explain what you do mean, because the way I understand it, the only man who would be interested in marrying me is one who is after my dowry."

Mr. McDonald threw up his hands. "I cannot win this debate. Tony simply wanted to know why you would keep it a secret from the family."

"It's no one's business but my own. I really thought I could trust you."

"Juliet, it just slipped out. Really, he would have found out regardless."

"What do you mean?"

"When you finally marry, your funds become your husband's property. The man you marry will no doubt be crowing with joy."

Juliet had to acknowledge that fact. What did Tony want, then? "Was he angry?"

"No. Not even surprised. He knows you too well."

Tony paced the library, waiting for Juliet. He wasn't sure what he was going to say to her. Maybe ask why she kept her talent a secret. It wasn't just the money. He was fascinated by her ability to amass a small fortune just by reading his brother's journals. He read them religiously, but nothing similar had ever occurred to him.

Along with the twinge of guilt he felt, he didn't like the feeling of Jules keeping secrets from him.

For some reason, seeing her again here, in her natural environment, forced him to see Juliet Townsend in a new light. They'd been friends for years, but now he wanted more. He wasn't sure what *more* was, but he wanted to pursue it.

"Tony?" Juliet closed the library door behind her. "You wished to see me?"

"Why didn't you tell me you had amassed a fortune?"

"Excuse me? I hardly see how it affects you."

Her hair glowed dark red in the bit of light provided by the fire. Her skin was pale. She was so pretty. She pushed her spectacles back up her nose nervously. Tony forced himself to focus.

"Where did you learn to invest?"

"From books and journals, mostly. The library has a wealth of information."

"Does Bartleby know?"

"No."

"There has to be something else, then, that is causing Bartleby's interest in you." He knew it was the wrong thing to say the instant the words escaped his lips.

Juliet remained perfectly still, and she was never still. "No. I understand. You mean the only reason any man would be interested in marrying me is because of my fortune. Honestly, Tony, the amount is a pittance." Her voice was calm but her eyes stormy.

"You are twisting my words."

"No, I completely understand your meaning. Thank you for being honest with me. Now, if you will excuse me, I'll return to the parlor."

"Jules, stop. I'm an idiot. I'm sorry."

"If men are only interested in me for my supposed fortune, then why are *you* so suddenly interested in me?"

Tony took a step back. Nothing he could say would be right, and he couldn't tell her the truth because he didn't know what that was. He only knew he was drawn to her in a way he'd never been drawn to another woman.

So for a moment he said nothing and simply watched the pain chase across her pale features.

"Jules, please." He grabbed her arm and she winced. He released her immediately. "I didn't mean to hurt you."

She grimaced and rubbed her arm. "It wasn't you."

"Let me see your arms."

"That is highly improper." Juliet backed away from him.

"Now," he demanded. He reached for her and pushed her shawl from her arm. Deep bruises encircled her arm. "Is the other like this?"

She nodded.

"Mr. Bartleby must have been severely disappointed with your answer to his proposal to hurt you this way."

Juliet removed his hand and pulled the sleeve of her dress back down.

"Does he know about your dowry?" asked Tony.

"Probably. I don't understand why he was so angry."

"I've visited the tenants and they all say the same thing about Bartleby. They think he's demanding higher rents and pocketing the extra."

"Penelope was right, then." Juliet pushed her spectacles from where they'd slipped down her nose.

"What did she find out?"

"She heard her father arguing with Mr. Bartleby about raising the rent. She confronted Bartleby because she was worried about her father. He was still healing from the accident. Bartleby attacked her."

"Did he rape her?"

"No. Aaron came and pulled Bartleby off her. She is terrified of him."

"You are trying to protect her. He could hurt you too."

Juliet shot him a hard look. "He wouldn't dare."

"Desperate men do desperate things, and he has already hurt you twice. Next time, it could be much worse."

"None of this makes any sense. Why would he do this? He is ill suited to be a steward. He considers the work beneath him. He considers all of us beneath him."

"You need to tell Nathaniel about this, Jules. He needs to know what Bartleby did to you."

She shook her head. "I can handle Bartleby."

Sharp anger speared through him. "No!"

"If I tell Nathaniel, he'll keep me here at the house. I can't abandon Penelope. I won't abandon her." Her voice held a note of desperation.

"Better that you are safe." He pulled her into his arms. "The man knows your habits. He knows where you walk, what days you go calling. He'll be waiting for another chance. If he compromises you, you'll have no choice but to marry him. Have you thought about that?"

Juliet shuddered in his arms.

He tipped her face up to his. "I will protect you."

She leaned her body against his for one glorious second and then stiffened. She pushed out of his arms. "Please, you must stop."

He wanted her back in his arms. He wanted her by his side. Safe.

But there was a quiver in her voice that held him back. He frowned. "You aren't afraid of me, are you?"

She shook her head but pulled a nearby chair between them like a shield. "I'm grateful you've taken an interest in the plight of the Williams family. I truly am."

"But?"

"You shouldn't toy with me like you'd tease a cat with string."

"I'm not toying with your affections."

Her smile was sad. "Aren't you? Spending this much time alone with me is going to cause talk. It probably already has. "

"I didn't think you cared about the talk."

"It's one thing when I act like a hoyden in company. It's another when I'm seen in the company of a gentleman unaccompanied. If the talk gets out, we'll be forced to marry. You don't want that." She walked to the door.

"How do you know what I want?" Tony growled. Everyone seemed to claim to know what he wanted but him.

"I don't want it either."

Juliet's words were like a dull knife in Tony's gut. Did she mean it? Could she mean it? "Jules—"

"Good night, Tony."

The door closed with a finality that echoed through his mind. Tony stood there, numb, as her words beat through his brain like a drum.

He stumbled over to the table and poured a brandy, then tossed it back, slamming the glass on the tabletop.

Tony hadn't realized how much he cared until just now. He'd change her mind. He'd find a way. He'd show her that he was honorable, worthy.

He closed his eyes and tried to fight against the pain in his chest. He wasn't honorable yet, but he'd find a way to be what she needed.

Chapter Eight

Juliet pulled weeds from the ground and watched as Tony and Aaron Williams worked with the sheep. The sun was hot today. Tony had removed both his coat and his waistcoat. His linen shirt clung to his sweaty skin.

"Miss Townsend, you're pulling out the vegetables, not the weeds. Pay attention," Penelope said with a laugh. "He's going to see you staring at him."

Juliet turned back to the garden and replanted the seedling she'd just yanked out. She needed to tell someone. She glanced back at the men. "The truth is that I think I care for him a great deal."

"That's wonderful, Juliet. Mr. Matthews is a good man." Penelope grinned. "And he's very handsome."

"He's a rake and a gambler."

Penelope wiggled her brows. "Yes, please!"

Juliet laughed. She glanced back at Tony for a long moment, watching the way his muscles moved under the damp linen of his shirt. He bent over and his buckskins tightened over his hips. *Oh, dear God!* Her mouth suddenly went dry.

"He does look well in those buckskins," Penelope whispered.

Indeed he did. Juliet turned back quickly as Tony turned around. Penelope waved.

"What are you doing?" Juliet whispered frantically.

"The man cannot stop looking at you," Penelope said. "Aaron says that Mr. Matthews glares at him every time he brings up how good you look in your breeches."

"I am tossing those in the rubbish bin."

"I wouldn't if I were you. Mr. Matthews might like them as well.

He is also very protective of you. He chastised Aaron for ogling you so much."

"If he's protective, it's because of Bartleby. He proposed yesterday. I refused him."

"How did Mr. Bartleby take it?" There was fear in Penelope's voice.

"I have bruises on my arms where he grabbed me. I think he took pleasure in causing me pain." Juliet pulled with both of her hands on a particularly stubborn weed.

"Miss Townsend, you should have told your brother-in-law. He would put a stop to it."

"If I did that, we would never get the chance to figure out what Bartleby is up to. Have you heard anything else from the other tenants?"

"Louisa told me that he tried to coerce her, the same as me. Her betrothed just happened to come by and put a stop to it."

"Are they afraid of retribution?" There had already been one family who'd been evicted because they had crossed the man. Juliet had personal experience with the viciousness of Mr. Bartleby.

"Louisa's betrothed isn't from this area," Penelope said. "Part of me wants us to leave this place. Take our chances in Lancaster. Aaron and I can get factory work. Papa can have another surgeon look at his leg."

Juliet grasped Penelope's hand. "Your family belongs here—as they've always been."

"If Papa had the chance to see a surgeon from Lancaster, perhaps he'd improve. There would be more opportunity for me to marry. As it is now, I'm a burden to my parents. Were I to marry, it would be easier for them."

"No one here has captured your eye?"

"No one suitable." Penelope looked down at the row of vegetables. "It's past time I was married with a family of my own."

Juliet said nothing. What could she say? Penelope was right. Even if she could live off her dowry, Juliet also had no choice but to marry. What else was there for women but to become the property of men? "It's not fair."

"It never is, as Mother is always telling me." Penelope looked at Tony and smiled. "You won't have that problem, Miss Townsend. I suspect you'll have a proposal from Mr. Matthews before the month is out."

"You are wrong, completely wrong. Mr. Matthews is nothing more than a friend. He's just having a bit of fun, that's all."

Penelope leaned close. "He does not act like a man who is just having fun."

Juliet refused to get her hopes up. "What do you mean?"

"He is a gentleman. He wouldn't toy with you. Besides, the man can't take his eyes off you."

Juliet sifted her fingers through the loose soil. "You can't breathe a word of this to anyone."

Penelope crossed her heart. "It goes to the grave."

"He kissed me." Juliet kept her voice low. "He's always trying to kiss me."

Penelope grinned. "He's deliciously handsome."

Juliet looked up at her. "He has a reputation in London. He plays fast and loose at the gaming tables. What if he's like my brother?"

Penelope glanced back at the men. "I don't know that many gamblers would actually spend their spare time working on another man's property, especially a mere farmer's. Your Mr. Matthews seems to enjoy the work."

Juliet snuck a look at Tony through her lashes. He smiled and waved. She automatically waved back. Could it be? Could he have real feelings for her?

Her heart jumped a beat. She couldn't let herself go down that path without him initiating it. But hadn't he already? Didn't kissing her mean he cared? Or was it just something rakes did—go around kissing bookish women?

"My father says that a man's actions count more than words. Mr. Matthews likes you. A great deal."

Aaron Williams bounded toward them with a grin on his face. "Come quickly, Miss Townsend! The first of the ewes is starting to deliver her lamb."

Juliet smiled. "I've never seen anything being born before."

"You can't miss this. The lambs are so sweet," said Penelope.

Juliet removed her gloves and tossed them in the basket. She dusted the dirt from her old dress as she followed Penelope to the barn.

She'd never spent this much time on a farm before. She loved it all: the smell of the earth, the sun, the animals. It was so much simpler than her life. "Maybe I should marry a farmer," she said.

"It's beneath you and you know it," Penelope said. "Don't let all this bucolic scenery tease you. It's hard work."

"Still, it's honest." Juliet tucked a stray strand of hair behind her ear. It was more honest than what she had gone through in London. Pretending interest in the inane conversations on the dance floor. And God forbid a woman be learned at something other than needlework and music.

They entered the gloom of the barn. Juliet stopped and let her eyes adjust to the light. Penelope and Aaron leaned on the stall railing.

"Jules, come look," Tony said in a soft voice.

Her heart started its thudding again. She fought to control her emotions.

He took her hand as she drew closer. "Stand right here. She's about to give birth."

Tony moved Juliet to stand in front of him, his hands resting on her shoulders. She could feel his overheated skin, feel his breath as it teased the back of her neck.

"When is it going to happen?" She really wasn't sure how any of this worked.

"Just watch. She's in labor now. See—her head is up and she's lying down." His voice was soft and close to her ear.

The ewe strained and a bubble of fluid appeared. It burst, and Juliet watched as the first lamb was expelled. It was tiny and covered in a film. The ewe bent to clean her baby.

It was amazing.

"Is she done?" asked Juliet, in awe.

"We'll have to wait and see. Many have two lambs," said Tony.

Juliet fought to keep her breathing normal and forced herself to stare at the ewe as she gave birth to another lamb. Tony's body was so near that she could feel his warmth.

The ewe was cleaning the other lamb. Both soon tried to stand on wobbly legs, falling down a great deal.

"We'd better get you back to the Lodge," Tony said softly.

She turned to face him. His hair was mussed and his shirt was open at the throat, revealing his chest. He had a smudge on his cheek.

She removed it with her thumb, feeling the roughness of his jaw. "Thank you."

"I thought you might like it," he said.

Juliet couldn't make herself move away. Dust motes floated around them in the dim light of the barn.

"Mr. Matthews, my father would like to speak with you before you leave," Penelope said from the barn door.

"Yes, of course." Tony stepped away from Juliet. "Give me a few minutes and we'll go."

Juliet nodded. She watched him go before turning back to the lambs. *God, I am so stupid.* She couldn't stop herself from touching him, no matter how badly he could hurt her.

"I told you," Penelope said softly, coming up beside her. "A man only looks at a woman like that when he loves her a great deal."

"In London, men have perfected that look to make a woman feel a certain way. It means nothing." Juliet sighed. "I apologize for my tone. He has me so confused."

"You need to just let things happen," Penelope said. "Mama says that's the only way love can occur."

"Your mother is a wise woman."

"She is that," Penelope said. "Isn't this the most amazing thing?"

Juliet glanced back at the two nursing lambs. "Do you name them?"

"Not usually. Papa doesn't think naming them is appropriate. It makes it difficult when we have to butcher them."

Juliet nodded. "It would be hard to kill a pet." Juliet took in the sight of the barn. "Every time I visit, I find another reason to long for a life like this."

"Miss Matthews, you have balls, gentlemen callers, parties, dinners, trips to London. I would love that." Penelope laughed. "We are a pair, both of us wanting what the other has."

Juliet said nothing. There were moments such as today, when she was watching Tony, that she wished things were different, simpler, that she could simply allow herself to love him. Not worry he would leave her again for London, for gambling. And there were moments when she sensed Tony felt the same.

Tony caught Miss Williams's knowing look as he brushed past her on his way to visit with her father.

Juliet had asked that he stop teasing her. This wasn't teasing. If he listened to his little-used heart, this was the opposite of teasing. His feelings were serious. The leg-shackling, set-up-home kind of serious.

Tony collected his waistcoat and jacket and slipped them on before stepping into the house to talk with Mr. Williams.

"Mr. Matthews, he's in his sitting room," Mrs. Williams said softly. "It's not been a good day, sir. He's been in a great deal of pain."

"I won't keep him long, ma'am."

"Shall I bring tea?"

"No. Thank you, ma'am," Tony said. He followed Mrs. Williams to the sitting room at the back of the house. The room was small and cozy with old, comfortable furniture. Mr. Williams sat in a chair staring out at the back garden.

Tony cleared his throat. "You asked to see me, sir?"

"Please sit down, sir." Mr. Williams motioned to a chair by the window, across from him.

Tony sat and waited for the man to speak. Pain had etched new lines in his face.

Mr. Williams got directly to the point. "My son tells me that you've been visiting the other tenants."

"Yes." While the other tenants had confirmed what Mr. Williams had said about Bartleby, few were ready to confront him to make things right. "They aren't ready to commit to confronting Mr. Bartleby."

Mr. Williams sighed heavily. His shoulders slumped. "I was afraid of that. Did you have any luck finding out who the new owner is?"

The business of lying was getting old. "Not yet."

"I hope he's more interested in the tenants than Mr. Chelsworth. This land could be much more productive and provide a good living with the right management."

"Has Mr. Bartleby called lately?" Tony needed to change the subject before he gave anything away.

"No." Mr. Williams leaned back in his chair. "Do I have you to thank for that?"

"Unfortunately, no."

Mr. Williams gave him a direct look. "Be careful with him. He could be very dangerous."

Given the bruises on Juliet's arms, Tony believed it.

"He is aware that you're asking lots of questions. He knows that you're talking to the tenants," Mr. Williams said. "I would be careful if I were you."

Tony stood. "Thank you, sir. I appreciate it."

"Thank you for the help, Mr. Matthews," Mr. Williams said.

Tony walked out into the sun. Mr. Williams was correct. The estate could provide a good living with proper management. The tenants were fair, hardworking, and aware of the agricultural advances being made. Crop rotations were done on a regular schedule. The land was left fallow when it needed to be. Several of the farms were already sheep farming with great success. Nothing seemed out of order.

Tony walked up to Juliet and Miss Williams. They were giggling but quickly broke it off before he got close enough to hear their conversation. Given the color in Juliet's cheeks, they were talking about him. Good—he knew Penelope Williams was on his side.

"Ready to leave?" he asked.

Juliet nodded. She clasped Miss Williams's hands. Penelope whispered something to her and she shook her head emphatically.

Tony assisted Juliet into the cart and then joined her, taking the reins from Aaron.

"Will you be back tomorrow, sir?" Aaron asked.

"No. It might be several days. Send me a note if anything happens or if you hear from Bartleby."

"Yes, sir."

Tony waited until they were out of earshot before saying, "That boy likes you."

"I suppose." Juliet was sitting perfectly straight, about as far from him as she could get without falling out of the cart.

"You might want to move a bit closer. If we hit a bump, you'd bounce right out."

"I'm fine."

God, he hated the word *fine*. Any time a woman used it, it never boded well. He couldn't stop himself from asking, "Are you certain?"

Juliet focused on the row of trees framing the overgrown lane. She was keeping her side of the bargain by not encouraging his attentions.

"What were you and Miss Williams discussing?"

"Nothing of consequence."

Tony almost groaned aloud. She was driving him crazy. He wasn't going to spend time guessing what was wrong. He'd just get to the point. "What have I done now?"

She turned to him. "We need to get home, Tony."

"Not until you tell me what's wrong."

"You've done nothing. May we go now?"

He hung his head. Juliet Townsend was going to drive him completely insane. "Is this about what almost happened in the barn?"

He watched the color flame in her cheeks.

"What do you mean?" Her voice was cold. "Nothing happened in the barn."

He moved closer to her. "You wanted me to kiss you."

"I did not."

Tony chuckled. "You think I cannot tell? Your breathing became erratic. Your pulse was racing. You kept licking your lips."

"I do not wish to discuss it."

He forced her head to face him. He wanted to see her eyes. "Juliet, my intentions are honorable."

She pulled in a breath and held it. He watched her for any reaction. She wouldn't look at him. "Did you hear what I said?"

She let out the breath she was holding. "Your voice was quite clear."

"And?" He winced at the impatience in his tone. *Damn it.* He was putting his heart out there and she wasn't reacting the way he thought she should. She should be happy—shouldn't she?

Juliet turned her head and met his gaze. "I'm confused. Why me? Why now?"

What the hell was she talking about? "I don't understand."

"Honestly, Tony. I am bookish. I wear spectacles. I do not dance well. I cannot engage in small talk. I am too thin. Why would you select me, especially when you could have Sophia?"

He looked down at his hands again. He could feel the trap closing around him. What was it about women that they twisted everything into an attempt to get compliments? "Juliet, you know that Sophia and I would never suit."

She glared at him. "I do not understand you. Of all the words I said, you focused on Sophia." She faced forward, her lips tightening. "I would like to go home."

"As you wish." Women were so strange. How was a simple man supposed to understand how their minds worked?

He went back over what she had said. *Bookish.* Yes, he got that, but he didn't mind. Juliet had the capability to learn anything by reading. It was a skill he wished he had. She didn't dance well, but he hated dancing, so that wasn't a problem. He hated small talk.

Too thin? Her old faded dress did little to emphasize her slight curves, but he remembered how she looked his first day back in Beetham. The current fashion might not play to her curves, but she had them. To him she was fine-boned, with curves in the right places. "Believe me when I say this: there is nothing wrong with your looks. I like your looks."

Juliet gaped at him.

"That's what you wanted to hear, yes?"

"Tony, you cannot arrive home and start acting like some lovesick fool within a few days of being here. It doesn't make sense."

"What about my being attracted to you doesn't make sense, Jules?"

"Why now?" she cried. "You barely paid attention to me in London."

He frowned at her. "I've always liked you, Jules."

"As a sister."

"Never as a sister. Ever. Let us look at the evidence. While in Town, I was at every single ball you attended. I danced one dance with you. I may have danced once or twice with Sophia, but I only waltzed with you."

"Those were pity dances," she sputtered. "You felt sorry for me for being stuck on the wallflower wall."

"I don't pity dance," Tony growled. "I danced with you because I wanted to."

The look on Juliet's face would have been comical if Tony wasn't so twisted over his feelings for her.

"You could have any woman you want," she whispered. Clearly she wasn't aware of her own appeal. "Rumors of your mistresses are legendary."

Tony wondered how she'd react to the truth. His way of handling mistresses was different. They were paid for being on his arm and for their silence. He'd never made love with any of them. They were there to support the impression he wanted London to have of him.

At some point he was going to have to tell Juliet it was all pretense. All of it. "I'm no legend."

"Is your current mistress awaiting your return to London?"

"We parted ways before I left for Beetham."

"You're still a rake and a gambler," she muttered.

"Only in London."

"I don't understand."

Tony stopped the cart on the road again. He stared at the reins in his hands, searching for the right words. Words that would tell her the truth without telling her all of it. "What I am about to tell you cannot be repeated."

"I would never."

"My reputation in Town is a lie. I made it up to keep up with Society and make certain I could sit at the table with the wealthy men we wanted to invest in our ventures." He glanced over at Juliet, who gaped at him.

"Mistresses too?"

He cleared his throat. "I paid them to be my mistresses in name only. I never. I haven't—" He couldn't finish his sentence. It was a very uncomfortable conversation to have with a lady.

Juliet's expression was one of shock. "You mean you're a . . . a virgin?"

He nodded.

She laughed.

"It's not funny," he growled.

"Yes, it is." She giggled. "That was the last thing I expected you to tell me, Tony."

She held her stomach while she laughed some more. "Deuces, Juliet, what did you think I was going to tell you?"

"I don't know. Maybe that you'd gambled away your income. Or ruined some other gentleman at the gaming hells. Not that I think you would. You have too much honor for that." She patted his hand.

Juliet was too close to the truth to suit him. She thought he was honorable. The weight of his lies bore down on him. Tony was beginning to regret ever opening his mouth and spilling part of his secret.

"Besides, didn't my father do that to your father?"

The sick feeling intensified. There was nothing he could say that wouldn't make it worse. She didn't care if he was a fake rake, but she would care that he'd ruined a man and took his estate. He started the cart toward the Lodge.

Only he would fall for the one woman who didn't care if he had mistresses but cared that he was a gambler. He could see her point, given what her brother had put her family through.

He couldn't disclose the truth now. She'd hate him, and Tony wasn't convinced he could bear it if she hated him.

Chapter Nine

The next morning, Juliet was still reeling from Tony's declarations. His intentions were honorable. Would he propose? And if he did, what would she say? His revelations did not necessarily mean he was in love with her. Could she marry him without a declaration of love?

Then there was his admission of never having been with a woman. Juliet understood that women had to prize their virginity but for a man to do so was unheard of. Why had he waited?

Juliet crept down the stairs. She intended to go out the kitchen door in order to avoid Anne. If she could get to the kitchen, she stood a chance of escaping the day's callers. She hated sitting there listening to the Beetham gossip. They had to be constantly inventing stories. There just wasn't that much happening in the village to talk about.

"Not so fast, Juliet," Anne said from the drawing room doorway. "You're not getting out of calls today. The vicar's wife, Mrs. Dellwood, is coming."

"Anne, please, not Mrs. Dullwood."

A smile twitched on Anne's lips. "It's Dellwood."

"She is the worst gossip, Anne." The woman had a high-pitched voice to go with her mousy appearance.

"I expect you to be in the drawing room with a smile on your face when she calls," Anne said. "Why are you always calling at the Williams farm? I'm beginning to think something inappropriate is occurring."

"If *inappropriate* means being covered in dirt—she's usually caked in it when she sneaks back in with Tony," Sophia said, coming down the stairs behind Juliet. "I'm glad you caught her before she left."

"Is this true, Juliet? You're sneaking out with Tony?" Anne asked with a frown.

"We aren't sneaking," Juliet defended. *Sneaking* made it sound as if they were up to something nefarious. "He's helping the Williamses with their farm. You know Mr. Williams had that horrible accident."

"I didn't know Tony was so interested in the neighbors."

"You can't possibly believe her story, can you?" said Sophia.

"What do you think they are doing?" Anne asked.

Juliet glared at Sophia. If she told Anne about the book, all bets were off; Ian McDonald would be spending every waking moment in Sophia's presence. Juliet would lock the two of them in a closet just to make sure of it.

"Nothing of importance," Sophia said.

"I wish you'd wear the nice dresses we purchased for you in Town," Anne said to Juliet.

She looked down at her old dress. "There's nothing wrong with this."

"Only if you were going back in time," Sophia said. "That dress is so old-fashioned."

Juliet hated the puffed sleeves of the new gowns she'd been stuck with for the Season in London. "I'll change, but I must first let Tony know I won't be accompanying him today."

"Please be quick about it," Anne said.

Juliet didn't waste a moment. She could hear Anne's voice echoing "Don't run!" through the hallway. The sun was already hot. It was a beautiful day, too beautiful to have to sit inside with the village gossip. She shaded her eyes from the sun and located Tony, already waiting by the cart.

He looked very handsome this morning, dressed less formally than if he were staying at home. His collar was open at the neck. His blond hair was tousled by the soft breeze.

"You're late," he said with a smile as she approached.

"Unfortunately, I can't go with you today. I'm stuck at home with Anne and Sophia. The vicar's wife is calling."

"Sounds like fun," he said with a chuckle. "We were going to start riding lessons."

The last thing she wanted to do was spend time with horses. She didn't like them and they didn't like her. It was better if they avoided one another. "I had hoped you would forget about that."

"No chance of that; a deal is a deal." His eyes danced with mischief.

"I've tried before and it's never ended well for me or the horse."

"I promise not to let anything happen to you—or the horse."

"I bet you end up saving the horse." Juliet looked back at the house. Sophia was staring at her from the window. "How long will you be gone?"

"Most of the day, unless you need me to come back early so we can start your riding lessons. I wouldn't mind a stroll to the Fairy Steps either."

Her gaze met his earnest one. "Gracious, you were serious about your intentions!"

"Why would I not be in earnest?" She winced as a hurt look chased across his face. "This is me, Juliet. We are friends; family, even." He stepped forward, took her hand, and pressed his lips against it. "I am serious, Juliet."

Could his feelings change so quickly? She would not let herself believe it. She hesitated, uncertain of what to say.

"When I come back from the Williamses, will you walk with me?" he persisted.

"I would like that."

He grinned that boyish grin of his. "I won't deny that I might steal a kiss or two, if we happen to be alone."

She smiled. She liked kissing him. "I'd be happy to walk with you later."

"Sophia is watching us. You're going to be bombarded with questions when you get back inside."

"I will deal with Sophia."

"Too bad she's watching or I'd kiss you right now."

Juliet's pulse quickened. "Shall I meet you later at the Fairy Steps?"

"I'll be there." He kissed her hand once more before departing.

Juliet walked back inside on a cloud. She couldn't hide her smile.

"What is between you and Tony?" Sophia demanded. "I saw him kiss your hand, touch your face. It's as if he's courting you."

"Maybe he is," Juliet said without thinking. *Oh, dear God, did she just admit that Tony was courting her to her mouthy sister?*

"What a good joke. Has he told you of his mistresses? Or his bad habit of spending too much time in the gaming hells?"

Juliet didn't want to acknowledge Sophia's questions. "Everyone wants to settle down sooner or later, Sophia. Perhaps he's finally ready."

"But with you?"

"Why not me?"

"You're bookish. You wear spectacles and old clothes. He's handsome." Sophia looked at her as if she smelled bad.

At least Sophia hadn't said outright that she was ugly. "What is your point?"

"He can have any woman in Town."

"I doubt that. He doesn't have a title or a great fortune."

"How am I supposed to avoid Ian McDonald if you're spending all your time with Tony?"

Juliet pitied Ian. He was a nice man with feelings for the wrong woman. "I think you should give Mr. McDonald a chance."

"Give who a chance?" Anne said, coming into the room.

"Mr. McDonald fancies Sophia," Juliet said with a grin. "I think he's rather nice."

"He is nice," said Anne, "but you can put your mind at ease, Sophia. Mr. McDonald left for Lancaster this morning."

"Mrs. Dellwood, ma'am," announced a footman as mousy Mrs. Dellwood breezed into the room. She wore a pelisse of puffed sleeves and far too many feathers in her hat.

"My dear Mrs. Matthews, and all you young ladies, wait until you hear my news," the vicar's wife said breathlessly.

"Mrs. Dellwood, it's delightful to see you. How is Mr. Dellwood?" Anne said, taking a seat.

Juliet sat where she could see out the window so that she would know when Tony came home. Her hope of keeping her heart from being attached to him was gone. Instead, she was surrendering to the feelings he stirred in her heart.

"Mr. Dellwood is fine," said Mrs. Dellwood. "He's off visiting the Williams farm today. Mr. Williams had that horrible accident, you know." Mrs. Dellwood smiled at Juliet. "Mrs. Williams has told me of your kindness to the family, Miss Juliet."

Juliet barely managed to squeeze in a quick thank-you before Mrs.

Dellwood spoke again. "You must be careful, though, dear, that people don't get the wrong impression from your connection to a farmer."

Juliet stared at the woman as if she'd grown two heads. What could she mean? "The Williamses are a very respectable family."

"For farmers," Mrs. Dellwood said. "The daughter of a baronet cannot be too careful."

"I've been telling Juliet just that, Mrs. Dellwood," Sophia said slyly. "We must be careful."

"Miss Townsend, you are so right," agreed Mrs. Dellwood. "But it isn't this that brings me to call today. I've news from Town."

"What news?" Anne inquired.

"It concerns Mr. Anthony Matthews and Mr. George Chelsworth."

"Mr. Chelsworth?" Juliet asked. The mysterious missing owner of Horneswood? What could connect him to Tony?

"Indeed. It is bad," Mrs. Dellwood said. "Rumors are flying through London that Chelsworth lost Horneswood to Mr. Anthony Matthews in a game of cards. Shameless."

Anger sparked inside Juliet. How dare this lady say such awful things? She moved to speak but stopped when Anne shot her a look. Juliet forced herself to sit and wait, tapping her foot impatiently.

Anne cleared her throat before speaking. "My husband would have heard this news from his brother if it were true."

"It's positively scandalous," Mrs. Dellwood said. "To lose an estate in a card game! Is this why Mr. Matthews is in Beetham? To claim his winnings?"

Juliet dug her nails into her palms. It couldn't be true. She knew men could be sucked so deeply into gambling that they lost everything. Tony's own father had lost everything to her own father years ago, leaving the Matthews family destitute. Surely Tony would never do the same to another man.

He was innocent; Juliet was certain of it.

Anne stood. Juliet followed, along with Sophia. "Mrs. Dellwood, I would advise you not to spread a story so outrageous about a member of this family. I appreciate your bringing it to my attention, but I can guarantee you that this is a complete falsehood."

"I really thought you should know," Mrs. Dellwood stuttered.

"Thank you," Anne said. "I will consult my husband about the matter."

Juliet waited until Mrs. Dellwood had left the house before she turned to Anne. "There's no truth in what she said! Tony wouldn't do that."

"I know it seems completely out of character, but we both know how men can carry things too far. I'll speak to Nathaniel," said Anne.

Juliet needed to warn Tony. He'd put an end to the rumors immediately.

The stone was cold beneath Tony as he sat and stared out at the village over the trees. A light breeze played along the stones and whistled down the steps.

The truth was catching up with him. He could feel it, just as he could tell when he had a losing hand.

"There you are," Juliet said, her chest heaving, as if she'd run the whole way.

Tony jumped to his feet and went to her. "Jules, what's wrong?"

She bent over, resting her hands on her knees, trying to calm her breathing. "Have . . . to . . . tell . . . you."

Good God, what could it be? He took her arm and led her to the edge of the stone steps. "Rest, please."

She sat silent for a long moment. She was rarely quiet like this. Tony watched her, feeling the worry rise up like a lump in his throat. His luck had run out. He could tell. Hell, Chelsworth was back in Beetham. There was no telling when the news would get out. "Are you able to talk now?"

"Yes." She looked up at him. "I'm sorry. I was so furious. She had no right to say what she said. I mean, what proof could she have?"

"What are you talking about?"

"Mrs. Dellwood, the vicar's wife, has just returned from London overflowing with *news* from Town." Juliet stood and started pacing. "I cannot believe she came to our house to repeat idle gossip. How dare she spread such awful lies?"

Tony went still. It had happened. The news had finally reached Beetham. "What did she say?" he forced himself to ask.

"She said you won Horneswood from Chelsworth, in a card game! Doesn't she know your family history?"

Tony looked down at the ground, listening to her defense of him. He didn't deserve her. He really didn't. She assumed he was honorable. It made him want to *be* honorable, to become the man Juliet saw when she looked at him.

That thought alone made it difficult to lie to her, but even more difficult to tell her the truth. If he lied, he'd lose her eventually. If he were honest, he'd lose her now. Either way, the truth was going to rip Juliet out of his hands and tear away his happiness.

"Who was there? In the room?" His voice sounded faraway, even to his own ears.

"Tony, are you all right?"

He nodded.

"Anne, Sophia, and I were there for Mrs. Dellwood's call. Anne is going to talk to Nathaniel about it," Juliet said.

Tony sighed heavily. It was worse than he'd thought. Nathaniel would confront him. This just got worse and worse. Damn; if he'd only had a chance to talk to Chelsworth—but Bartleby's intervention had made that all but impossible.

Juliet squeezed his hand. "I knew you could never do what she accused you of."

Juliet's faith in him squeezed his heart. He pulled her close. His mouth took hers as if she offered the last sip of available water. His last hope.

He needed her to believe in him, in the person she was so convinced he was. His hands moved over her back, pressing her into him, wanting to imprint her body against his.

Juliet moaned into his mouth as she wrapped her arms around his neck and pressed herself even closer.

Her scent, of lemon and flowers, filled his head. She tasted of vanilla and tea. "Thank you for believing in me."

"I knew you couldn't have done it." She hugged him, tucking her head under his chin. Even her hair smelled sweet.

Tony winced, knowing he couldn't tell her, not now. Not when he'd just found her again. He had to try to fix things first.

"You didn't do it, did you, Tony?"

To keep from answering her, he kissed her again, this time taking it deeper, letting some of the desperation he was feeling feed into the kiss.

Juliet responded, clutching his coat in her hands.

Her mouth, hot and moist against his, caused his heart to beat faster. He wanted her, wanted to be inside her, to feel her wrap around him. He moved his hands up to cup her small breasts.

"Well, isn't this nice?"

Simon Bartleby sat on a horse at the foot of the steps. Juliet gasped and tried to move away from Tony, but he wouldn't release her. Bartleby would need to get used to seeing Juliet with him.

"If I'd have known you preferred less gentlemanlike behavior, Miss Juliet, I would have been happy to accommodate you," Bartleby sneered.

"Just follow my lead," Tony whispered to Juliet. "Mr. Bartleby, you are the first to know. Miss Juliet has done me the very great honor of agreeing to become my wife."

Juliet began to speak, but Tony touched a finger to her mouth to silence her. He kissed her firmly on the lips.

"Rather sudden, isn't it?" Bartleby said suspiciously.

"We've known each other for years, Mr. Bartleby," Juliet said.

Despite Juliet's composed tone, Tony saw the anger burning in her eyes. Doubt curled through his belly. He had assumed by the way she'd responded to him that she felt something genuine for him. It had never occurred to him that he might be the only one with deeper feelings.

"Congratulations to you both," Bartleby said curtly, then tipped his hat and rode off into the woods.

Juliet waited until the man was out of sight. Then she punched Tony squarely in the chest. "What were you thinking?"

"What did you want me to do? I had my hands all over you!"

"But an engagement? It will be all over the village by tomorrow."

"We'll tell the family tonight at dinner. No one is going to be surprised. We've been spending a great deal of time together." He pulled her back into his arms. "Would it be so bad? Marriage to me?"

She played with the buttons on his waistcoat. "You live in London and I hate London."

Here was the opening he was waiting for, but thanks to the vicar's gossip of a wife, he couldn't take it. "What if I were to get a house here?"

She looked up at him with wide, hopeful eyes. "You'd do that?"

"I'm tired of Town. I came home to look for a place of my own. I want some of the happiness my brother has with Anne." Tony cradled her face in his hands. "Say yes. Please."

There were still questions in her eyes. Questions he thought she might be afraid to ask. Such as whether he loved her. He could. He was almost certain he was close to being in love with her. He just wasn't ready to tell her yet.

He had no idea what she felt, other than passion.

Tony kissed her deeply, his tongue tangling with hers, his hands running over her body. "Be my wife, Jules," he whispered against her mouth before kissing her again.

He was like a starving man where she was concerned. "If we are engaged, we can do the things pictured in your naughty books." He trailed his lips down the length of her neck, breathing her in.

Juliet pushed him back and stared at him in shock. "Is that all you're thinking about?"

"You started it when you tried to hide them in my room." Tony raised his eyebrow as a not-so-delicate curse slipped past Juliet's lips.

"Sophia threatened to tell Anne about the books!"

"Once we're engaged it will not matter." Tony traced a finger along the edge of her dress. She trembled beneath his hand.

"Yes, I'll marry you," she said. "But do not blame me if you come to regret it."

"This must be the oddest engagement ever," Tony said.

"Can you imagine what the marriage will be like?"

Chapter Ten

A s they walked back to the Lodge, Juliet's thoughts churned in her head like a whirlpool.

Tony had proposed to protect her reputation, but he'd seemed serious about it. He'd seduced her into a yes with his kisses and cajoling. He'd never denied anything about the gossip. He'd sidetracked her news with kisses, and very effectively too.

Oh, dear Lord. What had she done?

One kiss and she was a mindless puddle at his feet, incapable of stringing a sentence together. She wasn't sure she liked the fact that he could do that to her so easily.

Juliet had no doubt Tony cared for her. They'd been friends even before they'd become family. Surely that was enough with which to start a marriage.

But would marriage ruin their camaraderie? Would this passion they felt for each other ruin their friendship? Would they lose the ability to talk to each other and become like so many other couples she'd seen in Town?

Relationships like Anne and Nathaniel's were the exception rather than the rule.

Passion was a bright flame that dimmed over time. Wasn't that why men took mistresses—to experience the hot fire of passion before going home to a tepid wife and duty?

It would kill her to become just a duty to fulfill. She'd rather be a spinster.

Juliet's dashed curiosity was going to get her into deep trouble. The thought of being able to put her hands on Tony's body made her tingle in places she didn't know could tingle.

"You're quiet."

His voice was hesitant, but he still gripped her hand in his, as if he couldn't let her go. She looked at their joined hands. His swallowed her smaller one. He made her feel safe. He made her feel pretty. But was this enough to build a marriage on?

"I'm just thinking about how to tell the family."

And so the lies and half truths began. She closed her eyes for a few moments. How could they be husband and wife if they couldn't be honest with each other? "Tony, are you sure this is what you want? To marry me?" She forced the words out.

Tony looked down at her. "Are you changing your mind?"

His voice held a note of something she couldn't quite put her finger on. She wished she knew how he felt, but getting him to admit his feelings would mean she would have to admit her own. And she had no idea yet what her feelings even were.

Juliet liked Tony a great deal. She was probably well on her way to being in love with him, but if she admitted it now, Tony would have more power over her. Already she was lost the moment he touched her.

Juliet pulled her hand away from his. She couldn't think properly if he were touching her. "Tony, what if this is a mistake? I couldn't endure it if our friendship was hurt in any way."

He stared at her, searching for the right words. "Maybe being friends is what makes this such an easy decision. For me. I knew it was time to marry—"

"I don't want it to be something you feel you have to do because you're of a certain age." Her voice was harsh.

Tony winced. "You misunderstand. I only meant that I longed for what Nathaniel and Anne have. Perhaps it was our friendship that started me thinking about marriage. I always knew that I wanted to be a part of your family. I've always admired how close you are to your sisters. I've wanted to be a part of that closeness. Not even Nathaniel and Anne had this when they started."

"They loved each other."

"Who's to say that love won't grow the closer we become? Our beginning was different from theirs. We have a relationship already. In my mind, our engagement was inevitable. Look how well we have worked together at the Williams farm. Can you not imagine what it will be like when we have our own home?"

Inevitable. Tony thought their marriage inevitable. Juliet wanted so badly to have him admit his feelings for her, but she was terrified of the answer. It was too soon. "I suppose we should announce our engagement before dinner."

"That's as good a time as any. It will give the gossips something else to chat about."

She groaned. "Wait until Mrs. Dullwood hears this."

Tony laughed. "The vicar's wife?"

"Anne is always warning me not to give people nicknames. One of these days, I'm going to embarrass myself and call her by that name to her face."

"I'm sure she deserves it."

"But after the other rumor—"

Tony placed a finger gently on her lips. "Let's not bring up that unpleasantness. It will work itself out; trust me."

He wouldn't meet her eyes. A feeling that something wasn't quite right ran through her, but she nodded her head and let him pull her along toward the Lodge. "Mr. Bartleby wasn't very happy."

"He knows what he lost."

"You mean my dowry. I never thought the man had any real feelings for me."

"The man would have hurt you," he said tightly.

Pain lanced through her. Maybe being truthful was overrated. Still, she couldn't stop herself from asking, "So you proposed to protect me from him?"

"Yes . . . no, damn it. No." He struggled for words. "Remember the bruises on your arms? He is one of those men who takes pleasure in hurting women." He looked away from her. "I was going to talk to Nathaniel about it tonight. There was no way he would have allowed the match if he knew the kind of man Bartleby is."

"I had planned on mentioning it to Anne but hadn't found the right moment to do so."

"Now you won't have to worry about it. I won't allow the man anywhere near you. I'll tell Nathaniel when we return to the house," Tony continued. "The sooner we get the family on our side, the easier it will be to dispel any gossip."

"Heaven forbid that there be more gossip about us."

"If you don't want to marry me, just say so, Juliet." There was a tone in his voice that pulled at her, almost as if she had hurt him.

"I'm sorry, Tony. I just didn't think it would happen like this. Frankly, I didn't think I'd ever marry."

"Why would you think that?"

She laughed. "Outside of your attentions and those of Mr. Bartleby, there have been no other gentlemen interested in me, here or in Town. There certainly isn't a line of suitors waiting to call upon me."

"So your only concern is that you don't think you're worthy of my notice?" He chuckled. "Sweetheart, I've not been able to stay away since I arrived."

Juliet's heart skipped a beat.

"I attended those balls to play cards with investors. It was my job to keep them engaged and interested in investing in the business plans Nathaniel, Ian, and I came up with. The only joy I found at those events was my one waltz with you. Feeling you in my arms."

Juliet tripped over a tree root. She knew her mouth was hanging open at his confession.

"But I'm happy to show you how much I desire you. Only you, Jules."

Juliet's pulse raced. He wanted her. Too bad her clothing hid a multitude of inadequacies. He'd soon see for himself how truly unattractive she was, and she'd be left alone in a tight ball of pain.

Dinner had been torture, the announcement worse. Tony didn't know why everyone had been so surprised that he'd proposed to Jules. True, she was a great deal too good for him, but Anne was too good for Nathaniel. What was the difference?

All he knew was that this engagement was tenuous at best and he needed to make certain Juliet couldn't wiggle out of it once the truth was revealed. And it would be revealed sooner rather than later.

Tony's conversation with Nathaniel had been strained. Anne had informed Nathaniel of the gossip the vicar's wife had delivered. He had so many questions. Was Tony still gambling? Was it true?

The only thing that held Tony together through the entire conversation was the fact that Juliet had believed him. Her faith in him, though unwarranted, gave him hope that he could resolve the difficulty.

After enduring the lecture about the dangers of gambling, the announcement that he wanted to marry Juliet had been easy. He had been honest with Nathaniel about that. He was blunt about Bartleby and the bruises he'd left on her arms. Once that was said, Nathaniel's consent had been readily offered.

Tony now stood with Jules in the drawing room. She was quiet, stiff with nerves. Her sisters were firing questions at them both, but Juliet was only nodding in reply. He could feel her distancing herself from him. He did not like it.

Propriety would dictate that he wait until after the wedding to make Juliet his. It would be the honorable thing to do. He had waited this long—but how could he wait any longer?

Tony was tired of waiting. He wanted to taste every inch of her smooth skin. Show her how pretty she was, how desirable. He was ready to end this damned virginity business for both of them.

"I, for one, am happy to see you settle down, Tony," Lady Danford said. "I couldn't have picked a better lady for you to have by your side. I'm glad you were smart enough to snap her up."

"Thank you, Lady Danford," Jules said. Her voice was soft and tremulous. Very out of character.

"You two must have fallen in love during all those trips to the Williams farm," Sophia said.

"I'm happy for you," Ian McDonald said. "But I can't say I'm surprised."

Sophia looked a bit shocked. "Why do you say that?"

"Didn't you notice that while you ladies were in Town, the only time Tony would come to the balls was to dance with Miss Juliet? He would arrive, dance with his lady, and leave shortly after. I think there were wagers about it at White's."

Tony grimaced. Juliet was looking at him with those big dark eyes wide with hope. "It's true."

"I cannot say that it's much of a surprise to me either. Juliet was always watching for your attendance. She's held you in high regard for a long time," Anne said.

"Anne, please!" Juliet protested.

Tony watched as the color crept into Juliet's face. "High regard?" he teased.

"It wasn't as if it was a secret," Sophia said. "She followed us around like a puppy."

"I was there as chaperone," Juliet defended herself.

"You liked me even back then?" he asked.

"It was before I knew you well," Juliet muttered.

Tony glanced at Ian, who was, in turn, watching Sophia when she wasn't looking. The man was setting himself up for hurt. Sophia craved the attention that marrying into Society could give her.

Seeing Ian's lost cause gave Tony hope. He had found what he wanted. He'd found a woman who made him want to be a better man. He squeezed Juliet's hand.

She looked up at him and he smiled. She was truly the best thing to happen to him. Tonight he'd prove it to her.

"So, do you think Chelsworth lost the estate in a card game, Tony?" Nathaniel asked nonchalantly. Too nonchalantly.

Tony exchanged a glance with Ian and said, "It's possible. He's spent more time in Town than he has at his estate."

"You and Ian have been making the rounds to the tenants. What are they saying?"

"Most are barely scraping by," Tony said. "Bartleby is supposedly managing the estate, but he's running it into the ground."

"I've been looking into Mr. Bartleby's background. It seems he's been cast out of his own family for gambling and womanizing." Ian looked at Juliet. "He's ruined several young women on the way, and managed to avoid marrying them."

Juliet shivered. "He threatened Penelope Williams and others in the neighborhood."

"I'm just glad he didn't get his hands on you," Anne said. "I don't know why we didn't see this side of him."

"He's very smooth," Juliet said. "I didn't see it either until Penelope pointed it out."

Tony caught a pointed look from Ian. He frowned, not understanding, but said nothing.

"Perhaps, you should check into the possibility of purchasing the estate from Chelsworth?" Ian said carefully.

Why hadn't I thought of it? God bless Ian for helping me out of this predicament! thought Tony. "I wouldn't mind purchasing Horneswood. It would keep Jules close to her family."

Juliet rewarded him with a smile. "Is it possible?"

"I won't know until I ask. McDonald, perhaps you'd ride over with me in the morning. I hear Chelsworth is back in Beetham." Tony strove to keep his voice even. Finally, he would get the opportunity to speak with Chelsworth.

"I'd be happy to," Ian said, "but right now I'm in the mood to dance with the bride-to-be. Mrs. Matthews, would you play for us?"

Tony felt a tinge of jealousy as Ian led his fiancée away to waltz around the room.

"Come, Tony, surely you can dance with me as well," Sophia said.

"Of course." He took her into his arms for the waltz. "Are you happy for me?"

"I don't know yet," Sophia said. Of all the members of the family, she was the hardest to fool. Not that he had to fake his feelings for Jules.

"Why not?"

"It all seems so sudden, that's all," she said as he whirled her around to the music. "I knew you and Juliet were friends, but I thought it was more of a brotherly affection."

Far from it, but he didn't want to let on how much he had cared for Juliet.

"You do know about her penchant for naughty reading material, don't you?" Sophia said. "It's scandalous."

"I didn't know about it, but now I'm curious." Sophia didn't need to know that the books were actually now in his own room. "Is there something wrong with a woman wondering about that side of the relationship?"

"It's better we don't know, don't you think? There's less chance of disappointment that way."

"Perhaps you should set higher expectations."

Sophia blushed as she pulled out of his arms. "Don't hurt my sister," she said in a low, terse voice. "I will make your life a living hell if you do."

Juliet watched as Tony danced with Sophia. How well they looked together.

"Come now, I'm not that bad of a dancer, Juliet," Ian teased.

"I've always enjoyed dancing with you."

He whirled her away from Tony and Sophia. "I imagine you weren't expecting Tony to propose."

"As he will probably tell you, he did it to protect my reputation. He didn't need to."

"Perhaps there is more to it than that. He truly cares for you. Or can't you imagine someone feeling like that for you?"

She grimaced. He had hit the mark closer to home than she liked. "You do know how to get to the point, don't you?"

"I'm a Scot. We're used to dealing with reality."

She was quiet, allowing Ian to lead her around the room. She was terrified to trust her instincts and place herself into Tony's power. She could so easily lose herself in him if she wasn't careful.

"He won't hurt you. Not intentionally," McDonald said.

"Perhaps it's the unintentional hurt that I'm worried about. He's hiding something and I don't know what it is."

She glanced up and spotted the surprise in McDonald's eyes. "You mean I'm right?"

"This is a discussion you should be having with your fiancé," he said sharply. "Judging from your expression, I would say that you've already tried. Got distracted, did you?"

Juliet grimaced. She didn't want to admit that the minute Tony touched her, she was a puddle of longing, but there it was. This was what came of reading those types of books. She had fantasized about what it would be like to have a man do those things with her. Now she had a man who wanted to, a man she wanted as much as any man she'd ever met. "You don't know what you're talking about, Mr. Mc-Donald."

Ian laughed. "I know more than you think, my dear."

Juliet watched as his eyes followed Sophia as she danced with Tony. "How well do you like my sister, Mr. McDonald?"

He looked down at her in shock.

"Don't worry. She knows you fancy her but nothing more."

"It's a hopeless case."

She watched him for a long moment. He would be good for Sophia. He would ground her and make her realize that the world didn't revolve around London Society. "Do not give up just yet."

"And set myself up for more pain? I don't think so. Miss Townsend is not destined to marry a cantankerous Scot. Time will allow me to get past these feelings."

"Things change."

"However, I doubt very seriously that her affections for me will change. I have no illusions on that front." He whirled them to a stop and bowed. "Thank you for the dance, Miss Juliet."

She dropped a curtsy just as Tony came up to claim her.

"Come, darling, let us dance," Tony said, pulling her into his arms.

"There's no music." Juliet laughed as he spun her around the room.

"Who needs music?"

Juliet soaked up the boyish joy on Tony's face. He was so handsome he took her breath away. His sparkling blue eyes, his smile, the warmth of his hand through her gown. She wanted this man who made her smile, who teased her out of black moods. This man who wasn't afraid to dance without music.

What more could a girl desire?

Chapter Eleven

Tony looked in the mirror, then wiped his hands nervously on his trousers. The hour was late. The clock in the entryway had just gone through its never-ending midnight chimes.

He'd left his dinner trousers on, along with his linen shirt, uncertain of what to wear for a midnight tryst with a lady. He should have paid more attention to this aspect of life, but he couldn't bring himself to risk getting the pox and doing to another woman what his father had done to his mother.

His father had brought the illness home. It had cost his mother too many stillborn children to count, and her eventual demise, when she couldn't handle the pain of carrying and losing another child.

There was no way he would expose the woman he took to be his wife to such horror.

Except now he was engaged and had no experience with this side of love. He'd seen enough debauchery to know what the basics were. He knew where to put what. But he didn't know much more than that.

Deuces, so much was hanging on this! If he ruined this, it would color his and Juliet's whole life together. Tony took some deep breaths and cracked his neck. He felt as if he was going into the ring with Gentleman Jackson, not about to spend precious moments with the woman who would be his wife. He looked at the naughty book on his bedside. He picked it up and tucked it into the pocket of his dressing gown.

Perhaps he'd just get her to pick something from the book. He didn't want to guess what Juliet wanted; Tony wanted her actively involved.

He'd never been more nervous in his entire life. He blew out the candle in his room and then opened the door silently, checking to make sure the halls were clear. The last thing he wanted was to be caught sneaking into Juliet's room.

Tony quashed the nagging voice in his head that cautioned him to wait. He was tired of waiting. He was tired of being in pain from wanting her so badly. He was sick of having to stand behind chairs to disguise his want.

He needed Juliet.

He made his way to the other side of the house and scratched on her door, then opened it and stepped inside. The room was lit only by firelight. Juliet was in her bed. She sat up and clutched the quilt to her chest, then pushed her spectacles back onto her nose. An open book lay on the bed beside her. She must have fallen asleep reading.

Tony locked the door behind him and moved into the room. He removed his dressing gown and threw it onto the chair by the fireplace. He could hear the book drop to the floor with a *thunk*.

Books were everywhere—on shelves, in stacks on the floor by the chair. She wasn't jesting about her love of reading. Tony would need to establish a proper library for Juliet in their new home.

"Tony?" she whispered. "What are you doing here?"

"I told you I would come." He sat on the side of the bed. "You fell asleep reading?"

Juliet laughed softly. "I usually do."

She looked so young, her braided hair hanging over her shoulder, a dark rope against her white gown. Her thin nightgown had slipped off of one shoulder, revealing creamy skin. Tony didn't know where to start. "Is it all right that I am here?"

Juliet nodded, though her eyes were wide.

He felt foolish. It had seemed a good idea at the time, but now that he was here, Tony didn't know where to start. He couldn't just pounce on her. That would scare Juliet to death.

Tony hated feeling like this. "I brought the book—the one with the pictures." He handed it to her. "Which ones did you like?"

"You're serious about this?"

He bent and kissed her. "Yes. I am. I want you, Juliet. I've never wanted anyone like this."

Juliet let the quilt drop as she accepted the book from him. Tony gulped. He could see her nipples through the fabric of her nightgown. "You are so lovely."

"You've been drinking."

Tony stood and walked over to the other side of the bed. He tossed the quilts aside and tugged on her hands. "I want you to see what I see."

"Tony," she protested as he pulled her up from the bed.

The gown hung down to just past her knees. He pulled her in front of the mirror with him behind her. Her head just came to his shoulder. Tony took her braid and released her hair, spreading the dark waves around her shoulders.

"I love your hair." He brought a few strands up to his nose. "It smells so good. Like flowers and candy. As good as your skin." His hands touched her shoulders.

"Tony, no."

"See what I see, Jules. Look at this hair. So soft, so silky. Look at how it clings to my fingers." He threaded his hand through her hair, brushing it from her shoulders. "Your skin is the same, incredibly soft. My skin isn't like that."

Tony pushed the nightgown further off her shoulder and kissed the skin he revealed. She shivered beneath his mouth. "So pretty."

He could feel her breathing grow shallow. Her eyes met his in the mirror. "Shall I keep going?"

She nodded and bit her lip. Her eyes were wide but not frightened.

His hands moved down her chest slowly, until he could cup her small breasts. Her nipples were hard. He smoothed his hand down her body, molding over her slim hips. "Lovely."

She leaned closer against him.

"May I remove your gown?" Tony whispered, his hands on the tiny buttons on the front of her gown.

"Remove your shirt first," Juliet murmured. "I want to see you."

Tony stepped back from her and pulled his shirt over his head, tossing it on the floor. He faced Juliet and waited for her reaction.

She licked her lips and he hardened. If she touched him for too long he'd explode. She ran her hands over his chest, curling her fingers in the hair on his chest. She pressed her lips to his skin, her tongue tasting him. She made a noise of pleasure as her fingers found his nipple.

Tony groaned. "If you keep that up, I'll lose control. We have a ways to go before that can happen."

He turned her back to the mirror and unbuttoned her nightgown. He brushed the edges off her shoulders and let it fall to the floor.

Now she was naked. Juliet moved to cover herself.

"No. Don't. I've never seen anything so beautiful." He fondled her breasts and thumbed her nipples, drawing them tight.

She was slightly built. Small breasts and slim hips with skin like satin. Dark curls shielded her femininity from his eyes.

Juliet turned in his arms and faced him. A blush covered her skin. She pressed herself against him and Tony couldn't stop another groan. Her breasts against his chest was the most pleasure he'd ever felt. He wrapped himself around her, pulling her closer as his mouth found hers.

His tongue tangled with hers as she stood on tiptoe to better reach his mouth. Her fingers threaded through the hair on his chest. He moved his hands down her back and grasped her bottom. She wiggled closer to him, pressing herself against his cock.

He ravaged her mouth as he carried her back to the bed. He pulled the covers back and lay Juliet down. He wanted to savor every inch of her.

His mouth grazed the soft skin of her neck before dipping into the indention at the base of her neck. Her pulse beat fast and strong. Tony continued his quest down her body until he found her breasts. He pulled her breast into his mouth, sucking hard.

Juliet clutched his hair. "Tony!"

"Too much?"

She shook her head. "More."

Tony pulled the other breast into his mouth. She tasted so good. He trailed his hand down the curve of her stomach to the curls at the juncture of her thighs. He parted her folds, teasing her nub. Juliet pushed herself against him.

"Oh, Tony. What are you doing to me?"

Tony looked up and blew on her nipple as he pushed one finger into her. She was so tight, so wet. He knew he wasn't going to last long once he was inside her.

Juliet was out of her mind. She'd never known feelings like this. The pleasure of Tony pulling at her breast, his fingers playing with areas of her body she'd been afraid to explore. Oh, dear God, she should have explored herself before this.

"Am I doing it right?" he whispered in her ear as his fingers circled between her legs.

She squirmed under his playing fingers. "How should I know? Just don't stop."

Tony chuckled and kissed her belly. He moved down her body, pressing his mouth to her skin. She couldn't stop quivering each time he nuzzled her skin with his mouth, with his hands.

"Does this feel good?" He nipped the flesh of her hip.

"Yes."

He nipped her inner thigh, spreading her legs wider. "This?"

"It all feels good."

He was kneeling between her thighs now, looking at her. "I saw this picture in your book and wanted to try it."

His breath on the intimate place between her legs gave Juliet pause.

"Tony, I don't think—"

His mouth found her center, brushing against the knot of nerves. Juliet couldn't stop herself from trying to move away from him as his tongue laved her folds. It was too intimate, too much, even as desire flushed every thought from her head.

Tony held her hips, his thumbs caressing her skin, as his mouth continued to do wicked things to her. Juliet gripped the sheets with her hands, feeling so out of control that she needed to hold on to something. The heat built inside her. She needed more, needed something. "Tony?"

"I've got you."

Juliet couldn't hold back any longer. She pushed against him, shaking like a leaf in the breeze, and then collapsed on the bed as waves of pleasure rolled over her.

Tony kissed her between her legs one more time. He made his way up her body, leaving smacking kisses along her skin. "I hope you liked that as much as I did."

He kissed her mouth softly, pressing his erection between her legs.

"You're still—" she whispered. She reached down and palmed his cock through his pants with her hand. How was this going to fit inside her? It seemed impossible, but she still wanted it. She was empty and needed him to fill her.

"Not tonight, love."

"But it's your turn." He had given her so much pleasure; he deserved the same. She remembered one particular picture in the book that showed a woman gripping the man as he relaxed on the bed. Perhaps this was something she could try.

"Lay back," she whispered as she pushed him over on the bed.

"What are you doing?" He looked a little panicked.

She kissed him softly on the mouth before turning her attention to the buttons on the front of his trousers. She released his cock and wrapped her hand around it. The skin was silky soft against the hardness beneath. A drop of fluid appeared at the tip. She spread it with a finger, then took him in her hand and squeezed.

Tony groaned. "Easy, love. Like this." He placed his hand over hers and showed her how to move her hand and how tightly to grip him.

Juliet watched Tony's face as he squeezed his eyes shut and gripped his hands over hers, moving with her.

It didn't take long, a few tight strokes, and Tony climaxed. He fell back against the bed with a sigh while Juliet continued to stroke him, curious.

"Better?" she whispered as she stretched out beside him.

Tony brushed her hair back from her face with his hand. "Yes." He kissed her softly. "I need to clean up."

Juliet watched Tony go to the basin in her room and wet a cloth. He cleaned himself and then refastened his trousers. Tony approached the bed and picked up her gown. "As tempting as you are lying there, you must be getting chilled."

She smiled, loving the way he was looking at her, like a starving man. "Not really."

"Then put it on for me, before I lose my head with you." He tossed the gown to her.

Juliet pulled the gown over her head. "Why didn't we . . ."

Tony settled in the bed beside her and pulled her into his arms. "I want to take my time."

Juliet brushed his hair from his forehead. "I'm not sure I'm going to be able to wait."

"Nor me. I want you too much."

"Will you stay the night?"

"I shouldn't. We've already played fast and loose with your reputation."

"Will you at least stay until I fall asleep?"

"Sleep. I'll be here."

Juliet nestled into his side, her hand playing with the hair on his chest. She closed her eyes.

"Don't forget we have a riding lesson tomorrow," he reminded her.

Juliet groaned. "I was hoping you *would* forget about that." She truly hated horses.

"Wear your breeches. I think it will be easier to teach you to ride astride rather than sidesaddle. I won't risk anything happening to you."

Juliet cuddled next to him, listening to the steady beat of his heart. He stroked her hair softly, tenderly, coaxing her to sleep. Her eyes grew heavy as his warmth wrapped around her. "Thank you, Tony."

He pressed his lips to her forehead. "Sleep, my love."

Juliet relaxed in Tony's arms, finally succumbing to sleep. He continued to stroke her hair, letting the curls catch in his fingers. He couldn't allow himself to fall asleep in her bed. He didn't want any more damage to Juliet's reputation. And while it would better serve his purposes to tie Juliet to him by any means necessary, he couldn't do that to her.

Just as he couldn't make love to her tonight. He'd wanted to. He'd needed to sink his cock into her wet tightness. Her scent, her taste was still tart-sweet on his tongue.

But he couldn't do it. He had to give her a choice when the truth finally came out. At least he had held her naked in his arms. It had been heaven.

Juliet was sound asleep now, softly snoring as she drooled on his chest. He kissed her forehead and eased her back onto her own pillow. She stirred before turning away from him.

She was so delicately made. And she was his. How did he get so very lucky to have captured her heart?

Tony rose and pulled the quilt over Juliet. Her naughty book fell to the floor. He picked it up and flipped through the pages until he stumbled upon a particular picture. He tilted the book to look at it better. It would take more flexibility than he had, but it would make her smile.

Tony went to her desk and pulled out paper and pen. He quickly penned a note, suggesting they try it after her first riding lesson. He tucked the note in the book, marking the page.

He crept over to where Juliet was curled into her pillow, fast asleep. How the hell was he going to tell her the truth?

How was he going to survive the heartbreak when she jilted him?

Tony bent and kissed her, then tucked the book next to her, where she'd find it when she woke.

He slipped into the hallway and made his way back to his room.

Chapter Twelve

Juliet had stalled as long as she could. Every morning this week Tony had asked about the riding lesson and she had escaped with some excuse. There was the assembly Anne was planning as their engagement ball. There were calls to make, shopping for her trousseau, calls to receive.

But Juliet had run out of excuses. If she was going to spend any time with Tony, she was going to have to learn to ride. All her recent activities had kept her from him. There had been no more nightly visits, either. Each night he walked her to the stairs, squeezed her hand, and kissed her mouth sweetly.

Drastic measures must be taken.

Juliet dressed quickly and resigned herself to touching a horse. The thought of even being near one terrified her. She hated horses. They were big. They smelled. They didn't listen to her commands. They bit. They ran away with her, and they threw her off.

They were a necessary evil, given that horses pulled the carts and carriages she used to get around the village and Town, but that didn't mean she had to *touch* them. Someone else drove the carts, and held the horses still so she could enter and exit them.

Juliet pulled out the book Tony had left behind after his nighttime visit and opened to the page he had marked. She smiled, just as she did every time she looked at it.

That night had been wonderful. Every day since, Tony had been attentive and affectionate. It wouldn't take much more before she succumbed. She was already well on her way to falling completely in love with him.

Hence, Juliet would attempt to learn to ride. Tony was the only man on the face of the earth who could get her near a horse.

She pulled in a deep breath and fixed her hair, then made her way down the back stairs and through the kitchen.

She stopped long enough to grab two buns from a platter on the table and wrap them in a napkin. If Tony was going to expect her to deal with her terror, she was going to eat first.

She made her way to the stables and found him leaning against the outer wall. Waiting for her. Juliet handed him a bun. "You are really going to insist that I do this?"

"Good morning to you too," Tony said before taking a bite from his bun. "Thank you for breakfast."

"Cook just removed them from the oven."

Tony pushed away from the wall. "Are you ready to lose your fear of horses?"

Juliet's stomach twisted. "I don't know if I'm able."

"You've nothing to fear. We aren't going to ride today. We're just going to go into the stable and give the horses a few treats. I want you to see that you can touch the horse, pet it, reward it. I have the perfect horse for you. She's a sweet mare."

"I don't know, Tony."

"Trust me."

She allowed Tony to take her hand and lead her into the gloom of the stable. He paused at the entrance. "Do exactly what I tell you and how I tell you to do it."

"You're frightening me."

"Horses are large animals. If you treat them well and approach them correctly, you have no reason to be afraid of them."

Juliet fought the urge to run back to the house. Her hands trembled and were sweaty beneath her gloves. She swallowed.

"Don't show fear," he said softly. "Keep your voice down. Talk softly and approach so that the horse will see and smell you, as well as hear you."

She gulped. "You'll go first?"

"Of course." He took her hand and led her into the gloom of the stable.

The grooms were mucking out the stalls, adding fresh hay. The air smelled of horses, dirty straw, and feed. Juliet wrinkled her nose.

Tony stopped and she almost ran into him. "Talk softly. Her name is Lucy. She'll need to hear your voice and see you as you approach."

Juliet squeezed her hands into fists to still the trembling. "Can she tell that I'm . . ."

"Scared spitless?" Tony laughed. "Yes, you are, but don't worry— Lucy is a sweet old lady. She's dying to make your acquaintance."

Juliet stood in the shadows of the stable and watched as Tony crooned nonsense to the horse. Lucy stuck her head out of the stall and sniffed him, looking for something. Tony held out his hand with a piece of apple in his palm. Lucy gobbled it up. Tony stroked her nose and patted her. The horse nudged him in an affectionate manner.

"Your turn," Tony said. "Talk softly as you approach."

Juliet took a deep breath. "What do you want me to say?" She kept her voice low. "Does it matter?"

"No. It's all in how you approach. Relax your face. Smile."

"Smile?" Juliet didn't think she was capable of smiling just then.

"If you look terrified, she'll get nervous," Tony said, still stroking the horse. "Lucy is a sweet girl. She'll be fine."

Juliet forced herself to relax. She could do this. The horse was in her stall. Tony was there to keep her safe. She walked forward slowly, crooning nonsense.

Lucy was watching her closely, her ears pointing forward. Juliet stopped. "Her ears moved. What does that mean?"

"It means she's watching you, listening to your voice. You can walk a bit faster."

Juliet frowned at the humor in his voice. "You told me to go slow."

"You can walk a bit faster, just not quite your normal pace."

Tony was having way too much fun at her expense. She advanced until she was just outside the stall. The horse dipped her head down toward her and Juliet jumped back out of the way.

"Careful. Lucy just wants to say hello." Tony pulled Juliet close, tucking her under his arm. "Stroke Lucy's nose with your hand. No quick movements."

"I have to touch her?"

"Horses like to be stroked, petted. They want affection." Tony's voice dropped low. His hand moved to stroke the horse's muzzle again. Juliet couldn't control the shiver of awareness. "Go on; then we'll give her a treat."

Juliet looked up at him in shock.

"You can do this, Juliet. Lucy just wants a bit of attention."

Juliet pulled in a fortifying breath, pushing away the nightmares of what her brother had done to her when she was a child. She'd been young, too young to be on such a large horse, but her brother had put her on the horse to stop her from crying about being left behind. Her screams of fear must have spooked the horse. She remembered clinging to the horse's mane before the long fall to the ground. She reached out with her hand and gently touched the white spot on Lucy's muzzle.

When she moved her hands, Lucy's head followed her. Juliet jumped back toward Tony, who caught her by the shoulders. "Careful. She's just learning your scent. Ready to give Lucy a treat?"

There was no chance of Juliet feeding anything to this animal. Big teeth, big mouth, and her small hand? Juliet was not going to risk the horse nipping her fingers. "Do you usually bribe horses when you ride?"

"Horses respond well to bribes. Lucy is like a pet. She's been worked with and trained to accept our attentions. She's rewarded with treats."

Juliet took a carrot and presented it to Lucy who took it from her hand. "She does like it." She brushed her gloved hand down Lucy's nose.

Tony leaned close and whispered, "I think she likes you."

"Is that important?"

"There should be some trust between you and the horse." His voice was serious. "There might be a day when you need that trust. You'll depend upon it."

"Has that happened to you?" Juliet asked as she stroked Lucy slowly.

"There have been several times when I was thankful to have my horse, Thunder, with me." He patted Lucy. "This old girl could be your friend."

Juliet couldn't imagine it.

"Want to feed her a piece of apple?"

"Not really."

Tony laughed. "Just remember, talk softly. Horses don't like loud, abrupt noises. Make sure she sees you approach."

Juliet nodded. "If the lesson is over, I'll just go to the Williamses'."

"Oh, no, the lesson's just beginning. Let's take a ride."

Juliet blanched. "You mean get on the horse?"

Tony laughed again. "You can do this. I'll be right here."

"No. No I can't."

* * *

Tony asked a groom to saddle Lucy. She was older, but she should be able to handle the weight of both of them. He'd never seen anyone as afraid of horses as Juliet. Even now she was growing more agitated and pale. He hoped she didn't faint.

"I can't do this. Please don't make me." Her voice was breathy and high.

He pulled her close. "Sweetheart, it will be all right. I shall be with you." He tucked a strand of hair behind her ear.

She shook her head erratically. "She will just run off with me and I won't be able to stop."

Juliet's fear was making Lucy nervous. "You trust me, don't you? Relax. Miss Lucy here is an old lady; she's not going to want to go anywhere unless she has to. Come, we'll wait outside for Lucy to be saddled." He guided her out of the stable.

She crossed her arms. "I'm not doing it."

Juliet was so damnably cute when she was angry, but he couldn't let her give in to her fear. "You and I are going to take a ride around the yard."

"I'm not getting on the horse by myself."

She was starting to try his patience. Fears needed to be faced, overcome. There might come a day when she'd need to ride. "Juliet, the groom will hold the horse and I'll get on behind you."

"I can't."

"What if you just try?" Tony said, wincing at the tone of irritation in his voice. Bloody hell, what had they done to her as a child? He'd never seen anyone who was this afraid of an animal. Except for him and snakes, but that was different. Snakes were not something one encountered every day.

The groom brought out Lucy, saddled and ready to go. "Here you go, sir."

Juliet looked at the horse and went a bit pale. "It's a really large horse."

Tony studied her wide eyes and pale skin. There was no talking her into this. He'd have to take the decision out of her hands. "Her name is Lucy, Juliet. Address her as such."

He grabbed Juliet's waist and heaved her astride the horse. Juliet squealed and Lucy moved beneath her nervously. "Lower your voice. You're frightening her." He barked out the command. The last thing he needed was for the horse to rear up and dump Juliet off. He'd never get her on another damn horse.

Juliet snapped her mouth shut and gripped the pommel with white knuckles. Lucy moved beneath her and Juliet whimpered.

"Careful; I'm mounting Lucy right behind you. Lucy might not like it with both our weights on her," Tony said carefully.

"What do you mean, she won't like it?"

He glanced at the groom, who was struggling to keep from laughing. He shot the man a quelling glare.

Tony mounted the horse behind Juliet. She immediately leaned against him. He could feel himself responding. Only this woman could make him hard while she struggled with her fear of horses.

He took the reins from the groom. "I'm going to start the horse moving. Feel the way she moves back and forth. Move with her, not against her."

Juliet nodded, her hair tickling his nose. Lucy lurched beneath them and Juliet squeaked.

Tony held the reins still. "Steady, girl."

"Me or the horse?" Juliet said in a tight voice.

"Both." He chuckled. "You're doing fine, Juliet. Let's take a few turns around the yard."

Juliet gripped the pommel harder as the horse moved. She was stiff, fighting the rhythmic movement of the horse.

Tony gripped the reins in one hand. He took the other arm and wrapped it around Juliet, just under her breasts. He pressed her back flush with his body so that she could rest her head back on his shoulder. "Close your eyes, Jules, and relax against me," he whispered in her ear. He started the horse moving slowly again. "Feel how my body moves. Move with me."

Every breath she took pressed her breasts against his arm. He could feel her relax as her body settled against him. She had to feel his erection against her bottom, but she said nothing.

"Shall we take a short ride?" He kept his voice low and intimate.

"Where to?" Juliet said, her own voice much less tense than it had been before.

"I was thinking of the pond. It's a hot day." He'd love to swim today, especially with Jules. "The pond is nicely shaded. It will be cooler."

"If you think we should."

"You can dip your toes in if you want." Tony guided the horse onto the lane and forced her into a light trot.

Juliet tensed up again as the horse picked up speed. "Do we have to go so fast?"

"If we want to get there and back before tea, yes." Tony tightened his grip around her. "Don't fight the movement of the horse."

Juliet settled against him again and they rode for a while in silence. Tony guided the horse into the woods near the pond, then stopped. The shade was cool, but the pond shimmered in the sun.

Juliet looked around. "Is this part of Horneswood?"

"I don't know, really," Tony said as he dismounted. "Easy. I'm just tying the reins so she can graze."

Juliet was back to holding on with a death grip, though not quite as hard as she had when she first mounted the horse. Progress. Eventually he might actually get her to ride on her own.

Tony stepped beside the horse and held out his arms to her. "Just slide off the saddle and into my arms."

"You won't let me fall?" Her voice was all quivery again.

"I promise." He caught her against him as she dismounted. She slid down his body slowly. When her feet touched the ground, she stared up at him. She was trembling.

"You did well, Jules." He couldn't keep the gruffness from his voice.

She smiled, finally starting to relax. "I wasn't too much of a baby?"

Tony shook his head, unable to tear his eyes away from her face. He could feel the warmth of her body through the thin layers of the clothes she wore. He moved his hands to grip her hips.

Juliet licked her lips. It was more invitation than Tony needed. He bent his head and kissed her softly, brushing his lips back and forth, teasing. He tasted her with his tongue. She melted against him.

Juliet's fingertips touched his face, rough against her skin. Her lips parted and her tongue found his and rubbed against it.

Tony ached for her. Never before had he been unable to resist a woman, but this slip of a girl fired his blood like no other.

But he wouldn't take her here, on the ground, not their first time. Juliet deserved a soft bed and a bit of romance. Frankly, he wanted the same: a quiet, firelit room where they could explore each other thoroughly, love each other gently.

Tony put a more appropriate distance between them, the intensity of his feelings threatening to overwhelm him. Removing his cravat, he said, "I'm ready to cool off."

Juliet's eyes widened. "You can't be serious. What if someone comes along?"

"I only meant to dip my cravat into the water," he teased. "What were you thinking I was going to do?"

She blushed but said nothing.

"Do you have a riding habit? You'll need one for our next lesson."

"No, thank you."

"Sweetheart, you need to learn to handle a horse on your own. What if you were out with the cart and a wheel broke? How would you get back home?"

"I've managed so far without much difficulty."

"You will learn."

"No, Tony, I won't. I've done as you've asked. I sat on a horse. I gave her a treat."

"I won't have a wife of mine who cannot ride a horse. You will continue your lessons."

"Just because we're engaged does not give you the right to ride roughshod over me. If I choose not to learn, it's up to me."

Tony stared down at the angry woman before him. The stubborn set of her chin dared him to say something. He couldn't intimidate her. What did that say about the kind of marriage they'd have?

He would not yield. Juliet needed to learn to ride. He wanted the opportunity to ride through the countryside with her so they could enjoy each other's company away from the servants and cares of the day. She was just going to have to deal with her unreasonable fears. "You're going to learn to ride, Juliet. I insist upon it."

"Or what?"

"Or this." Tony picked her up and swung her over his shoulder and walked toward the lake. She was itching for a fight and he needed to cool down. He wrapped his arm around her kicking legs. "Be still."

"Put me down, Tony."

Tony walked to the edge of the pond and swung her around and into his arms. "We need to cool our tempers, dear."

Juliet paled. "No. Don't—"

Tony laughed and swung her over the water, only meaning to

tease her out of her anger, but she twisted in his arms to avoid being thrown in.

As he juggled her, his boots slipped on the moss-covered stones at the edge of the pond, and they both went into the water.

Icy water froze his limbs for a moment as Tony struggled to the surface, fighting the weight of his boots as they filled with water. He reached the surface and glanced around, expecting to see her gasping from the cold as he was.

She wasn't. Panic filled him as he dove down, looking for her pale dress in the murky water. Her dress and petticoats would have weighed her down, but she should have been able to swim against it toward the surface, unless she could not swim.

She was struggling to reach the surface. He dove and caught her around the waist. In her panic, she fought him, nearly pulling them down deeper. Tony wrapped one arm underneath her arms and swam as hard as he could.

He pulled in deep breaths of air as he broke the surface. He turned so that Juliet's head would be above the level of the water. She was still fighting, still panicked. "Shh. I've got you."

They went under again. He wrapped a tight arm around her waist and pulled them back to the surface. "Juliet! Stop or you'll drown us both."

Tony swam to the stones edging the pond and stood in the shallower water. Juliet was trembling; from cold, from fear. Her bonnet sagged down her back, her glasses were askew. He hauled her out of the water and onto a stone before heaving himself out of the water. Juliet coughed up water, breathing heavily.

Tony was shaken. Never in his life had he felt such fear. Juliet could have been gone from him by his own stupidity. It made him realize there were things about this lady that he didn't know. Facts like her not knowing how to swim. Didn't young ladies learn to swim? He had just assumed. "I'm so very sorry, Juliet. I only meant to tease."

She looked up at him, distrust filling her eyes. "What were you thinking?"

He hung his head. "I wasn't thinking, apparently." He removed the bonnet and tossed it aside. He couldn't even offer her his coat. They were both soaked to the skin. "I am sorry."

Juliet looked down at her wet clothes. "How are we supposed to explain this to my sister? Or to anyone else who might see us on the lane?" Her teeth were starting to chatter.

"We can sit here in the sun until we dry off a bit before we go home," Tony suggested. "I for one would appreciate the chance to catch my breath."

Juliet removed her leather gloves and plopped them beside her bonnet. She was wet and cold. Everything squished, including her half boots. Her spectacles were wet and there was nothing to dry them with.

If she had a stick, she'd beat Tony with it.

Tony found his cravat in the grass, where he had tossed it. "Allow me to remove the water from your glasses." She passed him her glasses. He dried them and made to replace them on her face.

"Don't touch me. I'm angry with you," she said.

He took her hand anyway and raised it to his lips. His lips were cold against her skin. He pressed a kiss to her palm. Heat spread through her and she shivered with awareness but blamed the icy water of the pond.

"You are cold," he whispered against her skin.

"The water was freezing."

Tony looked down at his own clothes. "I'm going to have to get new boots."

"Had you not been playing games, your boots wouldn't be wet."

"You were being unreasonable."

"Me? You were ordering me around as if you owned me."

"We're going to be married," Tony said in a softer voice.

"That does not give you the liberty to treat me thus. Nor does it give you the right to force me to do something I do not want to do. If I decide to learn to ride, then I'll do it. I won't be bullied by you or anyone else."

"I'm sorry, Jules. I just wanted you to be able to ride to safety, if you needed to. I won't always be there to protect you. I also thought it would be nice to share something with you. I love riding. The wind in my face as I gallop along. The power of the horse beneath me. It's exhilarating."

Juliet's anger drained away as his words sank in. "It's going to take me a while to face my fear of horses. I've been afraid for a long time."

"I had no right to force the issue. I just thought you'd like it once you had the chance to try it in a safe way."

"If you promise not to push, I'll try again." Juliet removed her Spencer, wrung it out, then smoothed it out on the rock to dry. She tried squeezing some of the water from her skirts.

Tony had gone still, pausing in the removal of his boots. He was staring at her breasts. Juliet looked down. The water had caused her clothes to become transparent. She snatched her Spencer to cover herself, even as she was hit by a wave of longing.

"You're all I see when I close my eyes. You're my first thought and my last each day. I want you so badly, Jules."

Juliet blinked away the sting of tears at the emotion in his voice. He cared something for her. Her heart tripped a beat, then swelled with its own flood of feelings. "Here?"

He laughed. "Damp clothing and a hard rock are not what I want for our first time."

She smiled. "It does not sound romantic to me either."

Juliet let her eyes fall closed as Tony pressed his mouth to hers. Her hands caressed his face, his skin slightly rough from his beard. The kiss was sweet, gentle, as if Tony was determined not to let things go too far. She needed more.

Juliet teased the seam of his lips with her tongue, taking charge as he had done in the past. As his lips parted, she swirled her tongue in his mouth, enjoying the taste of him, the warmth.

She loved the firmness of his lips against hers. She curled her hands into his wet hair and tried to crawl into his lap, needing to be close, even if their clothes separated them.

"Well, this is embarrassing," Simon Bartleby said. "I keep finding you both in compromising positions."

Juliet gasped and Tony wrapped his arm around her, preventing her from moving away. "Your dress is transparent, Jules."

His voice was soft in her ear. Juliet blushed as she buried her face in Tony's shoulder.

"Bartleby, what are you doing here?" Tony's voice was hard.

"I saw the horse tethered. I thought that perhaps someone was trespassing."

"So this is Horneswood land?" Tony asked. "I didn't know."

Bartleby laughed. "I'm surprised, given the interest you've shown in the property. You've been riding all over the county talking to the tenants."

"I have been looking for an estate to purchase, now that I'm ready to take a wife."

"Your engagement has been the talk of the county."

"Yes. Miss Townsend has made me the happiest of men," Tony said.

Juliet raised her head and met the disdainful gaze of Mr. Bartleby.

"From the look of things, I'd say she's made her bed. Let's hope she will still want to marry you as time goes by."

Juliet stiffened against him. "What is he talking about?"

"I'm sure you'll discover it, my dear." Bartleby tipped his hat. "Good day."

Juliet sat back once Bartleby disappeared. "Discover what, Tony?"

"Nothing." He gave her the waistcoat she'd discarded. "We should get back to the house and get out of these wet things. We've already been gone too long." Tony stood and walked to the horse.

He had retreated into himself, so far from her that she hardly knew him. A few words from Mr. Bartleby and Tony had disengaged from her, closed himself off.

Juliet tugged on her Spencer as best she could and picked up her ruined bonnet to stumble after him. "So you're not going to explain it to me."

Tony looked down at her. "Explain what?"

She stepped back from the hardness in his eyes. Something was going on between Bartleby and Tony. "What's going on between you and Mr. Bartleby? I know there is something."

"Get on the horse, Jules."

Juliet let him lift her onto the horse without complaint. He mounted behind her and started toward the Lodge.

"Does this have to do with the Williamses?" she asked.

"Juliet, it isn't your concern."

"If we are to be wed, it damn well is my concern."

"We aren't wed yet."

"Nor are we likely to be if you keep secrets from me." Juliet gripped the pommel in front of her.

They rode the rest of the way in silence. She was too angry to speak to Tony and unwilling to listen unless he offered up an explanation. Her heart hurt. She had thought Tony had changed. He wasn't the rake everyone in Town thought he was. He was kind, loving, funny, and honorable. He was hers.

The horse came to a stop at the stables. Tony dismounted and then helped her down. He didn't allow her body to touch his. He released her immediately. As if he couldn't bear to touch her.

Juliet stared up at him, willing to him look at her. She stood there like an idiot, waiting.

He turned and walked to the stables. Her heart cracked. She turned and ran into the house. She had to put as much space between them as possible. She raced up the stairs and past Anne.

"Juliet, what on earth?" Anne called out.

Juliet couldn't keep the tears from falling down her cheeks. Disappointment shook her to the core. She'd let her guard down again with Tony Matthews, with the same result as before. She shook her head at Anne and continued to her room. She closed the door softly and leaned against it.

The illusion she'd allowed herself to believe in crumbled at her feet like dried-out cake. Tears fell as Juliet leaned her head against the closed door.

If Tony could keep secrets from her, then he didn't love her. Love meant telling each other everything. That was what people did in novels. He obviously felt he had to hold a part of himself back.

Unlike her, who gave him everything. She even got on a horse for him.

Juliet had done it to herself. Again. She had given her heart to Tony Matthews only to have him smash it beneath his boot as if it was a bug.

Chapter Thirteen

There weren't enough curses to utter to allow Tony to feel better about his actions. He'd made a huge mistake with Juliet. What could he say? Anything that came out of his mouth would be a lie.

He would not lie to her outright. Omission was a given, but not an out-and-out lie. For some reason, simply saying nothing seemed like less of a sin.

Tony had stood there in front of her like a dolt, afraid to say anything, terrified that the truth would come tumbling out. The pain on her face had said it all. He'd hurt her with his silence.

There was a small part of him that had hoped she'd be able to handle the conflict, the dark moods men were subject to when cornered. Tony was disappointed that Juliet still believed love happened as it did in the pages of a Jane Austen novel.

The truth would come out soon, either from him or from Bartleby. If Juliet dissolved into tears over a bit of anger, what chance did he have of her feelings surviving the truth?

She'd never forgive him. She surely wouldn't marry him. The bleakness that arose from that one thought tore at Tony's heart. Somehow this one small woman had gotten past his defenses. Juliet could lay him bare to the world with one word. He didn't like being vulnerable, not one bit.

He needed to change out of his wet clothes. His boots were ruined, and probably his coat as well. He stepped inside the house to make his way up the stairs.

Anne came out of the parlor. "Tony, a moment, please."

Tony closed his eyes. He didn't need any more guilt. He didn't need any more lectures. "Of course." He followed Anne into the parlor.

"What's going on with Juliet?" Anne asked.

Tony wiped all the emotion from his face, for Anne could read him like a book. "We argued."

"She was in tears and soaking wet. What were you two doing?"

"I was teaching her to ride."

Anne's jaw dropped. "You put Juliet on a horse?"

He nodded.

"She actually got near enough a horse to get on it?"

Tony had to smile at the surprise in Anne's voice. "Yes, and we rode to the pond. Why doesn't Juliet like horses?"

Anne crossed her arms and looked down at the floor. Tony had a feeling he wasn't going to like what he heard.

"My brother put Juliet on a horse when she was but four years old," Anne said.

"Alone? She was too small. Unless it was a pony."

"Sophia had the pony. Juliet was crying that she wanted to ride like Sophia. John had the brilliant idea of putting her on his own horse, who had a bit of a wild side."

"Where was the nanny? Your parents? You?"

"Mother had just died. Father was grieving. I was with him." She hugged herself tighter and looked out the window. "John slapped the horse's rump and it took off with Juliet on its back, her hands tangled in its mane."

"How badly was she hurt?"

"She broke her arm and had some bruising. She landed in a pile of leaves," Anne said.

"She's lucky to be alive."

Anne nodded. "That's why I'm surprised she agreed to ride again."

Tony felt lower than pond scum. "I didn't give her a choice. I put her on the horse."

Anne met his eyes for a long look. "That says a great deal about how she feels about you."

Hope stirred in him until he remembered that no one knew the whole story.

"Don't hurt her again, Tony," Anne said.

"I don't want to hurt her." Juliet meant too much to him. Hell, he didn't even want to contemplate what he'd do when Juliet learned the truth. "Anne, would you mind if I went to change? I'm dripping on the carpet."

"Of course. How did you both get drenched? It's not raining out."

He could feel his ears heat. "We rode to the pond on the Horneswood property."

"You did know she can't swim, didn't you?"

He did now. "Uh, no."

"No harm done, I'm certain. Why would she be crying over that?"

That was a question he wasn't going to answer. This argument between him and Jules was their business, not Anne's.

"If you'll excuse me." Tony took the stairs two at a time. He paused in front of Juliet's bedroom door and listened. He heard a sniff. He cursed softly and then made his way to his room.

Damn, he couldn't feel worse. He'd fix this mess. He wasn't going to risk losing Juliet. Not now that he finally realized how much she meant to him.

Juliet stared at herself in the mirror. Her eyes were puffy. Her nose was red. She'd never get past Sophia noticing and calling her out. She leaned forward and banged her head on the bureau.

Love wasn't supposed to be this hard. Where was the happily ever after all the books talked about? She wanted that kind of love, not this painful variety.

God was punishing her for reading the naughty books. Burning in hell for looking at naughty pictures wasn't good enough—she had to suffer on earth as well.

Juliet needed an escape from the weight of the questions everyone would ask her, including the maids. Dinner was going to be sheer torture. She crept down the back stairs and out the kitchen door. The air was cool, but the sun was bright, mocking her dark mood.

Tony was driving her insane. How could they start a life together with secrets? If only he would talk to her. They could solve any problem if they did it together.

Juliet found herself by the old cottage, now just a stone shell. Ash from the fire that had almost killed her sister stained the stones, yet grass and vines grew in and around the rubble, a testament to their resilience. Could she also be that resilient?

"You used to live in this hovel, didn't you?" Mr. Bartleby said behind her.

Juliet jumped. "What are you doing here?"

"Would you believe me if I told you I was trying to find you without your lovesick beau, who seems to always be around?"

"I don't think that's likely, is it?"

He chuckled. "You have spirit. I admire that about you."

Juliet said nothing. She refused to show him that she was afraid of him. The only thing keeping her from running was the knowledge that he might have clues to Tony's secret.

"You look as if you've recovered from your dip in the pond."

"Yes, I have." The tension was thick between them.

"Was it truly an accident or were you pushed?" Bartleby asked.

"Tony wouldn't hurt me."

"There are many ways in which someone can hurt another, as you are well aware, Miss Juliet," Bartleby said with a sneer.

Juliet fought to keep her fear under control. What was it about this man? "I do not understand your meaning, sir."

"Oh, I'm sure you do, all too well," he said. "Perhaps you should ask Mr. Matthews? I'm sure he'll be forthcoming with all of his secrets."

"I'm sure if it's important, Tony will inform me."

"Such loyalty. It does you credit, but it will also be your downfall. After the trouble you've caused me, I shall enjoy seeing you fall, Miss Juliet."

"You are no gentleman."

"Neither is your precious fiancé. Are you sure there are no questions you wish to ask me? Or will you let your lover continue to lie to you?"

Juliet was tempted, more than she thought possible, to question Simon Bartleby, but she wanted to hear the truth from Tony first. "I had better return to the house."

"Are you afraid, Miss Juliet? Afraid of the truth about the man you've chosen to marry?"

He was baiting her, and it was working. "I trust Tony implicitly."

"Then you are more of a child than I imagined. Life is not a fairy tale, Miss Juliet. I hope you survive the truth."

Juliet fought to ignore Bartleby and turned to walk back to the house. Tony was coming toward them, a determined scowl on his face.

"Miss Juliet." He glared at Mr. Bartleby. "What are you doing here?"

"I was asking after Miss Juliet's welfare. She's had a nasty scare, thanks to you."

"It was an accident." Tony spit the words out like darts.

The tension increased between the two men. Juliet was afraid it would end in fisticuffs. "Mr. Matthews, Mr. Bartleby was just leaving."

"He shouldn't even be here."

"I was hoping for a chance to speak with Miss Juliet. She has a right to know the man she's chosen to marry."

Juliet placed her hand on Tony's arm, hoping to prevent a scene. "I explained to Mr. Bartleby that I would rather hear it from your lips than trust him."

Her words had the opposite effect than she'd intended; the animosity between the two men seemed to grow even worse. "Please escort me back to the house, Tony," she said quickly.

"Yes, please see your fiancée back to the house, Mr. Matthews. I shall take my leave," Mr. Bartleby said. "Perhaps during your romantic stroll you'll find the courage to tell the lady the truth."

Mr. Bartleby took the path through the woods, leaving Juliet standing beside Tony. An uncomfortable silence settled between them. She released his arm and wandered over to the old stone fence around the front of the former cottage. She desperately wanted Tony to speak, to finally tell her what was going on.

He said nothing.

"Please, can we talk, Tony?"

"We should return to the house. They will be ringing the gong for dinner."

Juliet blinked back her tears. "Is this what our life together will be like? You with your secrets and dark moods and me always guessing what is going on?"

"Are you ending the engagement?"

The harshness of his voice tore at her. Juliet didn't know the depth of his feelings, but he felt something. The pain in his eyes broke her heart. "I don't know yet."

"Don't. Please."

"Why?"

Tony moved to stand beside her. He leaned against the stone and looked back at the ruins of the cottage. "I miss the days when you lived here. Those were simpler times."

The change in subject didn't surprise Juliet. Tony always deflected the conversation when it suited him. There would be no learning his secrets today. Her shoulders slumped. "We had no money. Anne was so afraid we'd freeze to death in that drafty old cottage."

Tony looked back at her. "Trust me when I tell you, while things might be confusing at the moment, they will be all right. I would not do anything to hurt you."

Disappointment slid through her. "Of course."

She longed to rail at him about keeping secrets. She wanted a relationship where they shared everything, like the couples in the novels she read.

But Juliet was too frightened to say anything. She was afraid of losing Tony. She had to hope that whatever this secret was, it wouldn't destroy her.

"Allow me to escort you back to the house," Tony said and offered his arm.

Juliet placed her hand on his sleeve. She could not shake the feeling that their relationship had been tested, and that they'd failed miserably.

Tony stood by the fire in the parlor growing more discouraged by the minute. Juliet had refused to talk to him, except for a few polite words at dinner.

Now she was sitting in a corner not talking to anyone, hiding behind a book.

Lady Danford sat nearby, sipping her tea. "You're awfully glum this evening, Anthony."

Only his grandmother called him Anthony. "I'm perfectly well."

"Lovers' spats never last long. You'll be back in her good graces in no time."

"I don't know, Grandmother."

Lady Danford watched Juliet sitting across the room. "Too bad there's no music. In my day a dance with a lover was the perfect way to solve a dispute."

"I doubt one dance will do the trick this time."

Sophia wandered over to the fire. "You've really angered Juliet, Tony. I don't think she's ever been this quiet."

"Not now, Sophia."

"I encountered Mr. Bartleby earlier today in the village," Sophia continued, undeterred. "He had some interesting things to say. What were you doing at the pond?"

"Nothing," Tony muttered. Where was she going with this?

"He says he caught you and Juliet in a rather compromising position," Sophia said under her voice, glancing at Lady Danford.

"I'm old, I'm not deaf, child. They're engaged; people tend to overlook a bit of impropriety from an engaged couple."

"It's not the first time Mr. Bartleby caught them engaged in some inappropriate behavior," Sophia said.

"Bartleby is an ass," Tony mumbled.

"You have been spending a great deal of time with Juliet since you arrived," Lady Danford said. "I'm very happy with your choice of brides, but you didn't pay her any mind in Town. It does give one pause."

He'd been wrapped up in trying to win investors for Nathaniel. He'd been enthralled with being in London. "I do not know why everyone says that. I danced with her at every ball. I attended every function."

Sophia tilted her head and studied him for a long moment. "I didn't think that was why you were in attendance."

"I was in attendance to see Juliet." Those few minutes dancing with Juliet were the only times during his visits to London when he actually had felt as if he knew himself.

Lady Danford studied him for a long moment. Tony fought the urge to squirm. She had her way of getting information out of him. "She's liked you for a very long time."

Sophia pounced. "That's true. She followed us around like a puppy when you were courting me."

Tony winced. Sophia always brought that up. As if he were going lower by courting her sister. He knew now that marrying Sophia would have been a huge mistake.

Lady Danford stood. "I'm done in. I'm going up."

"Good night, Grandmother," Tony said.

She patted his hand. "Don't let the sun set on your anger, Son."

"I won't."

Tony made his way to where Juliet was reading by the fire. She looked up from her book but said nothing.

"What are you reading?"

"Just a novel."

"No agricultural tomes?" Tony picked up the book and looked at the spine. "*Rob Roy*—another romance."

Sophia joined them by the fire. "Juliet is always reading romances."

"Perhaps I like to escape into the story knowing that it will end happily," Juliet said.

"Real life isn't like that," Sophia said. "All that talk of romantic love. For instance, *Pride and Prejudice;* what was the point? Elizabeth should have known her place and accepted Darcy's first proposal. She would have had Pemberley and a fine life in Town."

"Sophia, you cannot be serious. Mr. Darcy clearly insulted her with his first proposal. You would not have accepted either," Juliet said.

"The point of the story was overcoming prejudice and falling in love," Tony said softly. "I thought the book was quite entertaining."

"What do you think of the books Juliet usually reads?" Sophia said. "I find them rather risqué."

Juliet's cheeks were flaming as Tony returned her book to her. "I have no objection to anything Juliet wishes to read. I rather enjoy reading Sir Walter Scott. If you will excuse us, Juliet has agreed to take a turn about the room with me," he said.

Tony took Juliet's hand and helped her to her feet. He tucked her hand in his arm and steered her away.

"What are you doing?" She tried to pull her hand away, but he wouldn't release it.

"We are taking a stroll."

"I'm not in the mood to stroll with you," she whispered furiously.

He glanced up and found everyone watching them closely. "Act as if we're making up."

"I'm still angry with you."

The woman was beyond stubborn. "Now you're just being foolish."

Juliet yanked her hand from his arm. "Foolish?"

"Jules—"

She moved closer to him and poked him in the chest. She was bloody furious. He only hoped she would keep her voice down.

"You are hiding something from me. If you plan to become my husband, you need to tell me what it is. I won't tolerate secrets."

He caught her hand. He wanted to deny it but couldn't. He *was* hiding something from her. And he would continue to do so until he had a plan to get around it. "We will discuss this later."

Juliet snorted. She turned and stomped out of the room without saying another word to anyone.

Damn.

"Haven't lost your touch, I see," Ian McDonald said, coming up beside Tony. "You can't tell her, can you? If she finds out from that idiot, you'll lose her for sure."

"She'll forgive me," Tony muttered. She had to if she cared about him. Didn't she?

"You know nothing about women. You lied to her."

"I did not lie," Tony defended himself. "I omitted."

Ian shook his head. "Tell her. Get it out in the open. Get it resolved."

Tony sighed heavily. "I just need a bit more time. I want to try to deal with Chelsworth first. Unfortunately, Bartleby seems determined to take it upon himself to tell Juliet."

"You don't have much time left."

Tony was afraid of that. He had to find a way to bind Juliet to him so she wouldn't leave him when the news broke.

Even telling her wouldn't keep him from losing her. She was just stubborn enough to end the engagement if she knew what he'd done.

"Tell her," Ian said softly, "or I'll do it. I mean it. I won't have her hurt because you're a damn coward."

"I'll do it." Tony would too, but first he'd find a way to make certain he didn't lose Juliet in the process.

Chapter Fourteen

Juliet barely slept that night and morning came all too soon. Tony had come to her door, but she'd refused to let him in. Had she let him touch her, kiss her, it wouldn't matter what his secrets were. She had no power to refuse him.

Juliet made her way down to the breakfast room. She needed tea desperately. Her eyes burned from lack of sleep. She found only her sister Anne in the room, nursing a piece of toast and a cup of tea.

"You look awful," Juliet said as she took some toast from the sideboard.

"It will pass—not soon enough for this assembly, though."

"I guess it's too late to cancel, considering how ill you are."

"Do you not realize it's only two days away?"

How had she forgotten? She thought it was still weeks away.

"You've been so wrapped up with Tony, you haven't noticed all the work around you for your own engagement ball," Anne said. "You will make up for it today. There are flowers to arrange, dresses to be fitted."

"I hate being fitted," Juliet grumbled.

Anne glared at her.

"Do we have to announce the engagement?" Juliet said

Anne set her cup down with a loud clatter. "What do you mean, not announce the engagement?" Anne's face was flushed, her eyes hard with anger.

The world was spinning out of control and somehow Juliet had missed the whole thing. "I only meant to keep it in the family for a while longer," Juliet explained.

"Are you or are you not going to marry Tony?" Anne demanded.

"I'd like to know the answer to that one myself," Tony said from the doorway.

Juliet sipped her tea. She refused to be intimidated by Tony, Anne, or anyone else. They could keep the assembly as just a late spring ball without having to announce anything. She didn't want all eyes on her. She didn't care if the engagement was never announced.

Tony stepped to the sideboard and filled a plate. He sat across from Juliet and motioned a servant for coffee. "You've not answered the question, Jules."

Juliet played with her cup. "I only meant that I don't need a ball to announce to the world that we are engaged. Having the banns read at church will be enough."

From the look in Tony's eyes, he knew she was hedging. Juliet didn't care. Until he quit keeping secrets from her, she wanted the ability to change her mind. While Mr. Bartleby might have caught them kissing twice, he had no idea it had gone any further. She might be labeled fast, but she wouldn't be ruined. Sophia had managed to get away with the same behavior for two Seasons now.

Anne pushed away from the table. "Regardless, there is a ball happening here the day after tomorrow and I expect you to do your share. No running off to hide at the Williamses' farm. The dressmaker will be here for your fitting at one. We've got to decorate the hall and get the house ready. Do. Not. Disappear."

"Yes, Anne," Juliet mumbled. Her day was ruined. There was nothing worse than dress fittings. The last time she'd had a fitting, she'd had to put up with jokes about her sunken chest. Why did that joke never die?

"I take it you object more to the engagement ball than the engagement itself," Tony said between bites of egg and sausage.

"I hate being the center of attention."

"Why? I thought all ladies loved to dance."

Juliet played with the edge of her teacup. "I don't mind the dancing. It can be quite nice."

"Then what is it you don't like about balls?"

"All those people, watching who you dance with, how close you are to each other, or worse, how many dances you dance with one person." Juliet loved being in Tony's arms. He waltzed beautifully and in his arms she felt beautiful, even special. At this ball they'd be watching and trying to discern why Tony had picked her. Juliet raised her eyes to find Tony regarding her with a curious smile on his lips.

"You haven't figured it out yet?"

Juliet suddenly felt breathless at the emotions chasing across his face. She dare not name it, nor believe it. "I think you were just tolerating me, Tony."

Tony chuckled. "Far from it." He finished his coffee and stood. "I'd best find McDonald."

"You aren't going to be around to help with the ball?"

"Good God, no. I plan on being as far from the house as possible until my presence is required," Tony said with a laugh. He came around to her side of the table, leaned down, and kissed her softly. "Behave yourself and help Anne. She's been feeling poorly lately." He kissed her again.

Juliet closed her eyes and leaned in to the kiss. Her hand softly brushed his face as her tongue teased his. Kissing Tony made her forget why she was angry with him. Kissing him made her forget her own name.

"Keep that up and you'll find yourself flat on the table and the wedding moved up," Tony said. He kissed her one last time, quick and hard. "I'm off."

Juliet watched as Tony left. She still had no answers to her questions. All the doubts came tumbling back into her mind like stones down a hill.

"Anything else, miss?" the footman asked.

"No, thank you," Juliet said, waving him away.

Anne stuck her head in the doorway. "Juliet, come help me cut flowers for the arrangements."

"Of course, Anne." Juliet pulled herself up from the chair to follow her sister out to the garden. As she walked around the house, Tony and Ian McDonald were leaving on horseback. She paused, watching them turn onto the lane toward the Horneswood estate. She frowned. Why would they go to Horneswood? Or were they? She supposed they could also be going to the Williamses' farm. It was in the same direction, but somehow, given how they were both dressed, she doubted they were heading out to do farmwork.

She was going to have to figure out what was going on. And something definitely was. Ian McDonald would tell her. She was sure of it.

* * *

Tony had waited at the stables for Ian. Seeing Juliet this morning, kissing her, had driven home that he wanted to start every day with her. Preferably in his bed. There was something right about marrying her. He couldn't lose her to his own stupidity. He could tell she was already questioning her decision.

"What's this about, Tony?" McDonald had said when he walked up. "I've not had my coffee yet."

"We're calling on Chelsworth."

"This early in the morning? He'll still be abed."

"I've tried to meet with him twice and he's always unavailable. I'll be pushing my way in today with your help." Tony had to get this resolved, sooner rather than later. Too many people knew the truth.

"Damn rude, if you ask me."

"The man won't meet with me. One way or another, I need to resolve this nightmare and move on. If that means finding another house and letting this one go, I will."

"This all could have been avoided—"

"Don't remind me." Tony was already reminded every minute he was in Juliet's presence that he'd made a huge mistake with that card game. The man had been in his cups.

Still he'd had no idea the man would gamble away a house just to win another game. While he hadn't been drunk, he'd had enough to make him more reckless than usual.

Tony had mounted his horse and accepted the reins from the groom. He'd spotted Juliet trailing after Anne with a basket, watching them with a frown on her face. The woman had an uncanny ability to uncover people's secrets. He'd tripped over it several times.

That latest stumble had almost ended the engagement. It still could. She was being stubborn about the engagement ball. It terrified him. Things could end badly in a trice.

"Let's get this done," Tony had said to Ian.

They left the house behind, trotting in silence down the lane toward Horneswood. It was a gorgeous spring morning. The trees along the lane provided shade from the new leaves.

"Now that we are away from curious eyes, what's the plan?" McDonald said. "I'm assuming you've tried to resolve this several times."

Tony blew out a puff of air. "The man is mad. He won't talk to me.

He won't answer any letters. I don't know what else to do. Bartleby is threatening to tell Juliet what really happened. I have to get this resolved."

"He knows he's ruined and is trying to avoid it," Ian said. "I'm not surprised at his reaction."

"This could all be over if I give him back his vowels. I wanted to offer to buy the house as well."

"This estate? It's a disaster. You said yourself that the tenant housing needs work. The land isn't being worked the way it should be. Why would you want to take that on?"

Because Juliet wanted it. Juliet was happy here. Because her friend was in trouble and Tony wanted to help.

But Tony couldn't tell Ian that. It wasn't a sound business reason. He knew better than anyone that you didn't make business decisions based on emotion. "I think I can turn it around."

Ian snorted. "I imagine Chelsworth thought the same thing."

Williams had said much the same. There'd been poor management for a very long time at Horneswood. "Still, if he accepts my offer, I'll have a house for Juliet and me."

"You still aren't going to tell her?" Ian didn't keep the disgust from his voice.

"I'll tell her. I'll tell her when this is over and we're married. We'll laugh about it."

Ian pulled the horse to a stop. "I can't let you do that to Juliet. You have to tell her before the wedding."

Tony glared at him. "This is none of your business."

"Juliet Townsend is my friend. I won't have her hurt."

McDonald was right. Juliet would be hurt by his omission. *Disappointed* would be a better word. It hurt him to think about it. "I won't allow it to come to that."

Ian said nothing, leaving Tony to his own thoughts, which was not a good thing. All he could envision was Juliet leaving him, or breaking off the engagement.

They paused at the gates of Horneswood. The iron was rusty and the stone crumbling.

"You will spend a fortune just fixing this pile," Ian said.

But it would be his. And Juliet's. It would be home. "What did you find out about Chelsworth?"

"Interesting case. Evidently he's been gambling and running up huge debts in Town for a long while. Creditors are getting nervous, especially with the rumors that he's lost the estate, which was collateral. The man should be desperate enough to accept any offer for the place."

"Is the house entailed?"

"No agreements were ever signed to keep it in the family. Chelsworth is the last of his line. He's unmarried, with no children, no other family members left. He owes more than the estate is worth."

Tony frowned. "I wonder if Bartleby had something to do with that. He's been doing some strange things with the tenants."

"I did some digging into him as well." Ian paused to look at the house. "His family used to own this land."

"You don't think he'd do something to drive the price down, do you?"

"I wouldn't put it past him, especially because his brother is anxious to get this old estate back. It was in his mother's family."

"How did it end up with Chelsworth?" Tony asked.

"I couldn't discover the particulars." Ian glanced at his pocket watch. "If we are going to barge in during the man's breakfast, we'd better just do it."

Tony nodded and led Ian up the long drive to the park. No groom came to take the horses. "I wonder if he's let the staff go."

"Perhaps they left because they weren't being paid." Ian tied his reins to a nearby bush. "If the worst happens, we can walk home, I suppose."

Tony did the same and they went to knock on the door. They stood there for a long time. Finally a maid opened the door. "We're here to see Mr. Chelsworth."

The poor maid went pale and looked behind her. "He ain't here, sir."

Tony glanced at Ian, who raised an eyebrow. "I think we'll wait inside, if you don't mind." He pushed open the door and walked into the entryway, then stopped.

"Sir, you can't—" the maid wailed. "Master is going to beat me."

Ian stepped into the empty entryway and pressed a coin into her hand. "If your master gives you trouble, let me know. I'll take care of it. Now, please fetch him for us."

"Yes, sir."

The maid disappeared to the back of the house, her steps echoing in the empty hall. Not one mirror or stick of furniture remained. The paintings were gone as well. Empty squares marked where they'd hung.

"Looks like he's sold off most of the furniture," Ian said, peeking into one of the rooms off the entry. "Not even a chair to sit on."

"Things are worse than I thought. I've not been able to get into the house before."

"Bartleby stopped you?"

"Most times, which was surprising. Where is he now?" Tony looked around. The place was like a tomb. "Do you think we might have to go look for Chelsworth?"

"He could be sneaking out of the house, thinking we are here to collect a debt."

"Aren't we?" Seeing how empty the house was, Tony was going to have to rethink his solution to this plan. Even if he forgave Chelsworth's debt to him, it wouldn't save the various tenant families who were relying on this estate for their livelihoods. Things had been so much different when Tony hadn't been involved with the tenants. Now that he knew the Williamses and some of the others, he couldn't just let this go. He had to ensure they were going to be taken care of.

"Perhaps. Let's walk toward the kitchens. I doubt he had a tray sent to his room. Not enough staff," Ian said.

"Wait. He's coming now." Tony noticed Chelsworth coming down the hall, an angry expression on his face. His clothes were wrinkled and his hair stood straight up, as if he'd run his hands through it regularly. He was a far cry from the gentleman Tony had met in Town.

"What are you doing here?" Chelsworth spat.

Tony noticed the maid hovering in the hallway. "Perhaps we can discuss this somewhere more private?"

"I've nothing to say to you." The man's face was florid, his nose and eyes red.

Tony could smell the alcohol. "We've a proposal for you that might solve all our problems."

"That I doubt," the man mumbled. "Come along. Bring coffee to the library, girl."

"Yes, sir."

"Damn girl should do a better job of screening callers," Chelsworth said, opening a door on the left of the hallway. "The library is one of the few rooms left with furniture."

Tony glanced at Ian as they followed the man. The room was dark and smelled of stale smoke and whiskey. That explained the wrinkled clothes. Chelsworth had probably spent the night there.

Papers littered the old desk. Two more chairs were in the room, but not much else. The shelves were empty of books and dusty. The curtains sagged in places and the carpet was threadbare.

"I'd offer you a brandy—"

Tony held up a hand. "A bit too early for me, but thank you."

Chelsworth sat in the chair behind the desk and shoved the papers aside. "What is this proposal you spoke of? Does it get me a ticket to America and money to start over?"

Tony looked at Ian. "There is the debt to be dealt with first," Tony said carefully.

"I have no money," Chelsworth said. "And you won the house fair and square. All I ask is that you give me some funds to start over."

"Where would you go?"

"America? India? The Continent? Don't really care much as long as it's away from here."

"Perhaps there's family—" Tony said carefully.

"There is no family," Chelsworth said. "I can sell it and let you dispute the gambling debt with the new owner."

"Has someone put in an offer on the estate?" Tony asked. His thought was to buy the house outright but deduct the gambling debt from the price.

"My land agent tells me he has a buyer," Chelsworth said. "I've not seen the offer." He leaned forward on the desk. "What's your offer?"

Tony glanced at Ian. "I propose to buy the house at its current value minus the gambling debt you owe me. That should leave you with enough money to do whatever you want."

Ian leaned forward on his arms. "The estate has not been producing as it should."

"Are you accusing me of mismanagement?" Chelsworth said.

Tony glared at Ian. "Not necessarily."

"You've been visiting the tenants, so my land agent tells me," Chelsworth accused. "For what purpose except to drive the price down?"

Tony paused. "Why would I drive the price down? You lost the estate in a game. You used it as collateral for your losses. Offering to buy out the house minus what you owe me is more than fair."

"Then why visit the tenants?"

"Just taking an interest in my investment," Tony said. "The estate is mine regardless."

"The rumor is that you're doing it for your fiancée. She's befriended one of the farmer's daughters," Chelsworth said. "You should have better control over your lady."

"My fiancée cares about the families in the village. As we are hoping to settle here after our marriage, I see nothing wrong with that."

Chelsworth sat back in his chair and crossed his arms but said nothing.

Ian looked at Tony. "The lady's charitable works are not a matter for discussion. We've made a proposal to purchase the estate for a fair price."

"You'd be deducting a fortune," Chelsworth exclaimed.

"Only to cover a gambling debt you incurred," Ian McDonald said. "A debt that, as a gentleman, you are honor bound to pay."

"The decision is yours, Chelsworth. Agree to my deal and walk away with money to either gamble away or escape to America for a new start."

"Or what?" Chelsworth chuckled. "What could you do from here?"

"I have letters notifying your creditors that this estate is no longer yours, and that you have no means with which to pay your debts. I believe that qualifies you for debtors' prison, does it not, Mr. McDonald?" He looked to Ian.

"I believe it does," Ian said with a smirk. "I hear Marshalsea is quite nice this time of year. The heat isn't so bad that it acerbates the smell of unwashed bodies and urine."

Chelsworth leaned forward. "I want the chance to win it back."

This was the last thing Tony needed. Nathaniel would kill him. Juliet would break the engagement. Given her family history, Juliet would never accept a husband who gambled like her brother. "No."

Chelsworth's eyes grew wild, his voice panicky. "A friendly game. Winner takes all."

"Isn't that how you got into this situation in the first place?" Tony said. "Accept the deal and you walk away with your honor intact and money in your pocket. Otherwise, I'll notify your creditors and see that you are no longer welcome in any of the gaming hells in London."

"Not to mention the clubs," Ian said. "No one wants to play with someone who can't honor his debts."

"You can't do that!" Chelsworth said. "I'll be ruined."

Tony almost pitied him. Chelsworth needed gambling to live. "The choice is yours."

Chelsworth sat back in his chair and covered his face with his hands. "You've given me no choice but to agree to your terms."

Ian pulled papers out of his pocket. "I have a bill of sale here. Let's sign this so you can move on with your life."

Chelsworth took out pen and ink and signed the document without so much as reading it. "I'll be gone by the end of the week. The property is yours."

"Thank you." Tony reached into his pocket and pulled out the bank note for the price of the property. "As we agreed."

"I'll inform Bartleby that the land is changing hands," Chelsworth said.

"Please tell Mr. Bartleby that I'll be by to meet with him in three days. Tell him to have his ledgers ready for me to go over." Tony wanted Bartleby gone from the property before he could do any more damage.

Ian took the signed documents and folded them. "I'll file the necessary papers to complete the sale of the property."

"Thank you for seeing reason, Chelsworth," Tony said.

"Reason? I had little choice," Chelsworth muttered.

"You have your new start. Try not to gamble it all away," Tony said harshly. "The next man you lose a fortune to may not be so easy to deal with."

Tony and Ian left Chelsworth sitting at his desk. They stood in the park of Horneswood and looked around. The house was Tony's. He had a home. He couldn't wait to show Juliet the place where they would raise their children.

"Nicely done," Ian said. "When will you tell Juliet of the purchase?"

"I don't know. I might save it as a surprise for the engagement," Tony said with a smile. Finally, things were as they should be. He could be open and honest about it. Mostly.

"I suppose Brighton is out of the question now."

"I'm afraid it is, unless Juliet wants to see it." Tony wanted to be married as quickly as he could. He was ready for his life to start. His new life, with Juliet.

"Damn, that means I'm going to have to go," Ian said.

Tony mounted his horse. "I'll talk to Nathaniel after the ball."

"I hope you know what you're doing. It will cost a fortune to repair the damage and neglect."

Tony already knew that. "Yes, but it has potential. A great deal of potential."

Chapter Fifteen

Tony was so excited about resolving the Chelsworth mess that he couldn't wait any longer to tell Juliet. While they couldn't tour the house until the sale had been finalized, he could drive her by and tell her about her new home.

It had been so long since the cards had been in his favor. Now he could be his own man, set his own destiny, and settle down with the woman he loved.

He loved her.

It had been coming on for so long, he hadn't really noticed. Tony wanted her with a fierceness that was beyond description. He felt tenderness when he touched her. Protective when she was frightened. He wanted to see her swollen with his child. He wanted to wake up beside her every morning. *Hell, it must be love.*

Tony wouldn't have to disclose how he came to buy the house. The gambling issue could be put in a box and sealed, and he could move on. It was exactly the solution he had been hoping for.

Of course there was still Bartleby to deal with. His meeting with the slimy land agent was set for the day after the ball. When Tony owned the estate he'd fire Bartleby, and that problem would be solved.

But today was about Juliet and him. It was time for a private celebration.

Tony had the stable master ready the curricle with Nathaniel's black stallions. He had Cook pack a picnic lunch. He would show her the house, tell her the news, and spend some quiet moments with her by the pond. He ached to feel her skin against his again. He ached to end the tension between them.

Juliet walked into the stable yard dressed in a simple dress and pelisse. She looked fresh and so pretty it made his heart skip a beat. She pushed her spectacles back up her nose.

"What's this?" she asked as she approached the curricle carefully.

Tony pressed his lips to her gloved hands. "I thought we'd take a drive. I've got a surprise for you." Tony handed her into the seat and he climbed in beside her. He accepted the reins from the stable master.

Juliet cut him a look and grabbed the edge of her seat as the horses took off at the touch of his whip.

"Where are we going?" Juliet said carefully.

"Just a few miles up the road," he said. "I think I might have found a house for us. We have to live somewhere, don't we?" Tony said.

Juliet didn't say anything for a few minutes. He glanced down at her face but couldn't see it due to the bonnet she wore.

"Of course," Juliet said.

There was a tone in her voice that gave him pause. "Did you think I wouldn't want to marry you?"

Juliet turned her head away from him, staring at the trees. "I thought you proposed so I wouldn't be ruined. Mr. Bartleby finding us like that . . ."

Tony pulled the reins to a stop and turned to Juliet. "I would have proposed anyway. Bartleby just precipitated the inevitable."

Juliet turned to him, her eyes anxious.

Tony took her gloved hand and raised it to his lips, his eyes never leaving hers. "Will you marry me?"

She gasped, and then covered it up with a laugh. "No fancy words? No poetry? You at least wrote Sophia poetry."

Tony damped down the disappointment. Juliet was stalling. He had no choice but to play along for now. "True, but I was young and foolish, with much to learn." He winked at her. "With the emphasis on the foolish, given the poetry I was writing at the time."

"It was awful."

"Careful. I might have to write some for you." He watched a blush touch her cheeks.

"Please spare me." She glanced out at the landscape as they approached the long drive to Horneswood.

"But isn't poetry the fruit of love?" he teased. "Aren't young ladies supposed to swoon over it?"

She laughed, and the feather on her hat danced with the motion.

"Poetry is the fruit of the nonsensical. I'd rather swoon over a good novel."

"I'm no novelist, but I can try, for you."

There was an unreadable expression in her eyes. "I'm not the sort of girl who inspires men to write."

His heart cracked open a little. "I will write you a poem, for our wedding."

"Oh, please, no." She laughed.

Tony guided the curricle down the lane to Horneswood. "I imagine you and your sisters had a good laugh at my expense."

"Only a small bit."

"Now I should definitely write a poem for our wedding."

Juliet sat up straighter in her seat. "This is Horneswood."

"I purchased it," Tony said. "The owner finally agreed to the price."

"If this is a joke, Tony, it's not funny," Juliet said.

He pulled the reins to stop the horse on the side of the lane, where they would be afforded the best view of the house. It was not as large as the Lodge, or as pretty, but it was his. Theirs. "I made the offer only this morning."

"What about the tenants? The Williamses?"

"It was Mr. Williams who gave me the idea of purchasing the place outright." Tony took her hand. "And you, of course."

Juliet turned her face to him. Her smile was wide, her eyes tear-filled. "I can't believe you did this for me."

"Are you going to be able to bear being married to a gentleman farmer? There won't be as many fine dresses or trips to London."

"I don't care about dresses or London." She leaned forward and kissed him. "Thank you."

Her gloved hand was cool and smooth against his hand, her lips soft. His pulse picked up as she pulled back.

"You've changed so much. You're settling down. You've given up your rakish ways," she said.

"Are you going to answer my question? Will you make me the happiest of men and become my wife?"

"I know that I've been uncertain about marrying you. I was afraid you'd fall back into gambling and I wouldn't be able to tolerate that. But you're not that man anymore."

He was right to keep the truth about the estate from her. Let her think he'd just decided to buy it. It was mostly true. She didn't have to know the circumstances behind the sale. Maybe he'd tell her in twenty years or so, and they could have a good laugh about it.

For now, the joy in her eyes was enough. "Say yes," he said. "Be my wife. Be my partner. Make a home with me."

Juliet's heart pounded at Tony's sweet words. It was like every dream she'd ever had finally came true. "Partner?"

"Of course. I can't do this without you, Jules. You are so much smarter than me in many ways. I'd be foolish not to take advantage of it."

No one had appreciated her brain before. She smiled through her tears. "Yes, Tony, I will marry you."

His blue eyes burned with emotion as he looked down at her. Juliet couldn't ever have imagined being this happy. "Shall we see the inside of the house?"

"Not yet. I've given Mr. Chelsworth time to remove his personal belongings. I should be able to take possession after the ball."

Juliet frowned. "What about Mr. Bartleby? Does he know?"

Tony turned the carriage around. "He probably does now. I'll meet with him after the ball."

"What will you do about him?"

"I will send him packing. I have enough evidence from the tenants to make sure he won't be a land agent again in this area any time soon."

Juliet bit her lip. Would Bartleby act out to hurt Penelope? The man was arrogant and mean.

"Don't worry. There won't be any repercussions, and if there are, he will find himself in gaol," Tony said.

Juliet relaxed and leaned against Tony. "Where are we going now?"

"The pond. I have a romantic picnic planned."

"You, romantic? I can hardly fathom it."

"I'm capable of being just as romantic as the next man."

"Is this what you couldn't tell me earlier?"

Tony stiffened beside her. After a long pause, he said, "I wanted it to be a surprise."

"Thank you."

"For what?"

"For explaining of course. I'm sorry I was angry about the secrets. I must learn to be more patient—"

"I can think of a few things we can do to teach you patience." He pulled the curricle to a stop near a large tree. He jumped down and tied off the horse before grasping Juliet's waist and pulling her into his arms. "It starts with kissing you. All over. Slowly."

Juliet gasped as her body slid down against his. "What if I don't want it slowly?"

He brushed his lips against hers. "Slow is good. Slow is thorough." He kissed her deeply.

Juliet surrendered to his kiss, her hands reaching into his hair. Her tongue tangled with his. Want and need thickened her blood and warmed her skin. She needed this man. *Now.*

Tony pulled away from her. "First lesson in patience: There is a time and a place for everything."

Juliet tried to pull him back, but he stepped farther away. "This is the time and the place," she said.

"We've both waited for that moment. I'd like it to be in a bed, not in a field where anyone could walk by."

"If you insist."

Tony reached behind the bench of the curricle and pulled out a basket. "Cook packed this for us. Are you hungry?"

"For food? Not really," Juliet said.

"You are going to be the death of me."

She grinned and took the blanket from him. "Where do you want to sit?"

"I thought in the shade by the pond," Tony said. He set the basket down in the grass. Together they smoothed the blanket over the ground. Once they were settled on the blanket, Juliet asked, "How did you manage to purchase Horneswood? Did you buy it from the new owner?"

"Something like that. Did you know Chelsworth?"

"He's never been here much. And when he was, no one saw him. In fact, when Mr. Williams had his accident, the man didn't even visit him to make sure he was all right."

Tony poured a glass of wine and handed it to Juliet. "Things will be different now."

"What are you going to do about the Williamses?" Juliet knew he had to deal with things in a businesslike manner, but her heart still hurt for the family that was so special to her.

"I think they can make up the rents. Despite Mr. Williams's injuries, he has some good ideas on how the estate should be run," Tony said, lifting his glass. "Enough of this talk. I want to drink a toast to my lovely bride."

Juliet smiled and clinked her glass to his. "When shall we have the banns read?"

Tony set down his glass carefully on the grass and unloaded strawberries, ham, and bread on the blanket. "I thought I'd get a special license so we could marry right away."

"That quickly? What will people think?"

"That I'm so besotted with my bride, I couldn't wait any longer." He kissed her deeply.

Juliet let herself fall into the kiss, her tongue tangling with his. She sighed as he pulled away. "You make me drunk with passion."

He grinned. "Good. You've been tying me in knots since I arrived. Shall we eat?"

"If we're going to eat, then we must talk of practical matters. Otherwise I'll be too tempted to kiss you again." Juliet smiled as he offered her a strawberry. She bit into it and let the sweetness fill her mouth. She closed her eyes and almost moaned. "This is perfect."

She opened her eyes to find Tony was watching her with his mouth open. Good. She wasn't the only one suffering. "How furnished is the house?"

"What?"

"How furnished is the house? I assume if Mr. Chelsworth was deeply in debt, we'll have to purchase furniture." Juliet took a bit of ham and cheese with her bread.

"The house appears to be pretty barren. I'll leave the decorating to you, but I'll have our bedroom ready before we marry."

Juliet's cheeks heated. He didn't play fair. She nibbled at her lunch. "What about the rest of the servants?"

"I think most have already left. I don't know when they were last paid. I'll have to rectify that matter."

"Mrs. Fellows at the Lodge can help us find good staff." Juliet was starting to feel a bit out of her depth. Anne had been lucky; she'd been running Lady Danford's house even before she married Nathaniel.

Juliet didn't have the same type of training. She'd never managed a house. She didn't even have her own maid. She shared with Sophia.

"What's going through that head of yours, sweetheart?" His voice was tender, understanding.

"I have no idea how to run a house, Tony." Her voice cracked. "What if I make a mess of it?"

"You won't. You're a kind woman, and people respond to that in you. I'm certain you will be fine. "

"Anne makes it look so effortless. And Sophia just orders people around."

"You treat people with respect. That is all anyone really wants. Respect their work and see how the servants respond."

Juliet nodded. She still had her doubts, but she'd figure it out. Anne would gladly help her.

"There is one thing I need to discuss with you, though."

Juliet frowned at the serious tone in his voice. He drained his glass of wine.

"What?" she asked.

"Your reading habits. Such naughty books, dearest." His eyes held a wicked glint.

She played along. "I thought you liked my naughty books. Though you did return one."

"Did you see the page I marked?"

She blushed. The page was one of a woman with her mouth on the man's privates. She couldn't stop herself from being curious but wasn't sure how it all worked.

"I see you do remember."

His voice rumbled along her nerve endings like ruts in the lane. Juliet was suddenly breathless.

"Are you finished eating?" Tony's voice dropped another octave.

Juliet nodded. "Shall I help you pack everything?"

"I'll take care of it." He placed things back into the basket slowly. He hesitated with the dish of strawberries and then set it back to the side of the blanket. "I might want dessert later."

Juliet could feel minor tremors from inside her body. She didn't know what to do with her hands. Should she remove her bonnet? Her pelisse?

Tony took the decision out of her hands as he slowly untied the ribbon of her bonnet. He removed it and set it aside. "You are so lovely."

"No. I'm not," she whispered automatically.

He tipped her chin so that her eyes met his. "Do not disagree with me. In my eyes, you are the loveliest of women."

"You haven't seen that many."

"I've seen enough to know that no other woman will do for me. Only you." His mouth met hers in a deep, soul-taking kiss.

Juliet let him guide her down on the blanket. His hands fumbled with the buttons on her pelisse.

"You have on too many clothes," he groaned.

"We are outside," she reminded him. "You were the one who said you wished to wait."

"I wanted to see the sun dapple your skin."

She shivered as he brushed aside the pelisse. One of his hands gently squeezed her breast through the thin muslin of her dress as his mouth took hers hungrily. She let herself get lost in his taste, his touch.

"Tony, touch me. Really touch me."

"As you wish, love." He pushed her bodice down and freed her breast. Her nipple tightened in the cool spring air. "Now time for dessert."

Tony took a strawberry and bit into it. He then rubbed the berry juice over her nipple, staining it red. "That's better." He pulled her breast into his mouth, suckling the juices from it. "Delicious," he whispered. "Shall we do the other one?"

Juliet's hands rushed to the fastenings of her dress. She needed so much more.

"Slowly, love." He loosened the dress and freed her other breast. He teased her nipple with the strawberry, then pulled it deeply into his mouth.

Juliet closed her eyes and moaned. She was never going to be able to eat strawberries again without remembering this.

She opened her eyes to find him staring at her. His look made her feel pretty, cherished, loved.

Tony pulled at the hem of her skirts until he could get his hand beneath. His callused hands scratched the tender skin of her thighs.

"So soft." His mouth found hers again and captured her cry as his hand found the juncture of her thighs.

He teased her with his fingers, barely touching the bud of nerves where she throbbed with want for him. "More, Tony. Please."

"As you wish, love."

He kissed her deeply as he inserted first one finger, then another inside her.

It wasn't enough. She needed more. She arched against his hand in a frantic rhythm, trying to force him to give her that sweet release.

"God, you're so beautiful," he said hoarsely against her throat. His mouth pulled again on one nipple, then another. "Come for me, sweetheart."

Juliet let the passion claim her as she arched against her release. "Oh, God."

Tony's touch slowed, soothed, bringing her down from the excitement. Her heart slowed, as did her breathing. She took her hands and pulled his face to hers and kissed him. "Your turn."

"My turn comes tonight." He tugged her skirts back down. "Will you let me come to you tonight? Will you finally be with me?"

"Are we going to act out that picture?"

"If you want," he said. "I think you're going to be the death of me, love."

"We'll die together next time." She brushed his hair from his forehead. "Tonight we'll be together."

"Let's get you tucked in and back home before anyone figures out what we've been up to."

Juliet fixed her bodice and allowed Tony to refasten her gown. "I had no idea you were so concerned about propriety, Mr. Matthews."

"I am where you're concerned. Now finish up getting dressed and I'll load the curricle."

"Yes, sir."

"Saucy wench." He kissed her again. He picked up the rest of the picnic things and loaded them into the basket. Juliet folded the blanket and followed Tony to the curricle.

She was so relaxed, so lost in her own emotions, that she didn't notice the popping sound until Tony knocked her to the ground.

Chapter Sixteen

Bloody hell, someone was firing shots at them. His arm burned in pain. He must have been hit. "Are you all right?" he asked.

"I can't breathe," Juliet said, her voice muffled by his chest. She shoved at him. "What's going on?"

He moved aside but placed a hand on her stomach. "Stay down. Someone shot at us."

"Who would do such a thing?" Juliet looked shocked.

Tony had his ideas but said nothing. He looked around for the curricle, but it was gone. The contents of the basket had been thrown over the ground after tumbling out of the runaway vehicle. They were going to have to walk home.

Unfortunately, they were in the open, so if they raised their heads, they'd likely be shot at again.

"Perhaps hunters don't know we're here."

"I don't think it is hunters. I'm going to get up slowly. Stay put until I can make sure the blackguard is gone."

Juliet went pale. "But he could shoot you."

"He already has."

Juliet gasped. "You're hurt? Where?"

Tony sat up slowly. "My arm. It's not serious." At least he didn't think it was serious; it felt like he'd only been grazed.

"We have to get you home." Juliet bent over and tore off a piece of her petticoat. "At least let me bind it."

"Thank you. Most young ladies would be screaming or crying."

"Just wait. I'll fall apart once the danger has passed," Juliet said with a wry smile. "You'll have to medicate me with brandy."

"There's brandy waiting at the Lodge." Tony allowed her to remove his ruined jacket. Blood had soaked into the linen of his shirt.

He pulled it away, tearing open a bigger hole. Juliet wrapped the piece of petticoat around his wound.

"It looks like a burn or a scratch," she said. "I don't think it penetrated the skin too deeply."

"I don't either. Luckily, the man is a lousy shot."

"I'm supposed to be home for my dress fitting. What do we do now?" Juliet asked, keeping her voice low. "The Williamses' farm is nearby. We can go there and have Aaron take us home in their cart."

"I don't want to take the lane. We'll be walking targets in case he comes back." Tony searched the woods for movement. The shots had come from the direction of the lane, but the man could have run into the forest. "Do you know a quicker way back to the Lodge from here?"

"There's a path through the woods that leads to the back pasture of the Lodge, by the river."

"We'll go home that way."

"What about the curricle and the horse?"

"The horse knows his way home. If not, someone in the village will return him. May I see your bonnet?"

Jules removed it and handed it to him. "What's wrong with it?"

He held it up, sticking his finger through a hole in the brim. Juliet went white and, for a second, Tony thought he'd have to carry her home in a dead faint.

"We must go. We're targets until we get to the woods," Tony said. He held on to the bonnet and rose carefully, ready to duck if he heard any movement. There was nothing. He pulled Juliet to her feet. "Do exactly as I tell you. Until we are away from here, we are not safe."

She remained pale but nodded.

He took her hand and led her into the woods, leaving the blanket and picnic things all over the ground. He wanted nothing to slow them down in reaching the Lodge. Someone would pay for this. The graze in his arm was one thing, but to shoot at a lady? Thankfully, whoever it was had missed. Had Juliet had been hurt, there would be nowhere the man could hide.

Juliet trembled beside him, but she didn't cry or scream. She had bottom.

"Tell me which way to go, love," Tony said softly, pulling her closer to him. He needed to keep her calm.

"Your arm is bleeding through the bandage."

"It will stop in a few minutes."

Juliet pointed to an old, barely distinguishable path at the far edge of the small clearing. He held the branches away from her face as she took the lead.

They walked silently, deeper and deeper into the woods. Juliet tensed as she heard the cracking of a branch, as if someone had stepped on it. He pulled her down behind some brambles until they could make out the sounds—probably animals, a deer or rabbit. They ducked down several times before they reached the edge of the woods, by the Fairy Steps.

"You know the way home from here," Juliet said breathlessly.

"I think we're safe now. Let's rest a minute."

They settled onto the first of the stone steps.

"I found you here, that first day you came back," Juliet said. "I always wondered if you were making a wish."

Tony chuckled. "I don't know about a wish. I knew I was ready for a change."

"I don't think someone wants you to change. Do you think it was Mr. Bartleby?"

He did, but he didn't want her thinking about it. "Why would he shoot at us?"

"He knows you purchased Horneswood. He has to know he is losing his position."

"I don't think he'd be stupid enough to fire at us. You look done in. Let's get you home."

Juliet leaned her head against his sore arm and he winced. She jumped back. "I'm sorry. We need to get a doctor to look at that."

"It's just a scratch." He stood and pulled her to her feet with his good arm. "And don't worry, it's not going to keep me from spending tonight with you, so don't get any ideas."

"Are we going to have more strawberries, Tony? Because I didn't get a taste."

"I think that can be arranged. In fact, I'll make sure we have strawberries ready, just in case."

"You know they are my favorite," she teased. Her lips traced his jaw.

"Behave or we'll never get home." He took her hand and raised it to press his lips against her glove. He pushed the glove from her wrist and pressed his mouth against the pale skin of her wrist. "Tonight, you'll finally be mine."

Juliet shivered against him. "Good."

They arrived at the Lodge without further incident. Tony wasn't happy when Juliet made a fuss about his arm, but she was worried about it getting putrid.

Nathaniel was the angriest she'd ever seen him. She sat through question after question about what had occurred. Things had happened so fast that Juliet couldn't remember much except Tony pulling her to the ground and protecting her. Her stomach gave a little lurch every time she thought about it. She hated that Tony was hurt, but she loved the way he had protected her.

She never thought of herself as being that kind of woman, who wanted to lean on a man. She wanted to be strong like Anne, but she liked knowing that Tony was there to protect her, to keep her safe from harm, to worry about her.

Which brought her around to the shooter. Tony seemed to think it was Bartleby. She'd overheard him talking to Mr. McDonald before she was rushed upstairs to prepare for her final fitting for the ball the next day.

Why would Mr. Bartleby take shots at them?

Why would the younger son of a peer take the position of a land steward in the first place? It would make more sense for him to have gone into the military or the Church. Mr. Bartleby could also marry an heiress. He'd courted Juliet for her money and she didn't have that much. Surely he could do better in London.

And there was the way he had treated Penelope, Mr. Williams, and the other tenants. He was capable of cruelty.

"Stand still, Juliet, and focus," Anne said in a frustrated tone. "You've kept Mrs. Jenkins far too long as it is."

"It's quite all right, Mrs. Matthews. It's not every day a girl finds herself in love."

Juliet fought the urge to roll her eyes. She hated fittings. "Thank you for staying, Mrs. Jenkins."

Mrs. Jenkins was fussing with the bodice. "Should we pad this a bit more, do you think, Mrs. Matthews?"

"No," Juliet said. "It's uncomfortable."

"But the dress will fit so much better if we do."

"You can't make the dress fit without it?"

"Not before tomorrow night," Mrs. Jenkins said.

"Fine." Juliet gave up. Tony knew the truth and didn't care.

Anne picked up the bonnet Juliet had tossed on the bed. "Do you realize there's a hole in this bonnet?"

"Anne—"

Anne went pale and tossed the bonnet back on the bed. "We'll talk about it later."

Juliet almost sagged with relief. She looked down at the dress. It was a pale, shimmering blue fabric trimmed in silver. It was quite pretty. "Thank you for doing this, Anne."

Anne's eyes welled with tears. She was so emotional when she was increasing. "I'm so happy for you. And for Tony. Who would have thought?"

Juliet smiled. "I didn't."

"I suspected when we were in Town. He would never miss any of the balls we attended, but he only danced with you; then he'd leave. I thought that was so strange."

"He bought Horneswood."

"I didn't know it was for sale."

"Neither did I. We went to look at it."

"Is that where you were?" Anne said, shooting a glance at Mrs. Jenkins.

"We had a picnic by a pond near the house."

"How romantic!" Mrs. Jenkins said. "It's so nice to see young gentlemen doing things like that. Though I will say that in his day, Mr. Jenkins could play the romantic fool quite well. I miss those days sometimes."

"I know what you mean, Mrs. Jenkins," Anne said with a sigh. "Daily life has a way of making us forget the romance."

Juliet frowned. "I hope not. I'm just getting used to it."

Mrs. Jenkins and Anne both chuckled.

"Romance is best in small doses, my dear," Mrs. Jenkins said with a smile. She turned Juliet toward the mirror. "There. The dress is perfect for you."

Juliet stared at herself in the mirror. *Dear Lord, she looked like a bride.* The pale blue brought out her brown eyes and the red in her hair. The silver added a bit of shine, catching the light as she moved. "It's beautiful."

"You'll be the belle of the ball," Mrs. Jenkins said as she undid the fastenings down the back. "Let me get the alterations done and I'll have it ready for you tomorrow."

"Perfect, Mrs. Jenkins," Anne said. "Thank you for waiting for Juliet to get back. I don't know what happened to cause their horse to bolt."

"No harm done," Mrs. Jenkins said. "It will be nice to have another young couple in the neighborhood. It's good to see Beetham growing."

"Thank you, Mrs. Jenkins," Juliet said, stepping down from the stool.

Anne had the maid escort the seamstress out and closed the door. She leaned against it. "Tell me everything."

"About what?"

"The house, the shots fired, everything," Anne said. "Nathaniel would keep me in the dark about all of it."

Juliet agreed with Nathaniel. Anne was in the early stages of pregnancy. She didn't need the worry.

"Don't behave as Nathaniel did. You're my sister and therefore on my side," Anne chided.

Juliet plopped on the bed, still in her petticoat with the tear in it. "We went for a drive and stopped on the lane to look at Horneswood. Tony told me he bought it for us."

"What else happened?"

"He proposed again. Properly this time. And then we went for a picnic." Juliet got up and went to the cupboard for another gown. "Are we dressing for dinner?"

Anne put her hands on her hips. "Don't play games with me, Juliet. Who fired the shots?"

Juliet frowned at her sister. "I don't know, so there's no point in getting upset."

"There's a bullet hole in your bonnet!"

Good heavens, when Anne wanted to raise her voice, she did it with a vengeance. "Anne, settle down—think of the baby."

"Who would shoot at you?"

"I don't know, honestly." Juliet pulled out a dress and tossed it over her head. She turned her back to Anne, who automatically fastened the hooks for her. "Tony will find out."

"Thank God for Tony. I don't even want to imagine what would have happened if you had been alone," Anne said. She tucked a strand of hair behind Juliet's ear. "You are certain you're all right?"

"Right as rain. Tony was the only one hurt, and it appears to be just a scratch." Juliet hadn't gotten the chance to even look at the wound. She had been ushered to the room for her fitting as soon as they arrived.

"Men always say that. God forbid they show weakness," Anne complained. "I swear, the only time I saw Nathaniel squirm was when I was in labor with Nat. I thought we were going to have to pour brandy down his throat to get him to calm down."

Juliet chuckled. She remembered realizing how much Nathaniel loved her sister in that moment. He couldn't fix the pain and he was having none of it. "Do you think Tony will be the same?"

Anne smiled for the first time. "I think he will. He loves you, you know."

Juliet looked down at her hands. "He hasn't said so."

"I've watched him since the ball we had before Nathaniel and I were married. That night was the first night he realized you were not a child any longer. He couldn't take his eyes off you."

Tears welled in Juliet's eyes. She so wanted to believe that he loved her, had loved her as long as she'd loved him. "Really?"

"At every ball in London he only had eyes for you. I was beginning to wonder if he'd ever act on it when he came home this time."

"Do you think he came home because of me?"

"I think that was part of it."

"Perhaps I'll ask him."

"I wouldn't," Anne said with a chuckle. "Men don't know their own minds when it comes to love and softer emotions. One day they awake and realize they are in love. Tony will tell you when he's ready."

Well, that was true, Juliet thought. She picked up the bonnet and stuck her finger in the hole left by the bullet. "Shall we dispose of this? I think it's quite ruined."

"Yes, let's. We need no reminders of unpleasantness. These next few days are all about you, Juliet." Anne smiled wistfully. "I wish Mama could see what a lovely bride you'll make."

"Perhaps she's looking down from heaven watching. I hope she'd be pleased."

"She would be, dear. She would be."

Juliet let Anne wrap her arms around her and hug her tight, feeling strangely sad and happy all at once.

Chapter Seventeen

Tony paused in front of Juliet's bedroom, his hand on the door. He was hesitant. Afraid to turn the handle. Enter the room. Change their relationship forever.

His hands trembled. The way she had looked at him as she sat beside him, stroking his hand while they listened to music after dinner. He could barely walk from wanting Juliet so badly.

Tony drew in a breath. Once he stepped inside her room, there would be no getting out of marriage. She would be his.

She'd made up her mind. She'd said yes, he reminded himself. She never needed to know just how he had come to buy their house.

For the first time in his life, Tony felt out of his depth. If he ruined this moment for Juliet, it would be with them both for a long time. But he needed Juliet. He needed her warmth in his bed. He needed her skin against his. He needed her. It wasn't just passion. She was home. She was his future, and he was ready to take that first step toward it. No words said by the vicar were going to make a difference in how he felt about her.

He opened the door and stepped inside, closing and locking the door behind him. The click of the lock sealed their fate.

The fire burned low in the hearth, giving little light to the room. Juliet sat up in bed and looked at him, straining to find him in the darkness. "Tony?"

Tony cleared his throat. "I—uh—need you. I can't wait any longer. Please don't say no."

Juliet pulled on her spectacles, then pulled the sheets to her chin. Her hair was a dark rope hanging over her shoulder.

Tony walked toward the bed. He removed his robe and dropped it to the floor. Juliet's eyebrows went up and she licked her lips as she took in his bare chest.

"Am I welcome?"

Juliet said nothing, and Tony started to worry that he'd misread the messages she'd been sending in the parlor that night. He thought about reaching for his robe and making his escape, until she moved.

Juliet rose from the bed and moved toward him without saying a word.

Never had she looked more beautiful than at this moment when she came to him and put her hands on his body.

Her hands curled in the hairs on his chest and he groaned. "I take it that's a yes."

Juliet looked up at him and smiled. A wicked smile. "I waited and waited. I fell asleep debating whether I should come to you."

Tony took his hand and unbraided her hair, spreading it around her shoulders. He could feel the tremors in her body. "Would you have? Come to me?"

She pulled in a breath, as if she didn't have enough air. "Yes."

All the blood in his brain headed south at her words. *God, he needed this woman.* Tony pulled her into his arms and his mouth found hers in a hungry kiss. He wasn't capable of softness; he was wound too tight. That one yes had him aching to be inside her.

But she was a virgin, like him. He had to make it good. It was a tall order because he didn't have the first clue what to do next. He forced himself to relax, to go slow.

"Tony?" Her voice was breathless. "Can I see you?"

"Now?"

Juliet chuckled. "In order for this to work properly, don't we have to remove our clothing?"

"That would make it easier."

Juliet shrugged, causing the loose night rail to fall off one of her shoulders. "In the book, it shows everyone naked." She looked down at his tented trousers.

The book. He'd forgotten the damn book. He stepped away from Juliet and fumbled with the buttons on his falls. He shucked off the trousers, smalls and all, and tossed them by his robe.

He stood before her naked, aching, hard, fighting for control.

Juliet examined him, her fingertips trailing his chest, his arms, and his arse as she walked around him. She lingered on his backside. "Very nice."

She moved around and stood in front of him, her hand on his abdomen, playing with the hair that trailed down to his cock. He wanted her to follow the hair down and grasp his cock in her small, soft hands.

"You don't mind, do you?"

"Please."

She took him in her cool hand and gripped him. He couldn't stop the groan that erupted from him. She was a fast learner.

"Am I hurting you?"

"No, sweetheart." He took her hand away. "But I'm afraid if you keep doing that I won't last long."

Juliet frowned, puzzling over his comment.

Tony framed her face with his hands. His mouth took hers and she responded, as hungry as he. She stepped closer, wrapping her arms round his neck, lifting up on her toes to better meet his mouth with her own.

He grabbed the fabric of her night rail and tugged it over her head, then tossed it aside. He pulled her to him, groaning at the feeling of skin against skin.

Juliet gasped. Tony groaned. She felt so damn good. His hands played along the silky skin of her back to cup her bottom and fit her against him. "You said yourself that you had to take your clothes off to do this."

Juliet looked up at him with slumberous eyes. "I did, didn't I?"

"You're so soft, so smooth." He pressed his mouth to the skin at the base of her neck. "You smell so good."

Juliet tilted her head to let him kiss her further.

Tony trembled. If he didn't get their bodies horizontal shortly, he wasn't sure his legs would support him. He walked her back to the bed as he kissed her, twirling his tongue around hers.

She had her arms wrapped tightly around his neck, her skin plastered against his. He placed his hands on her small waist and lifted her onto the bed and went down with her.

Tony lay beside Juliet, one hand running down her body with an awe he knew showed on his face. She was lovely. Rose-brown nipples tipped her small breasts that were sensitive to his lightest touch. He flicked one with his thumb. His hand trailed down over her soft stomach and he circled her navel, causing her to squirm.

"You're ticklish."

She blushed. "A bit."

"Good to know." His hand traced the curve of her waist to the flare of her hips. She'd bear his children one day. He trailed his fingertips over her thighs.

Juliet parted her legs as he caressed her inner thighs. He kept his touch light, until she opened her legs further.

Tony combed his fingers through the hair at the juncture of her thighs, his eyes watching Juliet's face. He parted her folds, continuing to torment her. He pressed a finger inside her. She was so very tight. He wasn't going to last more than a few seconds once he was inside her.

Juliet gazed at Tony through the foggy lenses of her spectacles. If the look in his eyes were any indication, he didn't care if her bottom was too big and her breasts too small. He made her feel pretty, wanted, with the heat of his eyes.

The stroke of his work-roughened fingers against her skin intensified the craving she had for him. When he touched her between her legs, she couldn't stop herself from pressing into his hand, silently begging for more.

"I want to make this good for you, Juliet."

"I'd like that too."

Tony moved over her, nestling his hips between Juliet's legs. He bent down and kissed her, his tongue tangling with hers. She nipped his bottom lip lightly, then licked it. He growled against her mouth.

Tony moved his mouth down her neck to her breasts, pulling one into his mouth. Heat pooled low, and she could feel her heart pounding hard in her chest and lower.

Tony switched to the other breast, pulling it into his mouth. She squirmed, needing to move. He moved down her body, his lips nipping at the skin of her stomach. He bent between her legs, his eyes fixed on her, as if asking for permission.

"Please, Tony," she whispered.

Juliet rested her head back against the pillow and gave in to a frenzy of emotions. His tongue licked, tormented her. His fingers moved in and out until Juliet couldn't control the movements of her own hips.

Pleasure built. She needed him deeper, harder, until the pressure burst and she collapsed, boneless, against the bed linens, her spectacles askew on her nose.

Tony moved over her, bracing himself on his elbows. He removed her spectacles and set them on the bedside table. "I don't think you need these right now."

"But I can't see."

"Then I'll have to get closer." Tony lowered his body to hers, positioning himself at her core.

Juliet raised her hips in invitation, her eyes not leaving his as he pushed into her. She winced. He was too big—this was never going to work.

"I'm hurting you." He paused. His voice was deep, rusty. His arms trembled as he held himself over her. "Do you want me to stop?"

"No. I'm fine," Juliet whispered.

Tony's face above her was tense as he tried to ease inside her. "Relax, sweetheart." His lips moved down her throat. "Please."

She squirmed beneath him, trying to adjust.

"Wrap your legs around me. That might help."

Juliet did as he asked and he slid inside her, deep. She gasped as her body adjusted to the invasion. He was still above her, inside her. Tense, waiting. She raised her eyes to his.

"All right?"

She nodded. He pulled out of her, then sank into her again. He kissed her hungrily as he repeated the movement. She raised her legs higher to accommodate him and felt the stirring of the passion that she'd felt before.

She caressed his back, her fingers moving over smooth, damp skin. Her palms slid lower to the curves of his backside. Her hips lifted with each stroke, seeking something just barely out of reach. "Tony?"

Tony slid deeper inside her, increasing the pace of his thrusts. She was starting to enjoy it as she felt him pump himself into her and then with a grunt collapse against her.

Surely, this couldn't be it. Juliet lay there, a bit disappointed, trying to breathe from the weight of Tony on top of her. Was this what put the smile on Anne's face most mornings? If so, Juliet thought they must be doing it wrong. She poked at Tony. "Can't breathe."

Tony rolled off her with a groan and pulled her into his arms. He brushed her hair from her face and kissed her softly, his fingers tracing circles on her skin.

Juliet liked this part. She had liked the first part too, but the middle not so much. She hoped it got better. No wonder they didn't want women doing this before they were married.

"Sweetheart, are you all right?" Tony whispered against her skin. "I didn't hurt you too much, did I?"

What was she supposed to say? "I'm fine."

He grinned. "I cannot wait to do it again."

Good Lord, no. "Perhaps later," Juliet said softly.

Tony frowned and leaned over her, looking at her face. "You didn't like it."

She glanced away from his knowing look. "It wasn't bad."

"But it wasn't good either."

"The first part was good. And this is quite nice." Juliet tucked her head back on his shoulder. "I like this a great deal."

Tony tipped her face to his. "It won't hurt next time. I promise."

Of course he was going to want to do it again. Juliet said nothing, fighting to keep the contented smile on her face. "It's very late."

Tony yawned and pulled her into his arms again. "That it is."

"You're sleeping here?" Juliet tried to keep the shock from her voice.

Tony opened his eyes and frowned at her. "You want me to leave?"

"Well, no, but isn't that what people do?"

"I don't want to go. Not yet," Tony said softly. "I want to sleep with you in my arms."

"But what if we're discovered?" Juliet didn't want either of her sisters to find Tony in her bed.

"The door's locked, and I'll go back to my room before the maids get up." He pushed her head back onto his shoulder and kissed her forehead. "Go to sleep."

Juliet watched Tony close his eyes. He fell asleep in minutes. Clearly, the exercise had proven too much for him. He relaxed against her. Once he finally succumbed to sleep, she crept out of the bed, cleaned herself, and put on her night rail.

Juliet studied him as he slept. He was so handsome, and he didn't look quite so large now that he was asleep. Unfortunately, she was going to have to find a way to like having relations, as it appeared Tony really enjoyed it.

She climbed back into the bed and pulled the covers over them both. She snuggled against him and closed her eyes, finally letting sleep take her.

Tony woke hard and wanting, curled around Juliet. When had she put her nightgown on? He nuzzled her neck softly. She smelled warm and sweet. He could envision his future, waking every morning with this woman in his arms.

She stirred slightly, turning toward him, still asleep. One shoulder was exposed, having slipped free from her gown. Her hair was a wild tangle across the pillow. Her long lashes formed shadows on her cheeks.

Tony needed to be inside her again. His hand edged her gown out of the way and caressed her sex. He moved his finger over the nub of nerves between her legs.

Juliet moaned softly in her sleep and her hips arched to meet his fingers. He slipped first one and then two fingers inside her. She met the thrust of his fingers with tiny pulses. Tony moved over her and slid inside her easily.

Juliet was having the most amazing dream. She was making love with Tony and it felt really wonderful. He was leaving little bites along her neck. She opened her eyes and found Tony's body over her and inside her. He was moving slowly, deeply.

"Good morning," he whispered against her mouth.

Juliet captured his lips with hers, kissing him hungrily. He was deep inside her, and this time it didn't hurt; there was only fullness and this delicious passion. She raised her hips in time to the rhythm of his hips. She could feel the fire building inside her, as it had when Tony had his mouth on her. "Oh, God."

Tony deepened his thrusts as she wrapped her legs around his hips, reaching for more of the excitement she was starting to feel. She wanted more.

Tony reached down with one hand and touched her between her legs, rubbing against her sex in concert with his thrusts.

Juliet closed her eyes and came. Tony joined her a few minutes later, collapsing against her.

"I like waking up like this," he said softly, his lips trailing over her skin. "Was it better this time?"

Juliet still had a silly smile on her face when she opened her eyes and gazed up at him. "Oh, yes."

He grinned and kissed her again. "Save the waltz for me tonight at the ball."

Juliet's eyes widened. "I'd forgotten all about the ball."

"Good, then I've achieved my objective of making you forget everything but me."

Juliet giggled. "What time is it?"

"Early; just past dawn," he said against her skin. "I'm going to have to leave you soon."

She turned into his arms. "Do you have to?"

He chuckled. "Well, that's a change from last night, when you couldn't wait to get rid of me."

Juliet snuggled against him. "I was stupid."

"I'm going to love waking up next to you every morning, but I do not care for this night rail. I want to feel your skin, not linen."

"I must have something to sleep in." Surely women didn't do that.

He chuckled again. "You look quite shocked. I assure you, many people sleep naked."

Juliet poked him and lay back down. She wasn't ready to concede this point yet. They weren't even married yet. "We'll see."

"Which means no," Tony said.

"That is not what it means," Juliet defended herself. She pulled a few of his chest hairs.

"Ouch, stop." He placed his hand over hers.

"It means that I'll think about it." She smoothed her hand over his chest.

Tony chuckled. "I'll just have to convince you." He rolled her over to kiss her. He was growing hard again.

She looked up at him. "Again?"

"You have that effect on me, love." Tony kissed her softly. "But as it is your first time, we'll slow down."

She brushed his hair off his face. "It was your first time as well."

"My first." He kissed her. "My last." He kissed again. "My only."

This time when his mouth met hers, Juliet was ready. She poured all the love she had for him into that kiss. Their tongues tangled and she held his face in her hands. His whiskers were rough on her skin, but his mouth was warm.

Tony pulled away reluctantly. "If I'm going to keep my word about not having you again, I'm going to have to go."

"I already miss you," she whispered. And she meant it. She would miss his warmth and the way he cherished her.

He got up and pulled on his clothes. Juliet loved everything about him, but his bottom was especially nice—firm and hard.

"Keep looking at me like that and you'll find yourself on your back again," Tony said as he leaned over her in the bed. "I'll see you at breakfast."

"All right." She savored one more kiss.

Juliet watched him leave and then lay back against her pillow. She smiled. He definitely loved her.

He'd never said the words, but it was in his touch, in the way he took care of her.

And the act had been so much better the second time. With practice, they could get quite good at it.

She chuckled to herself as she snuggled back into the blankets and fell back asleep.

Chapter Eighteen

"You look different," Sophia said after staring at Juliet for a full minute.

Juliet squirmed. Did her lips still look swollen from Tony's kisses? She had worn a high-necked gown to hide the rash his beard had left behind. "What are you talking about?"

"More relaxed, somehow. I would have thought the scare from yesterday would have left you unable to sleep, not to mention the ball tonight."

Juliet managed to swallow her tea without choking on it. "I slept well. Perhaps that's it."

"You were moving around a lot last night—how could you have been sleeping?" Sophia said grumpily. "I didn't get much sleep and now I'm going to look like a hag tonight."

Juliet snorted. Sophia couldn't look like a hag if she tried. "Take a nap before dinner."

"We can't," Sophia complained. "Anne has a huge list of things for us to take care of."

Lady Danford entered the morning room. "Good morning. I see we are all awake bright and early this morning."

Juliet looked down at her plate.

"Juliet, you look different," Lady Danford said as she waited for her tea to be poured. "Have you done something different to your hair?"

Juliet glanced at Sophia, who mouthed "See?" Heavens, she was never going to get through this day if everyone kept noticing how different she looked. "Perhaps I'm just happy."

"As you should be; it's your engagement ball."

Tony came in for breakfast and Juliet couldn't keep the smile off her face.

"Oh please, it is much too early to endure such happiness," Sophia groused.

Tony leaned down to kiss Juliet. "You are going to have to learn to live with it, Miss Townsend."

Juliet giggled as Tony stepped to the sidebar to fill his plate.

"I think I'm going to be sick," Sophia said, resting her face on her hand. "Not even Anne and Nathaniel kiss at the breakfast table."

"Maybe because they have breakfast in their room." Juliet would like to have breakfast in bed with Tony. They could get more strawberries.

"What are your plans for today, love?" Tony said as he sat beside her.

"Helping Sophia finish the flowers for tonight. And doing whatever Anne tells me to do. I'm sure she'll have a long list."

"So no sneaking away with me today?"

"Over my dead body," Sophia said. "You are not leaving me with all the work again, Juliet."

"Tony, I expect you to take Mr. McDonald to do whatever it is you men do before events like this. We don't need you underfoot while we try to get the house ready for our guests," Lady Danford said. "Besides, your bride-to-be will be busy preparing for tonight."

Ugh. Hours of bathing, hair styling, and dressing. Having an engagement ball wasn't necessary, but Anne insisted. Juliet would be happier to have the banns read followed by a simple service at church.

But she had to admit that her dress was lovely. She couldn't wait for Tony to see her in it. She also couldn't wait to dance with him.

"I cannot deal with this any longer. You two are positively sickening. I'm going to work on the flowers. The maids won't have time to work on them with their other duties. I'll be in the ballroom when you're ready, Juliet." Sophia stomped out of the room.

"We aren't that bad, are we?" Tony said with a grin.

"There's a time and a place for that kind of nonsense. The breakfast table is not it," Lady Danford said.

Juliet felt her face flush. "I'd better help Sophia. We have so much to do today."

Tony stood as well, leaning over to kiss her cheek. "Until tonight."

Juliet's heart skipped a beat. She ducked away from Lady Danford's knowing glance and escaped the morning room.

* * *

Tony returned to his coffee, ignoring the look on Lady Danford's face. It was all he could do to keep the grin off his own face. He felt so good that he thought his face might freeze in permanent happiness.

"So that's how it is," Lady Danford said between delicate bites of egg.

"What do you mean, Grandmother?"

"You just couldn't wait, could you?" Lady Danford set down her fork. "What is the matter with you young people today? Can't even wait for the wedding."

Tony was stunned. "I don't know what you're talking about."

"You have that look about you. And Juliet was blushing."

"What look would that be?"

"Don't be impertinent. You know exactly what I'm talking about. You've compromised her. Why you young people think you invented marital relations is beyond me. How do you think you got here?"

"It's between Juliet and me, Grandmother."

"If you're going to keep this behavior up, you might as well plan a trip to Gretna Green. Have you even set a date yet?"

Tony fought the urge to squirm. No, they hadn't set the date. They hadn't even discussed it, except that Juliet didn't want a special license but rather the banns read in church. He probably would get a special license now anyway, because he had in fact compromised her, quite thoroughly. "No date is set, but I'm sure that will be resolved once we're past this ball."

"There's something you're not telling me," Lady Danford said.

"Honestly, Grandmother, there is nothing to tell." Tony picked up his coffee and motioned for a refill.

"If you back out of marrying Juliet Townsend I will personally horsewhip you. Your rakish ways will not do for her. She's not prepared to deal with them."

"You'd be surprised," he muttered. "Trust me; I am marrying Juliet Townsend. In fact, it cannot happen soon enough for me."

Lady Danford must have been satisfied with his answer because she went back to eating her food. Tony tried not to sag with relief. Not that he had much to hide anymore, but he did not want to anger his grandmother. She had the power to make his life a living hell.

"Tony, in the library when you have a moment," Nathaniel said sternly from the doorway.

When was his brother going to treat him like an equal instead of a child? He downed his coffee and stood to follow Nathaniel to the library.

"One of the maids saw you coming out of Juliet's room early this morning," Nathaniel said with no preamble when they were both in the room. "I'm assuming you'll be going for a special license?"

"I had planned to, yes."

"Good."

"Might I remind you that you did the same with Anne? You two spent the night alone at an inn before you were married. Not to mention how many times you snuck into her room here at the Lodge," Tony said.

"I'm not denying it. I had every intention of marrying Anne," Nathaniel said.

"I will marry Juliet."

"Do you love her?" Nathaniel asked in a different tone of voice.

Tony rather thought he did, but he wanted Juliet to hear it first, not his brother. "I don't think that's any of your concern."

"Let me caution you against tying yourself to a woman you have no feelings for."

"Did it occur to you that I'd like the lady to be the first to know?"

Nathaniel smiled. "I suppose she has that right. Should we go over her dowry information?"

"If you wish. And just so you know, I've purchased Horneswood. I thought Juliet would want to be near her sisters," Tony said. He kept his stance casual, though inside his stomach was tightening as he waited for Nathaniel's response. He couldn't believe he still craved his brother's approval. "I plan to raise sheep for wool."

"Good. The estate needs some work, but nothing overwhelming. I think you made a good purchase. I take it Brighton is out of the question?"

Tony nodded. "I'm afraid so, with the wedding and all."

"You could always take her there for a wedding trip," Nathaniel said slyly.

"I'd rather spend my nights with my wife and not at the gaming tables with future clients."

Nathaniel chuckled. "I don't blame you there. It's not a bad thing, being married."

Tony allowed himself to relax. His brother knew his plans and approved. It was a huge relief. "You seemed so happy, I thought I'd try it myself."

"I can't recommend it more. Especially if you love her," Nathaniel said. "I've never been happier."

"I can only hope for the same."

Nathaniel stood and reached behind him, moving a painting away from the wall to reveal a safe behind it. He opened it and pulled out a jewelry box. "These were Mother's."

"I thought you gave Mother's jewelry to Anne."

"She insisted I save a set for you and your bride." Nathaniel pulled out a velvet pouch and handed it to him. "I think these will suit Juliet very well."

Tony opened the pouch and poured the contents into his hand: a necklace, earrings, and a ring of blue topaz and diamonds shimmered in the light. "Are you sure?"

"Do you think Juliet will like them?"

Tony had no doubt she'd love them. The settings were old, but not overly intricate. Juliet favored simpler things, so these were perfect. "Should I give them to her tonight?"

"I think she should wear them to her engagement ball, don't you? Mother would be proud of the man you've become. She'd approve of your choice of bride."

Tony's throat closed with emotion. "Thank you—that means a great deal to me."

"Now go fetch that special license before I have to force you to make a dash to Scotland."

Tony grinned as he put the jewels back into the velvet pouch. He couldn't wait to see them on Juliet. How beautiful she'd look wearing his jewels.

For the first time in years, he felt good about himself, about his future. He felt like the honorable man he wanted to be, like his brother was. He couldn't wait to start the rest of his life with Juliet by his side.

Juliet trimmed the thorns from the stem of a rose and placed it into a bucket with the rest. She was horrible at floral arrangements so she had been relegated to preparing the flowers for Sophia to arrange.

The beauty of having a spring ball was the abundance of flowers. Everything was in bloom. Peonies lay in piles on the long table, their scent heavy in the air.

"I hate the smell of peonies," Sophia complained as she jabbed another flower into the large arrangement she was creating.

"Where is that going?" Juliet asked as she passed her another rose.

"The entry hall, I think." Sophia turned the large urn and placed another rose into the center. She turned it again, looking for empty spots. "There. Done."

"I wish I could do that," Juliet said wistfully. "I'll never have flowers in my house if I have to do the arrangements."

"You can have a maid do it. So you really are going to marry Tony?"

"I love him."

"I heard you two last night," Sophia said smugly. "The bed was banging on the wall."

Juliet did not want to discuss this with her sister. "How many more arrangements do we need to do?"

"Three more, so you are going to have to answer my questions." Sophia pulled another urn over and poured water into it. "Hand me those pale pink peonies over there, and the ivy too."

Juliet did as she was told. Sophia was in her element. The woman was born bossy. "Will these work?"

"Yes, those are good. Are there any more of the yellow roses?"

Juliet picked through the piles of flowers and found a handful of stems. She trimmed them and handed them to Sophia.

"Was it good?" Sophia asked, her voice low.

"Was what good?"

"You know, last night with Tony."

"Why would you want to know?"

"Really, Juliet. Do you think Anne is going to tell me? I'd like to be prepared when my turn comes."

"Don't you want to fall in love?"

"Falling in love is completely up to chance. I have no wish to leave my future to chance. I want to live in London."

"I'll be happy to never see London again," Juliet muttered. "Except for the bookshops."

"I can't wait to go back. I hated having to come home early."

Juliet slid a glance at Sophia. "Will you dance with Mr. Mc-Donald tonight?"

"I won't have a choice." Sophia sighed.

"He's a very nice man." Juliet couldn't help but feel bad for Ian McDonald. He was doomed to be hurt by Sophia.

"He's not a peer—and you've totally avoided my question."

Damn. She did not want to discuss it. "It was nice," Juliet said reluctantly.

Sophia laughed. "Nice? I wouldn't tell Tony that."

Juliet giggled. "The first time wasn't so good, but the second time was really—quite pleasant." Juliet's face was burning.

"Pleasant?"

"I'm not comfortable discussing this with you."

Sophia stopped what she was doing and leaned close. "Did it hurt? One of the ladies in London told me she screamed with pain."

"It was like a pinch. It hardly hurt at all."

"I wonder why she said that, then. She was quite adamant. Of course she's married to some old man."

"That might be your fate, Sophia, if you're so determined to marry a peer."

"There are plenty of young men who will inherit titles. I don't have to marry a man with one foot in the grave."

Sophia was crazy to consider marrying someone she didn't really care for just to be part of Society. "I don't understand you, Sophia. Marriage is forever."

"Juliet, what you and Anne have is rare. I'm just not the same kind of person as you. I don't think I've ever been in love. I don't think I'm capable of feeling it."

"I wouldn't give up yet. There's someone special for you."

Sophia laughed. "I'm glad you think so. I haven't met him yet, though I did meet a very handsome heir to an earldom this Season."

"Really? Do I know him?" Juliet thought of the gentlemen Sophia had danced with. She'd had ample time to observe from the wallflower wall.

"I don't think so," Sophia said.

"What's his name?"

"You'll know soon enough. Until then, I'm not saying anything."
Juliet shook her head at her sister. "You are so strange."
"So are you, but I'm happy that you're marrying Tony."
"Me too. I'm really glad you didn't marry him first."
Sophia laughed. "Me too."

Chapter Nineteen

Juliet gawked at herself in the mirror. Who was this person staring back at her? Anne had told Juliet to allot three hours to prepare for the ball. Juliet had laughed. Surely putting on a dress and doing her hair wouldn't take three hours!

Staring back at her were the results of those three hours' work. Juliet had been poked, prodded, pulled, creamed, and powdered until she was ready to scream. If this much trouble was put into a ball, how much more effort would go into the wedding? Scotland and an anvil marriage were looking better and better. Perhaps Tony would consider it.

The gong sounded and Juliet couldn't put off going downstairs any longer. She turned to leave her room just as Anne came in with a velvet pouch.

"Tony sent these up for you to wear," Anne said softly. "They were his mother's."

Juliet took the pouch and opened it. In her gloved hand was a beautiful topaz necklace, earrings, and a ring. She looked up at Anne. "For me?"

Anne took the necklace and placed it around her neck. Juliet added the earrings and slipped the ring on her finger. She'd never had anything so beautiful to wear.

Anne hugged her. "You look so beautiful. You will outshine all of us."

Juliet laughed. "Doubtful, but I think I'll do."

"Tony will not be able to take his eyes from you," Anne teased.

Juliet wanted to see that look in his eyes when she walked into the room. He was such a handsome man.

"You love him, don't you," Anne said. It wasn't a question.

"I always have. He is perfect."

Anne frowned. "Dearest, don't put him on a pedestal. It's a long way for a man to fall. And he will fall eventually. I know you, Juliet. You see the good in everyone until they disappoint you." Anne brushed a stray hair from Juliet's face. "Think about Mr. Bartleby. You liked him well enough until he threatened your friend, Miss Williams."

"Tony's not like that."

Anne was quiet for a long moment. "Relationships are funny things. When you live with someone, you have to take the good with the bad. We make mistakes; we say things we don't mean. As long as you can forgive each other, you should do well together."

Anne was right. There were still so many things they didn't know about each other. "Anne?"

"Yes, dear?"

Tears stung Juliet's eyes "Thank you for everything."

Anne smiled, her eyes also welling with tears. "You've gone and done it now. Nathaniel will want to know why I'm crying again."

"Blame it on the baby," Juliet said with a smile. She looped her arm through Anne's as they went down the stairs to the parlor.

Juliet's stomach jumped with excitement. She tightened her hands into fists, then released them to relieve some of the tension she felt. Juliet hated being the center of attention, but tonight she'd be with the most handsome man in the room.

Anne and Juliet entered the parlor, where everyone was waiting. Juliet hung back, waiting for Tony. He was leaning against the fireplace, talking to Nathaniel.

His eyes widened as he took in her dress. He smiled broadly and moved toward her. Juliet couldn't keep from smiling back.

"You look so beautiful," he whispered. He touched the necklace. "Do you like it?"

"It's lovely, Tony. Thank you." Juliet took his hand. "You look very handsome, but then you always do."

"Save the waltzes for me, please?" he said. "I can handle you dancing with other men tonight as long as I'm the only one to hold you in my arms."

"I rarely dance at these things, so saving you a waltz or two will be easy."

"Tonight just might be different."

Juliet hoped not. She'd rather spend the evening with Tony than dancing with men she didn't really know. "I'm happy to just watch."

"You say that now, but when you're an old married woman, you are going to wish you'd danced more. I hate to admit that the thought of other men dancing with you makes me jealous."

"The others are going into dinner. Should we go?"

Tony waited until the room was empty and then leaned forward and kissed her softly.

The only places they touched were their lips and hands. Juliet wanted to feel his arms around her, but Tony held firm to propriety. He broke the kiss slowly, lifting his lips but keeping his forehead against hers.

Juliet leaned into him, wanting more of his touch. "Do we have to go? Can't we just sneak upstairs? Just you and me."

"Your sister will kill us, Jules," he whispered. "As tempting as that thought is, I want to show you off. Let everyone see what a lucky man I am to have won your heart."

Juliet laughed. "You are mad."

"Excuse me, sir, but Lady Danford has requested your presence at dinner," the footman said from the doorway.

Juliet beamed up at him. "I suppose escaping is out of the question now."

"It seems so. Shall I escort you to dinner, my love?"

Juliet took his arm and let him lead her into the dining room.

Tony glanced at the hall clock one more time. They'd been standing in the entry greeting guests for nearly an hour. From the looks of the ballroom, Anne and Lady Danford had invited half the county. There were people here he'd never even met.

He was tired of men ogling Juliet. They tripped over their tongues trying to converse with her. Tony had to give several men a direct glare to ward off their attentions. Most men had never even noticed she was in the room before tonight.

And she was his, only his. Always his.

Juliet touched his sleeve. "The music is starting, Tony. Shall we dance the first dance?"

"Of course, love. Let's show them how it's done." Tony took her hand and led her to the middle of the dance floor.

Tony turned Juliet in his arms as the waltz started. In this moment, she epitomized joy. He turned her to the beat of the music, pulling her closer than he was supposed to, but their engagement would be announced shortly. Let people talk.

He took the turn quickly as other couples joined them. McDonald had claimed Sophia, who didn't look too happy about it. "Look at who your sister is dancing with, love."

"She's been avoiding him this entire time."

"There's more to those two than meets the eye, I think," Tony said. He was happy and he wanted everyone else to be happy as well.

"Sophia wishes to marry a peer and be the belle of Society."

Tony leaned closer. Her heady scent filled his head. Tonight he'd remove the dress and leave the jewels and have her beneath him once more. He couldn't wait but had no choice. It would be nearly dawn before the last of the guests was gone. Tomorrow they were definitely setting a wedding date, the sooner the better as far as he was concerned.

The dance ended and he pressed his lips to her gloved hand. "Let the torture begin."

Juliet smiled. "What are you talking about, Tony?"

"My torture of having to watch you dance with every man in the room. No one waltzes with you but me." He escorted her off the dance floor to where Anne and Nathaniel stood.

"I don't have to dance."

"Yes, you do. You really didn't get to do much dancing in Town," Tony said.

"I didn't care, either."

Anne laughed. "Tony, I hope you realize that your Town days are numbered. Juliet never liked London."

That suited Tony just fine. The thought of spending the rest of his life with Juliet in the country raising children and sheep was more than he deserved. "Who will you dance the next with?"

Juliet sighed heavily beside him. "Mr. Thompson."

"And here he comes. Go have fun, my love." Tony pressed his lips to her cheek. "Find me when it's my turn again."

She nodded and wandered off.

"I can't believe you finally settled on a wife and it is Anne's sister," Nathaniel said.

Anne smiled smugly. "I don't know why you are surprised."

Tony looked at Anne in surprise. How could she have known

when he hadn't even known himself until he came home? "There's no way you could have. I didn't even know, Anne."

"Your head may not have known, but your heart did," Anne said smugly.

Nathaniel looked down at her. "That's just romantic nonsense, dear. I'm inclined to agree with my brother. How could you know?"

Anne tapped her fan against her hand. "Remember the ball Lady Danford held before Nathaniel and I were married? You and Sophia were arguing about something."

"And?" It had been the beginning of the end of his fascination with Sophia Townsend.

"That was the first time Juliet wore a dress befitting her age at the time. You danced two dances with her that night."

"I was avoiding Sophia," Tony defended himself. "And I didn't want Juliet not to dance."

Nathaniel crossed his arms now. "You are making too much of two dances, Anne."

Anne laughed. "It was the way Tony looked at Juliet. Like he'd been hit in the stomach." She turned to Tony. "You couldn't stop looking at her."

"I don't know, Tony." Nathaniel slapped him on the back. "I think Anne knows you very well."

Tony had to acknowledge that Anne did indeed know him well. Nothing could anger him tonight.

"Oh, dear," Anne said. "I thought Juliet was going to dance with Mr. Thompson. I made certain Mr. Bartleby was not on her card."

Tony turned to the dance floor and spotted Juliet dancing with Simon Bartleby. "How could you invite him?"

Anne was wringing her hands. "I sent the invitation before we knew his true character. I thought he'd have the good manners not to attend."

"It's a crowded ballroom. Bartleby will behave himself," Nathaniel said.

Bartleby knew the truth behind his purchase of Horneswood. He also thought Tony had cheated him out of getting the estate back into his family, and cheated Bartleby out of Juliet.

Tony felt gut punched as he watched Bartleby execute the dance, taking every opportunity to talk to Juliet and weave his lies.

Juliet looked shocked. The more Bartleby talked the more wooden her movements became. She glanced at Tony and his heart stopped. The pain and disappointment on her face cut him like a dull knife.

Bartleby looked past Juliet to meet Tony's eyes. He was powerless to do anything but watch as Juliet struggled to hide her pain.

Bartleby said something else. Juliet stopped in the middle of the dance, slapped him, and walked out of the room. Tony made his way to follow her as the tittering voices of the gossips filled the ballroom.

Anne's hand on his arm stopped him. "Let me."

Tony didn't want to let Anne handle it. He wanted to face Juliet himself, and what . . . ? Confess? Surely Bartleby had painted him as the villain.

Tony spotted Bartleby leaning against a post, waiting for him.

"What did you tell her?" Tony demanded.

"The truth. I must give you credit for doing such a good job of persuasion. Miss Juliet defended you through all of it. I imagine you educated her in other ways as well?" Bartleby looked bored.

"You bastard."

"Tony." Ian McDonald came up to him and placed a hand on his shoulder. "Not here."

Tony looked around and found everyone watching them. He jerked away from Ian's touch and stomped away. He had to find Juliet. He had to explain.

He was a thickheaded idiot for not telling her the truth before now. It was his own damned, cowardly fault. Now he was going to lose the best thing that had ever happened to him. Tony searched various rooms until he reached the ladies' retiring room. It was the one place Juliet would think he'd avoid.

He paced in front of the door, waiting for someone to come out, waiting for someone he could ask if Juliet was inside. Finally, desperate, he opened the door and peeked in.

The squeals of women had him backing out of the room with his eyes closed.

"You did not just go into that room, did you?" Nathaniel said from behind him.

"I have to find Jules."

"She's in the morning room with Anne."

Tony sagged with relief. She wasn't alone. "I need to get to her."

"Did the events Bartleby described to Juliet truly happen?"

"Yes."

"You took a man's livelihood in a card game. After what happened to our father, you went and did it to someone else. Have you learned nothing?"

"I really don't think this is either the time or the place for this discussion."

"I have no idea who you are."

Tony couldn't imagine feeling any worse than he did. "I need to find Jules."

"We're not done discussing this," Nathaniel said.

"I am well aware, but think on this, Nathaniel. I no longer need you to clean up after me. I'm capable of taking care of myself."

"It certainly doesn't seem that way," Nathaniel muttered. "Damn it, Tony, I thought you were above all of that."

"We'll discuss it later."

Tony walked away from his brother, desperate to find Juliet. Her opinion was the only one that mattered. How was he going to explain it all to her? Would she listen? Would she forgive him?

God, he hoped so.

Juliet leaned against the window, blindly staring at the garden in the moonlight. How could she have been so wrong about Tony?

"What is it with this family and our propensity to cause scandals at our own events?" Anne said. "Really, Juliet, I thought we were beyond this type of embarrassment."

"You shouldn't have invited Mr. Bartleby." Juliet wouldn't have known the truth until it was too late.

Mr. Bartleby had taken great pleasure in telling her everything, each word like a blade into her heart. She stood there taking it until he had the audacity to suggest she become his mistress. Her hand still stung from when she finally slapped him.

"You had no idea that Tony did this?" Anne asked.

"None." Juliet had suspected something was going on with Tony, that he had secrets, but he'd seduced her with strawberries and kisses. "How could he do it?"

"Give Tony a chance to explain. I'm sure it's not as bad as it seems."

"Was Nathaniel angry?"

"Heavens, yes, but he's always been afraid Tony was like their father."

Juliet nodded but said nothing. There were a great many things she hadn't noticed about Tony until now.

"I warned you about putting Tony on too high a pedestal. He's just a man. He makes mistakes."

"Big ones," Juliet muttered as she turned back to the window.

The door opened and Tony came in. She could see his reflection in the window. He looked haggard.

Nathaniel came in behind him. "Between Ian and I we were able to keep Tony from killing Bartleby on the dance floor in front of the guests. Bartleby has left."

"Good riddance," Juliet mumbled.

Tony crossed the room and went to put his hands on Juliet's shoulders.

"Don't," Juliet said as she edged away from him.

Pain etched Tony's face as his hands dropped to his sides. "Juliet."

"We must have the guests go in to supper. I had planned on making the engagement announcement right before," Anne said.

"There will be no announcement," Juliet said. "Not now."

"Please don't do this." Tony's voice cracked, and Juliet had to close her eyes against the tears welling up.

"I suppose we can postpone it until later tonight," Anne said.

"Don't make the announcement," Juliet said again.

"Juliet, everyone is expecting it," Anne said. "The rumors will ruin you."

Juliet laughed harshly. "It's a bit late for that now, isn't it?"

"Is this true, Tony?" Nathaniel demanded.

Tony turned and glared at his brother. "Don't make yourself a hypocrite, Nathaniel."

"Both of you stop," Anne said. "This is not helpful."

"I want to speak to Juliet alone," Tony said.

"I don't think that's a good idea," Nathaniel said.

"Now." Tony's voice was harsh, commanding.

"It's all right, " Juliet said. If things were going to get ugly, she preferred it be just the two of them. The situation was tearing the family apart as it was.

"We'll be here if you need us, Juliet." Anne took Nathaniel's hand and led him out of the room.

Juliet waited, watching Tony. How could one go from perfect happiness to deepest sorrow? She felt betrayed.

"What did he tell you?" Tony asked.

"That you won Horneswood in a card game in a gaming hell. He also said that you came back to Beetham to claim your prize. I take it this was what you meant when you said you 'purchased' the estate?"

Tony said nothing.

"Are you unable to argue against the truth?"

"There is no cause for sarcasm. Did he say anything else?"

"Only that he was interested in obtaining a mistress."

"I'm going to kill him."

"You have enough problems without adding murder to the list. All I want to know is why?"

"Because I was stupid and just a little bit drunk. Chelsworth was even drunker. I should never have let him play."

"You could have stopped it and didn't?"

"You have to understand—Chelsworth is sick with gambling. He would have played and given away the land to someone else if not to me."

"And that excuses your behavior?"

Tony held out his hands. "I came back to Beetham to make this right, Juliet."

It was some comfort to know he had a conscience. "How did you fix it?"

"It took me days to get to Chelsworth. By then I had evidence that Bartleby was stealing from him. He was making sure the land was worth a great deal less than it had been. He paid several of the tenants not to plant their crops."

"Why would he do that? Don't paint Mr. Bartleby black to save yourself."

"Ian discovered that the land used to be in Bartleby's family years ago. My guess is Bartleby wants the land back." Tony scrubbed his face with his hands. "I'm sorry, Juliet. I didn't mean for you to find out this way."

Had he told her himself she would have been angry, but she probably would have forgiven him. The fact that he had lied to her, withheld information, was what gave her pause. What else had he lied about? she wondered.

"I bought the house outright," Tony said. "Chelsworth agreed to the price. He gets to keep his honor as a gentleman."

"God save me from this warped sense of honor among gentlemen." Sarcasm dripped from her voice. "Is there anything else?"

Tony shook his head.

Juliet shook her head. "Is there anything else you've lied to me about?"

"No! Juliet, I never lied to you."

"Omission is still a lie, Tony."

"What do you want to do?"

"End our engagement."

"So you're breaking it off?" Tony's voice hardened. "Just like that."

"You've lied to me from the beginning. How can I trust you?" Juliet cried.

"You can trust me, Jules; you know you can. I would never do anything to hurt you."

"You already have."

"This is insane. There are a hundred people out there waiting for us to announce our engagement."

Juliet said nothing. She didn't care if the king himself was dancing the waltz outside the door. There was no possible way she could marry Tony now.

"We are going out there and announcing our engagement. We passed the ability to turn back last night when I was buried deep inside you," Tony said.

"No. We are not."

"Juliet, what if you're with child?"

She looked away from him and felt her face heat. "It is far too soon to tell."

"Even more reason why we are going to walk out there and announce our engagement."

"I prefer to wait."

Tony pulled her into his arms and his mouth came down on hers. She braced herself for a kiss of anger, but it wasn't. His mouth was soft, persuasive. He stroked his tongue along her lower lip.

Juliet couldn't stop her body from responding to his touch. She fought the urge to respond, but she softened against him despite herself. Tears welled in her eyes and trailed down her cheeks. He released her.

"I need time," she whispered.

"We are going out there and announcing our engagement before this entire county."

Juliet shook her head and wiped at her eyes. "I cannot go out there and pretend to be happy."

"Try."

"Why are you being like this?"

"Because if we aren't engaged and eventually married, Bartleby will ruin your reputation."

"He wouldn't."

"He's already planning it."

Juliet shook her head. God save her from men! Tony had lied and Bartleby would ruin her. How was a woman supposed to figure out which men were good? Were there any good ones? "I'll take my chances."

"I won't." Tony handed her a handkerchief. "Dry your eyes. We are going out there and we are announcing our engagement. You will smile and act like a woman happy to be getting married."

"What purpose will it serve?"

"I'm not taking the chance of you being pregnant with my child. We will be married." Tony's voice brooked no argument.

Juliet had never seen him act like this. "I feel as if I don't even know you."

"We'll fix that later," he said. "Right now, we're going out there and playing our parts. Understand?"

Juliet nodded, knowing she didn't have a choice. At least it would buy her some time until she figured out what she wanted to do.

Chapter Twenty

It was early the next morning when Tony finally made it to his room. The guests had stayed, danced, and drunk, waiting for scraps of the scandal like vultures.

Juliet had stood by his side while everyone drank to their engagement, her face as brittle as the glass she held in her hand. She'd escaped him after their final dance. He hadn't seen her since.

Nathaniel was shooting daggers at him. Anne glared at him as well. Lady Danford just looked disappointed.

Tony felt lower than a snake. He needed to talk to Juliet. He had to make her understand that this wasn't what she thought.

Or was it?

He'd gambled against a man and won his estate, effectively ruining him. Just as Juliet's father had ruined his own. He'd left a man destitute, as Sir John had abandoned his sisters.

If he hadn't been such a coward, he wouldn't be in this position. He should have been honest from the beginning.

Juliet had been concerned about his gambling when he first came home. Even in Town, she had always been nagging him about haunting the hells. Clearly, she had been wounded by her brother's actions.

Tony had won and lost fortunes without ever blinking an eye. But what of those men he'd beaten? He had never thought about them. Juliet had been the one on the receiving end of what happened when all the money was gone. So had he, but he had been so young when it happened. Nathaniel had covered much of it up. Lady Danford had shielded him from the worst of it. Tony had been blissfully unaware of the tragedies that gambling had brought to his own family.

He wasn't like his father, he'd told himself. He didn't lose often. He could quit any time.

But could he?

In the few weeks he'd been back at Beetham, he couldn't deny that he'd itched to go down to the public house to play a few rounds. He hadn't only because of Juliet. She'd kept him so busy that he hadn't thought about gaming. Even during cards after supper, he hadn't played. His mind had been occupied solely with her. Tony sat down on the side of the bed in shock.

All because of Juliet. She'd saved him.

God knew where he would end up if he didn't have Juliet with him. He couldn't let her go without telling her.

Tony pulled himself up. He walked over to the window and stared out at the back pasture, squinting to see the house that had caused all of this uproar.

A movement caught his eye in the garden. It was Juliet. She was alone.

Tony tore out of the room, down the stairs, and out the door to catch her. He circled the yard looking for her. *Damn, she could move fast!* He started down the path through the woods toward the Fairy Steps.

He didn't call out. If she knew he was looking for her, she'd run. He was the last person she would want to see, except maybe for Simon Bartleby.

Juliet was numb. She'd left the ball for the privacy of her room after the announcement. She couldn't pretend to be happy. She wasn't happy. She was destroyed.

She just didn't know what to do. She loved Tony, but she couldn't deal with the gambling. She'd seen it wreck her own family. It had wrecked his family.

She just didn't understand why Tony needed to keep doing it. She understood it was popular and the thing to do in Town but didn't understand the excess.

Could she risk marrying a man with such a sickness? What if he gambled away their house or all their money? Where would that leave them? Dependent on Nathaniel and Anne?

What if Nathaniel disowned his brother for gambling? It was clear Nathaniel hated it. He never even played card games for shillings. If he disowned Tony, where would they turn?

She'd almost reached the woods when she heard someone behind her. She turned and found Tony coming toward her.

Panic set in. She wasn't ready to talk to him. She wasn't strong enough to resist him. She turned and ran into the woods.

"Juliet! Wait!"

She was only prolonging the inevitable. She stopped and waited for him to catch up.

He was breathing heavily, still dressed in his evening clothes. "Thank you," he said between breaths.

She didn't say anything. Her heart tugged at how tired Tony looked.

"Juliet, we need to talk."

She hugged herself and backed away when he made a move to touch her. "I'm not ready to talk about it yet."

Pain etched his face in a way she'd never seen before. She stiffened her spine, fighting the urge to give in to the temptation to comfort him.

"Please let me explain."

"Tony, was anything Mr. Bartleby said untrue?" she asked carefully. "If so, tell me. Please."

Tony dropped his hands. "What he said was true."

Juliet nodded, then turned away to continue to walk.

"He painted the picture black." Tony defended himself.

She kept walking. She couldn't allow herself to be persuaded that he would change. No one changed that much.

"Juliet." He grabbed her arm. "Please stop."

She turned to Tony. "I can't do this now."

Frustration vibrated through him. "It had nothing to do with you. With us. Nothing."

"It has everything to do with us." She wiped at the tears she couldn't seem to stop. "My brother lost everything because of gambling. So did your father. How could you do this?"

"I'm not like my father." His voice was low, angry. "I am not."

"Can you quit?" Juliet said. "Can you walk away and never play another game, gamble another shilling?"

Tony ran his hands through his hair. "I've not gambled in weeks since arriving here."

"What about when we go to London? What about while you are at your club, or at a ball with gaming tables? Can you resist it?"

Juliet prayed that he'd say yes. Hoped he could indeed walk away from gambling. It was the only hope she had.

"I'm a man, Jules. I make mistakes, one of which was thinking you loved me enough to forgive me."

Juliet's head snapped back as if he'd slapped her. No, this was worse than a slap. This was blunt force.

She had no words, no pithy comment. His shardlike tone left her brain numb and her voice mute. She nodded to him woodenly and turned away. She moved absently past Tony.

He said something. Her name, perhaps, but she had to keep moving. If she stopped, she would shatter into a million tears. She refused to allow that to happen. She had that much pride still left.

She could do this. One foot forward, then another. Walk slowly. Don't let him know he's destroyed you.

"I'm not going to make a promise I can't keep. I can't promise to never play a card game again. But I can promise that I won't lose everything I own on the table. I won't ever do that."

The tone in his voice now haunted her. It was as close to begging as Tony could get. She didn't turn. She couldn't. If she saw his face she would give in to this urge to ignore her common sense and listen to her heart. "I can't risk it."

Juliet left him as quickly as she could, following the path back to the house almost automatically. She moved, head down, until she was in her room. Closing the door and locking it, she sagged against it, silently crying.

Tony watched as Juliet made her way down the path toward the house. Her head was down.

He had an uncontrollable urge to punch something. Hard. His hands fisted.

"Well done, Matthews," Bartleby said as he leaned against a tree, near enough to have witnessed the entire scene.

"Have you removed your belongings from Horneswood?"

"Of course," Bartleby said with a sneer. "You had the housekeeper watch while I packed. I'm on my way to the village inn for the night."

Good riddance. Tony was glad to see the back of Bartleby. He started for the Lodge.

"I want the chance to win Horneswood back," Bartleby shouted.

Tony stopped and turned. "What the hell are you talking about?"

"Horneswood. It was in my family until my father lost it in a bet. Ironic, isn't it?"

Tony hesitated but said nothing, waiting. There was always more to the deal, especially with a desperate man. Bartleby's tone had that note of desperation to it.

"The estate should have gone to me when my mother died. I want the chance to win it back."

Tony was out of his mind for even considering it, but the urge to ruin this man who had destroyed his chance of happiness was stronger than anything he'd felt before. He could stop Bartleby. Exact a revenge from which he would never recover. Temptation raged in him.

"If I win?" Tony was almost surprised when the words fell out of his mouth. He needed this game. He needed to squash Bartleby like the insect he was. Tony fought the urge to rub his hands together in glee. He could end this now. Leave Bartleby destitute, crawling back to his family with nothing. "What do you have that I want?"

"Money."

Money Bartleby probably had skimmed off the estate for the last few years he'd been in Beetham. Tony thought about what Bartleby had done to the Williams family and the other tenants on the estate. He thought of Jules and what she'd want. If he won, beat Bartleby, it would avenge everything the man had done. Temptation reeled him in like a fat fish on a hook.

Except Tony wasn't that man any longer. "No."

Tony walked away, leaving Bartleby sputtering in rage.

"I'll ruin you in this village, Matthews," Bartleby shouted after him. "I have connections that will ensure you can never show yourself in Town. I'll ruin your brother. He'll not be able to do business in England."

Tony turned toward Bartleby in a red haze of anger. He reared back and punched Bartleby, knocking him flat. "I don't give a damn what you do to me, but if I hear that you speak one lie about my family, I will have you thrown in jail for attempted murder."

Bartleby stood and picked up his hat, knocking the dirt from it. "I have done nothing wrong."

Tony laughed harshly. "Don't be too certain."

Bartleby went white, confirming Tony's suspicions. It had been Bartleby shooting at them that day.

"Get the hell out of Beetham, Bartleby. Get out before I change my mind and have you arrested."

Bartleby's face went red. "You have no proof."

"I have an eyewitness who saw you shooting into the woods. If you leave now, we'll forget the whole thing. If you choose to make trouble, I'll bring charges against you."

"My brother would never allow it," Bartleby shouted.

"Go ahead. Risk it, but I have it on good authority that your brother put you in this position as punishment for gambling beyond your means and other thefts."

Bartleby tugged his waistcoat down. "Go ahead and marry your whore, if she'll have you. I will have the house one way or another. It is mine by right."

Tony fought the urge to punch the man again. "If I see you in Beetham again, I will make your life a living hell."

He walked away from the man toward the Lodge. It was time he set the record straight with Nathaniel. It was time to get on with his life.

Chapter Twenty-One

Tony entered the gloom of the house, his hands shaking. Walking away from that offer of a game had been a close thing.

The urge to beat Bartleby had tempted him like nothing had before. He itched to sit down at the table and beat the idiot at his own game, ruin the man so badly he would have no choice but to leave England. Tony had wanted it in a way he'd never wanted anything else.

God, he truly had become his father.

Tony leaned against the wall and banged his head against it. How had he become so consumed by the games that he lost focus on what was important?

Juliet had saved him.

Tony had the sudden need to tell her, thank her, and beg her to take him back. With her by his side, he could fight off the temptation to gamble. With her, he had too much to lose to be willing to throw it all away on a deck of cards. With a sudden surge of energy, Tony started down the hall to the stairs to find her.

He collided with Nathaniel.

"Good God, you're still in evening clothes," Nathaniel said. "Have you even been to bed?"

Tony had been so busy trying to talk to Juliet and dealing with Bartleby, he'd forgotten how he was dressed.

"No matter," Nathaniel said. "We need to talk."

"Do we have to do this now?"

"Yes."

Tony felt like a schoolboy again as he followed Nathaniel into the library. "This really isn't necessary."

"What the hell were you thinking? You could have lost it all." Nathaniel pounded his fist on the desk.

"But I didn't." Tony realized that those words were the wrong ones to utter by the way Nathaniel's face hardened. "Honestly, I regretted it the very next day. I came back to Beetham to make it right. I bought the estate."

Nathaniel frowned, puzzled. "But you won it."

"I took advantage of a man who was deep in his cups and desperate. I couldn't keep it." Tony refused to be sorry for what he'd done. He'd made a mistake. He'd fixed it. He wasn't that stupid young man with his hand out for his brother to pay his debts. He'd done the honorable thing the best way he knew how. It might not have been perfect, but it was right.

"How much?" Nathaniel's low voice broke through Tony's thoughts.

"The value of the house minus what he owed. Chelsworth keeps his damned honor as a gentleman and has money to start again."

"How can you afford it?"

"Don't worry about that. I will handle it."

"You think you can run an estate of that size?" Nathaniel laughed. "What do you know of agriculture?"

Tony frowned at his brother, always so quick to judge him. "I may not know about running the estate, but I know enough to hire the right man for the job. Give me some credit."

Nathaniel's eyebrows rose.

"Williams, a tenant on the estate, happens to be an expert. I've hired him to help me turn the estate around and start raising sheep," Tony said. "Raw materials I can sell to you for our own textile mills."

Nathaniel was quiet for a long moment. "You have thought this through."

Tony finally sat in the chair across from the desk. He propped his arms on this knees. "For a long time. I need to get out of London. I can't do it any longer."

"Too much temptation?"

"I want what you have. Family, a wife who cares about me, purpose. London is filled with empty people living empty lives."

"What about Juliet?"

Tony met his brother's gaze, nothing hiding the way he felt. "I love her. With her I'm a better man. I'm the man I should be, not some shell of our father."

"Have you told her this?"

Tony laughed harshly. "I've tried. She thinks I lied to her."

"Lies of omission can be more damaging than straight-out lies with women," Nathaniel said. "What are you going to do?"

Tony hung his head. "I don't know. Give it some time? I need to move into the house and start the changes on the estate while it's still spring. Bartleby left a huge mess." He had to move forward. He couldn't, wouldn't, go back to the man he was.

If that meant he was alone, so be it.

Tony stood. "I need to change out of these evening clothes." And get started with the rest of his life.

"What about Bartleby?"

Tony laughed harshly. "With any luck, the bastard will be gone from Beetham. He's been ordered off the estate." Tony didn't mention the threat or the black eye Bartleby was sporting. "He's been stealing from the estate since he arrived. Turns out his father lost the estate in a bet years ago. It was from his mother's family."

"So he had ties to the place as well," Nathaniel said. "I take it he was trying to get the price down or run Chelsworth off."

Tony nodded. "He wanted a chance to win it back."

"And you said no?" Nathaniel stood and walked around the desk. "I'm proud of you, Tony."

Tony's eyes pricked with tears at the words. He had no idea that Nathaniel's approval would mean so much, but it did. "Thanks."

"Give Juliet time. She'll come around."

Tony had his doubts.

He made his way back to his room. The house was quiet, still. He passed Juliet's room and paused, his hand on the door. He wanted so badly to open the door, pull her into his arms, and kiss her until she forgave him.

He wanted to bury himself inside her until they were one. Until she admitted she loved him. Until she could forgive and forget.

His hand moved to the door handle and gripped it. Would she give him a chance, let him in, accept him? Or would it be locked?

Just as he realized who he really was and found his honor, he lost the one person who made it happen.

Tony let his hand drop to his side, realizing this was something he couldn't fix. He walked to his room and closed the door, the silence echoing like thunder in his head.

He leaned back against the door, remembering the times they were together. There would never be another woman in his life like Juliet.

She'd changed him.

But he couldn't change her. He realized that now. He couldn't make her see beyond the man he used to be.

If she didn't see the man he'd become, then there was no hope for them.

Tony pulled at his cravat and tossed it aside.

It was time to move forward. If Juliet wanted to cling to what was, there was nothing he could do about it.

Juliet sat in the chair by the fire as the room grew dark. The gong had sounded hours ago. She should have gone down, but she couldn't face Tony.

She knew she was acting childishly, but it didn't erase the pain of his deception. And it *was* deception.

Did he expect her to be happy about living in a house he's stolen from another man?

True, he'd won it fair and square, but did that make it right? And what if he did it again? Could she live with the anxiety of waiting for him to gamble away all they had?

Juliet tossed the book she'd been pretending to read aside. She hated these feelings. She hated missing Tony. Even the room itself reminded her of him. Of the times he had come to her, laughed with her, made love to her.

There was a knock at the door, and when Juliet answered a maid came in with a tray. Anne was right behind her. The maid set the tray on the dressing table and left. Anne closed the door.

"This is the last time you will eat in your room." Anne's voice was stern.

Juliet's eyes stung. "I won't see him again."

"You won't have to. He's gone."

Pain stabbed at her. It was what she wanted. Why did it hurt so much? "Where?"

"He moved to Horneswood. Chelsworth and Bartleby are both gone." Anne moved to sit on the side of the bed. "You're going to have to talk about this."

"Soon."

"I spoke with Nathaniel. There's something you need to hear."

"There's nothing more to say on the subject."

"Unfortunately, there is. Tony purchased Horneswood. He'd won the estate but couldn't ruin the man. He bought the house from Chelsworth."

"That doesn't change the fact that he lied to me."

Anne pinned her with a hard look. "Doesn't it? He made a mistake. He put it right. What more do you want?"

"He should have told me."

Anne shook her head. "You wouldn't have listened. I know you, Juliet. You put people on pedestals. You expect the best from them, then want to walk away when they disappoint you."

"I do not."

"You weaved this fantasy of happily ever after in your head, of how perfect life was going to be with Tony. We don't live in a romantic novel, Juliet. We're human. We make mistakes. We disappoint one another. It is part of life."

Juliet couldn't believe that was true, any of it. Certainly she expected the best of people. What was wrong with that? And how many times had they disappointed her? More times than she could count, if the truth were told. "That has nothing to do with this."

"That man loves you. Yes, he made a mistake, but he made it right. On his own and at great cost to himself, when he didn't have to."

"He should have told me." Juliet stubbornly clung to her anger.

"Don't blame the man for hiding something from you because he didn't want to see you disappointed. That's your problem, not his," Anne said.

"I disagree."

"Then you don't deserve him," Anne said. "You aren't mature enough, woman enough for him. Tony is a good man, a really good man. If you let that slip away, then you are not the woman I thought you were."

Juliet reared back, as if she'd been slapped.

"As it stands now, you're ruined. Only marriage to Tony is going to fix that. The rules are the rules in Society. All of us have to live by them.

"Now you need to face up to those mistakes as a grown woman would, and stop pouting in your bedroom like a child. Eat. Sleep on what I said. Tomorrow I expect you to come downstairs for all your meals and rejoin this household."

"What about the engagement?" Juliet asked. "How can I get out of that?"

"You can't. Accept the fact that you have to marry. If you end your relationship with Tony, you'll have to marry someone else," Anne said. "This is the world we live in, Juliet."

Juliet nodded. If she had to marry, then she'd marry someone else. She just couldn't join her life to someone who would gamble away the future.

Chapter Twenty-Two

The next day, Juliet walked down the lane mindlessly. Perhaps she'd call on Penelope Williams. She needed someone who would tell her she was right, with her family completely against her.

Lady Danford had put it succinctly by calling her an idiot. Perhaps she was, but she had her principles.

The signs had been there. Thinking back, she should have been paying more attention instead of living in a fog of love. Sophia had gone as far as accusing Juliet of being in love with love.

Perhaps it had been about being in love with love. Tony's touch had excited her, and his kiss was addicting. He was kind, considerate, handsome. He danced with her, laughed with her, made her feel like she was the only woman on earth. She'd been wrapped up in her own fairy tale.

Juliet felt as if she were seeing him for the first time now, as if she'd cleaned the smudges off her spectacles. She saw the flaws now, and those flaws scared her.

But God, she missed Tony. Juliet found herself vacillating daily; sometimes feeling the urge to run and beg Tony for forgiveness, at other times filled with the desire to scream at him for what he had done to her. Except she'd done it to herself. She'd allowed herself to believe in the fairy tale and had not paid attention to what was real.

Juliet had seen the loveless matches made during the Season, where having money was more important than love. She'd been escaping it for years, through her books. She had arrogantly thought heartache wouldn't happen to her. She'd thought she'd never have to choose between money and love. Now love was before her and issues of money had frightened the love out of her.

What if Tony gambled it all away? What if he didn't? What if gambling won? Marriage was forever, made longer by regrets. She'd die if she came to hate being married to him.

The what-ifs ran through her brain when she closed her eyes to sleep at night. They ran through her head as she walked the grounds each day. Juliet had discovered she was more like Sophia than she was comfortable admitting. She felt selfish and childish, but she had her principles.

But they weren't keeping her warm at night.

She ached for Tony when she flipped through the pages of the naughty book. She ended up putting it away, burying it in the bottom of the chest in her room, hoping out of sight, out of mind would work.

It was the same with the jewels. She'd stared at them, imagining Tony's fingers on her skin while she was wearing them. She had to give them back. She'd given them to Ian to give to Tony.

She found herself at the front of the Lodge again. Memories were everywhere. Juliet wrapped her arms around herself as if she could compact the pain into one small part of her heart.

"Miss Juliet," Ian McDonald called out softly.

She turned and found him walking toward her from the stables. He looked grim. "Yes?"

"I took the jewels back to Tony."

Juliet longed to ask how Tony was, but she didn't dare. She didn't want to feel worse than she already did. "Thank you. It wasn't right to keep them."

"He's hurting."

She didn't need to hear that. "I hope his pain will be of short duration."

"He came here to make it right. He had no intention of keeping the house or ruining Chelsworth."

"Anne told me." Juliet thought about saying she didn't care, but she did.

"He used all his savings. That's the part that Bartleby didn't tell you, Miss Juliet. Tony made sure Chelsworth walked away with funds."

"I hated thinking Tony could so easily ruin a man."

"If that's how you feel, then why give the jewels back? Unless you really don't love him."

"What if Tony does it again? I've lived through it once. I can't live through it again. Gambling is a sickness, Ian. I've seen what it's done to my brother. I've seen how my father ruthlessly exacted fortunes from men who lost to him in a damned card game." She looked at the house. "Everyone loses eventually."

"Yes, they do. But when Tony won that estate, it changed something in him. It forced him to look at his life. He didn't like it. He looked at this as a new beginning. He took it as a sign that it was time to take a different path." Ian looked at her long and hard. "He was strong and honorable enough to give Chelsworth a way out of his dilemma. He was smart enough to see where the road was going and get off."

"Why are you telling me this?"

"Because if there is the right woman for him, it's you. You make him a better man. He told me that."

"I can't."

"I never took you for a coward, Miss Juliet, but if you can't forgive him, then let him go. He deserves a woman who will stand beside him, not some girl who puts him on a pedestal. Perhaps you aren't woman enough for him."

Juliet watched Ian walk away from her. It was all she could do to keep standing, the pain was so great. She stumbled to the stables and leaned against the wall, closing her eyes against the pain.

Ian was right. Tony deserved better. Could she be better? She didn't know. She wandered into the stables and found herself at the stall where Lucy was kept. The horse watched her approach.

Juliet stroked the muzzle of the horse, for once not afraid of the large animal. Tony had taught her that. He'd taught her that her fears were unfounded.

Could this fear be unfounded too?

Tony sat in the dark library going through the ledgers, trying to figure out which accounts Bartleby had skimmed the money from. The man was gone, but Tony was stuck with trying to make sense of the accounts he'd left behind.

Juliet was so much better at this than he.

He quashed that thought quickly. Juliet wouldn't be here to help with the household accounts. Tony was just going to have to deal with that.

"You look like hell," Nathaniel said from the doorway.

"Why didn't someone tell me you'd arrived?" Tony said, closing the ledgers and setting them aside.

"It might have something to do with you biting everyone's head off every time someone speaks to you," Nathaniel said. "I remember feeling that way."

"I suppose you have a reason to be here?" Tony muttered. Part of him wanted news from home. Or rather, news of Juliet. Ian had little to say about her except that she was crying a great deal, which made Tony feel lower than low.

"I thought I'd come see what you've bought. You are going to need some furniture."

"Chelsworth sold what he could." Tony had intended for Juliet to buy what she wanted. "I haven't got around to looking yet."

"There are some things up in the attic at the Lodge, if you want them. Some old pictures too, to fill in the blank spots," Nathaniel said. "If you want to come over to look."

The last thing Tony needed was to see Juliet. If he did, he'd probably snatch her and keep her until she was pregnant or agreed to marry him, or both. Both sounded good to him. "How is Grandmother?"

"Giving Juliet hell every chance she gets."

"She ought to leave Juliet alone." Why bully the girl? It wasn't going to make things any easier.

"The gossip in the village has reached a fever pitch, so my wife informs me. Are those the jewels I gave you?"

Tony glanced at the velvet bag on the desk. He hadn't touched it since Ian had brought it by. "Juliet returned them."

"Are you going to sell them?"

"I've thought about it." He couldn't do it, though. But he also couldn't see giving them to another woman. Only Juliet. He picked up the bag and tossed it to Nathaniel. "Take them with you. Put them back in the safe."

Nathaniel frowned. "You might want to give them to someone else."

"Perhaps," Tony said, solely to appease his brother.

Nathaniel took the pouch and tucked it into his coat. "Do you want to show me the grounds? Frankly, I'm curious why you'd give up London for this."

"Are you serious?"

"I knew you were getting too deep in the wrong crowds."

"You never said anything."

"You're a grown man, Tony. At some point I had to let you take your own path, no matter how much I hated watching it."

"Did Grandmother make you say that?"

Nathaniel chuckled. "No, she just reminded me that I had no say in your life's direction anymore. You are your own man now."

Tony was silent for a long moment as he looked around the room. It was true that he felt pain that Juliet wasn't going to be part of his future, but he was excited about investing in the land. The house was smaller than the Lodge, but the land was perfect for what he wanted to do. "Would you care to take a ride through the pasture?"

"That sounds good. How did the tenants take the news that you're the new owner? I take it they were glad to see the last of Bartleby."

"I've had to invest in some of the housing. We've been working to fix some of the roofs before the next rain." Tony had been thankful for the work. The more physical the labor, the less energy he had to focus on other things.

"Nothing like hard work to take a man's mind off his problems. Who did you get to replace Bartleby?"

"Mr. Williams has agreed to take the position temporarily. He knows more about this land than I ever will." Tony knew the man felt bad about his disfigurement, but at least he could still work. There was nothing like work to make a man feel better about himself. He'd learned that from Williams himself.

"The Williams family is well liked in Beetham. I'm glad you could use his expertise. What fields were you planning to turn to pasture?"

"Let me show you." With that, the brothers headed outside and mounted their horses. Tony turned his horse in the direction of the back pasture. "The land that adjoins the Lodge was where I planned the first pasture. It hasn't been enclosed yet."

They rode in silence to the hill that overlooked the Lodge. A river ran between Tony's land and his brother's. He could see the house in the distance. It made him think of Juliet; her bedroom window faced his property. "How is Juliet?"

"I was wondering if you were going to ask."

"It hurts, but I have to know." He looked at his brother. "Does that make sense?"

Nathaniel nodded. "Be glad you have Horneswood to escape to."

Nathaniel had hidden in the library while he had worked through his own issues with Anne.

"What is it about these Townsend women, to make us feel this way?"

"I don't know, but I wouldn't have it any other way," Nathaniel said.

Tony stared out at the Lodge. "I just don't understand. I thought she saw me for who I was."

"Juliet has always been the imaginative one. Too many novels, if you ask me," Nathaniel said. "But I see her point."

Tony frowned at his brother. "In what way?"

"Let me ask you this: What was your wager when Chelsworth threw Horneswood on the table?"

Tony squirmed in his saddle. He hadn't told anyone about it yet. "Several thousand pounds."

"Bloody hell, Tony. What would you have done if you lost?"

"I didn't. Honestly, I think through what happened that night and know that someone was watching over me. It could have easily gone the other way."

"The fact that you didn't even think about throwing away a fortune is exactly what frightens the hell out of Juliet," Nathaniel said. "Her only memories of her father are of him winning and losing large fortunes. Then their brother left them destitute, living in the cottage, surviving on the charity of Grandmother and others."

"We have the same memories," Tony said. "Father shot himself because he'd lost it all in a game and couldn't pay."

"It always surprised me that you'd even consider sitting down to a loo table to begin with. I couldn't do it."

"I thought I was better at the game than Father. I wouldn't make the same reckless wagers he did. In the end, I was just like him."

"Luckily, you won. I don't think I could have come up with that much money to cover your debts."

Tony met his brother's gaze. "I wouldn't have asked for the money." He looked back at the house. "I didn't think much of it when Chelsworth wagered the house. I'd seen men do it before. Hell, it happened daily at some of the clubs.

"But when I won, I watched Chelsworth's face as all hope faded away. He needed to win. He'd risked it all and lost. I saw something of our father in his face at that moment and knew I had to stop."

"You plan on gambling like that again?"

"Never." The word exploded out of his mouth. "I have far too much to risk now. There are people who are depending on me. I wouldn't just be throwing away my money but the livelihood of ten other families."

"Did you tell Juliet that?"

Tony frowned and looked away. He'd tried. He'd wanted to. He'd needed to. "She never gave me the chance."

"This dilemma needs to be sorted out. While her brother is away, I have to act in his stead."

"Not that he really cared one way or the other about his sisters," Tony said.

"The fact remains that you and Juliet both were behaving in an inappropriate manner. All of that can be overlooked if you marry, but if you don't . . ."

"Juliet will be ruined."

"Could she be with child?"

"Yes."

"Have you given any thought to where that leaves her?"

"Every damn day."

Nathaniel shot him an angry look. "Did you know that Mrs. Williams will no longer let her daughter speak with Juliet because of her 'wild' ways?"

Tony said nothing. He hadn't known, but he wasn't surprised.

"If things keep up this way, I'll be stuck with both of Anne's sisters for the rest of my natural life," Nathaniel muttered. "Make it right and take the woman off my hands. Please."

"In other words, I have to marry her."

"Yes."

"The woman doesn't know her own mind. She can't forgive me or trust me. What kind of start is that?"

"A tough one, but you're a Matthews. You've charmed her thus far."

Tony sighed. "She's living in a fairy tale."

"Right now it's more of a nightmare. Not one person in that house has let up on her. Even Ian has taken to chastising her."

Tony winced. It was the last thing he wanted. "I didn't want to hurt her, but damn it, she should have trusted that I wouldn't do what her brother did."

"There was no evidence to the contrary, Tony. Now you're going to have to make promises, and God forbid you break one."

"I can't promise that I won't play cards again. It's not realistic. I am what I am."

"Can you promise to stay away from it for a long time until this passes? Gambling caused many terrible things to happen to the Townsend sisters. It's a wonder Juliet wasted time talking to you at all. Your reputation is legendary at the gaming hells. Juliet heard about it in London."

"I hate it when you're right."

"Just fix it. Please." Nathaniel turned his horse back to Horneswood. "It's a good house. It could be a great home with the right woman by your side."

"Rub a bit more salt into the wound, why don't you?"

Nathaniel chuckled. "That's what family is for. Trust me, it will be worth it in the end."

"How can you be certain?"

"I can because I've experienced it. On that note, I'm going home to my wife and child."

Tony watched his brother ride across the pasture. He looked at the Lodge again, and in a window he thought he saw a faint figure watching him.

Juliet.

Chapter Twenty-Three

Juliet fed a carrot to Lucy just as Tony had taught her. She petted Lucy carefully.

"Do you want me to saddle her for you, miss?" the groom asked. "You've been by every single day for a week."

"Not yet. Perhaps later." She hadn't yet worked up the courage. But if Juliet was going to prove to Tony she was able to overcome her fear, she needed to actually get on the horse.

"Juliet, what are you doing out here?" Sophia said from the doorway. "Mrs. Dullwood is here."

"It's Mrs. *Dell*wood," Juliet corrected. "I'm trying to overcome my fear of horses."

Sophia frowned at her. "Why?"

Juliet had no intention of explaining to Sophia what she was planning. "Should we go in?"

"Not until you tell me what's going on. You've been moping around all week since Tony left. Now you're spending all this time in the stables talking to a horse. You hate horses."

Juliet glanced at the groom, who was doing his best to ignore them. "Shall we discuss this inside?"

Sophia rolled her eyes. "Yes, of course."

Juliet followed Sophia into the house. She paused at the parlor door. Mrs. Dellwood stood in the parlor, a superior expression on her face. Lady Danford was frowning and Anne looked pale. Juliet slid into the room and took a seat as quietly as she could.

"What do you have to say for yourself, young lady?" Mrs. Dellwood said.

"Pardon?" Juliet looked at Anne.

"The whole village is talking about it. You walk around flaunting the rules. Wearing men's clothes and being seen without a chaperone."

"Mrs. Dellwood, I'm sure Juliet has an explanation for her actions," Anne said, struggling to keep her voice calm.

"Now the whole village is talking about Mr. Matthews walking away from the engagement. Not to mention that Mrs. Williams won't allow her daughter near this hoyden. It's a disgrace," Mrs. Dellwood said, her tone harsh.

"So much for the judge-not-lest-ye-be-judged part of the Bible," Lady Danford said.

Juliet wished she'd stayed in the stable with the horse. She felt herself shrink with every word Mrs. Dellwood uttered.

"I beg your pardon, ma'am, but what kind of example is she setting for the young ladies of the village?"

"Mrs. Dellwood—" Anne tried to interrupt.

"Poor Miss Townsend, you're doomed to spinsterhood all because of your sister's behavior." Mrs. Dellwood stood. "I think perhaps it would be best if Miss Juliet would refrain from attending church for a while."

Normally this would be welcome news to Juliet, but now it felt like a slap. What had she done that was so very bad? She had kissed a man. She wore men's clothes to help a family who needed it. Juliet was about to speak when she saw Sophia shaking her head. Sophia was urging caution? Juliet closed her mouth.

"I'm sorry you feel that way, Mrs. Dellwood," said Anne. "One must indeed be careful with whom one associates in such a small village. As the vicar's wife, you can't be too careful."

Mrs. Dellwood looked shocked but nodded her head. "I hadn't thought of it quite that way. You are quite right."

"And so I would not want to see your husband's reputation in the village be tainted by your visit today," Anne continued.

Juliet knew Anne was angry. Juliet folded her hands and ducked her head down, ashamed. She'd done this to the family. How disappointed they must be in her.

"Thank you for understanding, ma'am. Good day." She swept through the room and out the door.

Anne turned to Juliet. "What were you thinking? If you bothered to think at all."

"Nothing. I wore men's clothes to help at the farm. I'm supposed to do that in a dress?"

"You and Tony have flaunted the rules in front of the whole village. You had to know there would be consequences."

Juliet's jaw dropped. "I was helping the Williamses. Isn't that more of an example of charity than what Mrs. Dullwood does? Not one person from our level called on the family to check on them."

"Her name is Dellwood," Sophia said with a smirk.

"Be quiet," Juliet muttered.

"It was one thing when you planned to marry Tony . . ." Anne said.

"It gets worse," Sophia said with a slight smile. She pulled a book out of her pocket. "You should see this."

Oh, dear God, no! Juliet's eyes widened as the depth of her depravity was brought to light. "How could you?"

"Something needs to be done," Sophia said, mimicking Anne's tone.

Anne took the book and flipped through the pages, her eyes growing big. At one point she frowned as she turned the book to get a better angle. She closed it with a snap, her cheeks pink. "Where in heaven's name did you get this . . . this rubbish?"

"In the library," Juliet whispered. She felt like a child caught with her hands in the cracker jar. "It was behind some of the agriculture books I've been reading."

"You actually read books on agriculture?" Sophia asked. "No wonder you turned to that."

"Sophia, hold your tongue," Anne said.

"Let me see that book," Lady Danford demanded.

Anne reluctantly handed it over. A strange smile appeared on Lady Danford's thin lips. "I remember this book. I thought it was lost."

All three women looked at the old lady.

"It was my husband's." Lady Danford snapped the book closed. "Don't look at me like that. How do you think the three of you were put on this earth? Delivered to your parents by birds?"

Anne whipped her head around to look at Juliet. "Don't tell me you and Tony—"

Juliet shrugged as heat warmed her cheeks.

Anne plopped back into a chair. "Good God, are you with child?"

"I don't know." The waiting was killing Juliet. The baby would force a decision she was having trouble making. But it was wrong. She was a grown woman. She should know her own mind.

"You have to marry Tony now."

Juliet opened her mouth to speak when Lady Danford interrupted. "Let's not be too hasty, Anne. The girl doesn't know if she's with child. If there is no child, we can sweep it all under the carpet."

"Not with Mrs. Dellwood spreading gossip through the village," Sophia said. "It's just a matter of time before the entire county knows."

"The entire county doesn't care, Sophia."

"It's my reputation as well as yours. Not that I don't love you, but I wouldn't want to see my chances of making a good match ruined by your stupidity," said Sophia.

"You are too kind, Sister," Juliet bit back.

"What are you planning to do about this, Juliet?"

That was the question. What *was* she planning to do about it all?

He'd hidden things from her, but she wasn't exactly blameless in the whole game either. This time away from him, despite the pain, had made her realize she'd done him a disservice. She'd been so wrapped up in a fantasy, she'd missed reality.

Tony had been all the things a man in love was supposed to be. He had shown her his love by his actions every day, but she had been so blinded by waiting for something bad to happen that she'd missed the sweetness of it.

Juliet could see Tony's house from the window. Sometimes when she looked out she imagined him looking back. She could feel him watching.

What if he didn't want her any longer? What if her childish behavior had made him realize that she wasn't worth the trouble? Juliet sighed as the ladies behind her bickered about what to do to resolve the situation.

Juliet knew what she had to do. She had to prove to Tony that she wasn't afraid anymore, that she was brave enough to deal with whatever life gave them.

Sophia came up behind her. "I take it you've finally come to your senses. What are you planning to do about it?"

Juliet looked at her sister. "Do you have a riding habit I can borrow?"

Sophia grinned. "I like the way your mind works. Come. Let's get started."

* * *

Tony had to stop staring at the Lodge. It wasn't as if Juliet could see him gazing at her bedroom window, especially at night. He felt as if he was intruding on her privacy.

All he wanted was a glimpse of her. Was she suffering as he was? Was she craving him as he was craving her? Would he see her swell with his child?

He made his way downstairs to fuel himself with enough coffee to get him through the work he'd planned.

He'd hoped the long days of hard labor would help him sleep. It hadn't. He'd lie in bed trying to force himself to forget the feel of Juliet's skin beneath his hands, his mouth. His body raged for her. He woke up hard.

Tony took his coffee into the library. He was going to have to buy furniture. He was getting sick of eating at the desk in the darkness.

"Lady Danford to see you, sir," the maid said from the doorway.

Tony stood. "Grandmother, it's a bit too early for a call, isn't it?"

Lady Danford looked around the room and sniffed. "It's dreary in here. Don't you have a proper parlor?"

"Not yet. I need to buy some furniture."

"Still, the house has good bones. You did well, Son."

"Won't you sit down? Shall I call for tea?" Tony motioned to the chairs near the desk. He watched as Lady Danford wiped the chair off before sitting.

"When was the last time you had the maid clean in here?" Lady Danford said. "No tea. I won't be here long."

Tony prepared himself for the tongue-lashing he knew was coming. It had been nearly a fortnight since the ball and he hadn't spoken to Juliet since.

"I'm ashamed of you, Son. It pains me to say it. Do you know who called on us yesterday? Mrs. Dellwood."

"Who?"

"The vicar's harpy of a wife. She's hearing all sorts of gossip around town about you and Juliet riding around in men's clothes."

"I usually wear men's clothes, Grandmother."

She rapped her cane on the desk. "That's not what I meant! Then I find out about this book." She tossed a book on the desk. It fell open at the page he'd bookmarked for Juliet.

"Where did you get this?"

"Evidently, Juliet found your grandfather's private book collection."

That was a story Tony didn't need to hear. He waited for the other shoe to drop. His grandmother never did anything without a purpose.

"Juliet's reputation is destroyed in this village. You had your way with the girl and I expect you to make it right. The Matthews family name is at stake."

Tony doubted that, given the scandal Nathaniel and Anne had stirred up. "She doesn't want me. She's made that perfectly clear."

"The girl doesn't know what she wants. You sweep in and turn her life completely upside down. You shower her with attention. She's never had anyone, including her own family, pay attention to her. What did you expect? But you can't play fast and loose with her reputation as you have without paying the consequences."

"I asked her to marry me, remember? My intentions were honorable. I don't think hers were."

"What do you mean?"

Tony met his grandmother's eyes. "She was merely infatuated with me."

"Then you should have kept your hands off her," Lady Danford said sharply. "Really, Tony. You should have known better."

He had to agree with her. He shouldn't have given in to temptation.

"She's pregnant," Lady Danford said baldly.

"What?" Tony sputtered.

"You heard me."

"Why hasn't she told me?"

Lady Danford gave him one of those are-you-that-much-of-a-fool looks she was so good at. "How is the girl supposed to tell you? Ride up in a carriage, knock on the door, and announce it? Write a note, perhaps?"

"Well, yes, I suppose so." Tony pulled a hand through his hair. A thrill went through him. Juliet was carrying his child, the child they had created together out of love. At least love on his part. "How is she?"

"As well as can be expected."

"Does Nathaniel know?"

"As you are still walking the earth as an unmarried man, no." Lady

Danford sniffed. "Of course she won't be able to hide it for long. Nathaniel has been through two pregnancies with Anne. He's going to pick up on the symptoms rather quickly."

"Thank you for telling me," Tony said sincerely. He'd never have known otherwise. Now he could prepare for Nathaniel's reaction. He didn't want to start his life with Juliet like this, but if she was his wife, he'd have time to wear her down, get her to forgive him. She'd have to talk to him, wouldn't she? She'd have to make the best of it.

But if she didn't love him, how was he going to deal with that? She'd be stuck in a marriage she didn't want.

"I expect you to put in an appearance at the Lodge and deal with this within the next fortnight. I also expect you to get a special license. As it stands now, her reputation is in tatters. There's not much we can do about that save a wedding and years of good behavior. At least if we contain it now, it won't ruin Sophia's chances at marriage."

"I'll see to getting a special license. I'll have to ride to Lancaster for it," he said.

"See about ordering furniture while you're at it. And have the maids clean. You can't bring a new bride into this house the way it is." Lady Danford stood.

Tony got to his feet as well. "Yes, ma'am."

"Try not to make too much of a tangle this time, Son."

Tony stood staring in the doorway long after Lady Danford had left. His heart pounded in his chest. Juliet was pregnant with his child. He was half afraid, half hopeful. Providence had seen fit to let them have a child together—surely that meant something.

If he was going to be the man he wanted to be, he had to make this right. He had to convince Juliet that they belonged together. No child of his would be raised as a bastard. She would marry him, and that would be that.

He felt hope for the first time in weeks.

Chapter Twenty-Four

Juliet stared at herself in the mirror. She pulled at the gaping fabric at her breasts. "I look ridiculous."

"It's not my fault you stopped growing so early," Sophia said. "We can always stuff them again."

"Never. Again."

"Besides, it doesn't appear to be important to Tony." Sophia smacked Juliet's hand away from the bodice of the riding habit. "That's all that matters, isn't it?"

"Maybe I'll have something made."

"There's no time to have a proper one made. There is no time to lose. You and Tony need to make up and be married as quickly as possible. If you're pregnant—"

Juliet hung her head. "I'm not."

Sophia lifted Juliet's chin with a finger. "When did you find out?"

"The day after Mrs. Dellwood's visit." Part of her had wanted a baby to ease the way with Tony; the other part had hoped she wasn't, even though it made reconciliation harder for her.

She hated having to choke on her own pride.

Sophia had a calculating expression on her face. "Does anyone know?"

Juliet shook her head.

"Excellent. Then there's still time for this plan to work." Sophia grabbed the hat that went with the habit and jammed it on her sister's head.

"Ouch! What plan?"

"It's best you don't know. Come, I've had the horse saddled for you. Today you're going to be riding without the groom leading you around the park."

Juliet felt a bit dizzy. "Are you mad?"

"You're ready. Trust me."

Juliet had a very bad feeling about this. She didn't feel ready. Yes, she'd been on the horse by herself every single day. She'd even managed to walk Lucy around without the groom holding the reins. But that was it.

"I thought we'd take a ride through the back pasture," said Sophia.

Juliet blanched and shook her head. "No. I'm not ready."

"Of course you are. Don't worry about a thing. I'll be right there."

There was definitely something going on. Sophia was never this nice to Juliet unless she was planning something. "Do you swear?"

Sophia met her eyes in the mirror. "Really, Juliet, do you think I'd let something happen to you?"

"Swear to me that you won't. Swear it on Mother's grave."

Sophia looked away. "And they accuse me of being the melodramatic one!"

Juliet just stared back at her sister.

"Fine. I swear on Mother's grave that I won't let anything bad happen to you. Are you satisfied now?" Sophia picked up her gloves. "Now can we go for a ride? We are letting a beautiful day get away from us."

Juliet followed Sophia to the stables, still unable to shake the feeling that something horrible was about to happen. It wasn't that she didn't trust Sophia; surely she wouldn't do anything to really hurt her. Would she?

"Do you think we can postpone this until tomorrow?" Juliet hated the fear in her voice, but something inside her was screaming to be cautious.

"No. Now come on. We're late."

"For what?"

"If we don't get going we'll be late for tea. I intend to have a decent ride."

"You can always get Mr. McDonald to ride with you." Juliet refused to move off the steps.

"He's busy and it wouldn't be proper. See, you have taught me something."

"I'm not a dog to be ordered about," Juliet muttered. But she followed. She really didn't have a choice. This whole riding nonsense had been her idea.

A stupid idea, now that she thought about it. What was she supposed to do? Ride up to Horneswood without a chaperone and throw herself at Tony's feet? The more she thought about it, the more she hated the idea. Acting like a hoyden was what had gotten her into this mess in the first place.

Tony's feelings for her were probably gone now. He'd find a less childish woman. He'd find a woman with breasts that would fill out a riding habit. She fiddled with the bodice of the habit she'd borrowed. "I look foolish."

"Do stop worrying about it. There is no one here to impress. This is the final test. If you do well, we'll order a proper habit from the village. I think a nice dark blue would be lovely on you," Sophia said.

Juliet blew the feather drooping down from her hat away from her face. It kept tickling her nose. "No feathers in the hat. I hate feathers."

"But they are the fashion. You must be in fashion."

"God forbid I save some poor bird his feathers."

Lucy was already saddled and ready to go when they got to the stables. She nudged Juliet, looking for her treat. "Here you are, sweet thing." Juliet held pieces of apple in her hand for the horse to take. She rather liked having a horse for a pet. Lucy really was sweet and had proven to be an excellent listener over the past few weeks.

"She's taken a real shine to you, miss," the groom said, holding the reins. "Just take her real easy, just like I showed you. Miss Lucy will take good care of you."

Juliet smiled her thanks as she settled onto the horse's back and smoothed out the skirts of her habit. She accepted the crop from the groom. "I'll need this?"

"Just a gentle tap will do the trick. It's just to get old Lucy going. Don't worry about getting lost. This old girl knows her way home."

Juliet's eyes got bigger. "We aren't going that far, are we?"

"Just riding to the back pasture, that's all," Sophia said with a smile. "I want to let the horse have his head."

"I'll just watch and let Lucy eat some grass."

"Good idea, miss," the groom said. "Come on back when you've had enough. I'll be here."

Juliet tapped Lucy on the rump with the crop and the horse lurched forward. Juliet allowed herself to get used to the rhythm of the horse as she followed the mare Sophia was riding.

It was actually quite nice, ambling along like this. The spring day was warm and humid from the rain the night before. The fields were lush and bright green.

As they climbed the hill behind the Lodge, Juliet could see Horneswood. Where was Tony? Was he out helping a tenant? The estate and its lands needed a great deal of work before they could be profitable. Was he working too hard? Was he getting enough rest?

If he was anything like her, he wasn't sleeping well at all.

"It's not a bad house, Juliet," Sophia said. "Although a bit small for my taste and way too far from London."

"I never wanted the same things as you."

"For which I'm thankful, even as I question your sanity for wanting to marry a sheep farmer," Sophia said. "Now that you know you're not carrying his baby, you could walk away from this whole mess. You don't have to marry him."

The thought had crossed her mind. People would talk, but they had no proof that things had gone as far as they had. Juliet imagined her life without Tony and found it a very lonely road to nowhere. If she didn't marry Tony, she wouldn't marry anyone else.

"Do you have a plan?" Sophia said. "You really can't call on a man at his home without a chaperone. Even with a chaperone it is chancy."

Juliet sighed. That was true enough. She hated the rules that kept her from being able to be open and knock on his door, demand that he make things right. "I don't know."

"I don't see him out and about anywhere."

"Why would he be?"

"Oh, I don't know," Sophia said. "I guess I hoped we'd accidentally run into him if we rode this way."

Juliet's luck wasn't that good. She'd have to make a point of seeing him. Perhaps a note to meet at the Fairy Steps or by the pond, someplace special to them both.

A note might work. She thought about what she might say. Should she beg for forgiveness? Make a joke of it? Or just pour her heart out?

None of her ideas were appealing.

She was so lost in thought that she didn't realize until it was too late that Sophia had plans of her own.

Sophia's crop landed hard on Lucy's rump, causing the horse to jump and then take off like a shot. Juliet screamed and pulled hard on the reins.

Lucy raced down the hill, slinging up mud and grass into Juliet's face. She fought to control the animal, but her fears overwhelmed her—just like the last time she'd found herself clinging to the back of a racing horse.

They were headed for the river. If Lucy threw her into the river, she wouldn't be able to get out. The waters were still foaming from last night's rain.

Oh, dear God. She was going to die. She was going to die never having told Tony how much she loved him or how sorry she was for not believing in him.

Juliet closed her eyes and prayed for the first time in a very long time.

Tony had just returned to the stables when he heard a woman scream from the direction of the Lodge. He turned his horse and galloped until he saw something that stopped his heart.

Juliet was on the back of a runaway horse heading toward the river. If the horse didn't kill her, the water would. It would take her and his child.

Tony spurred his horse faster, leaning forward to make more time. He had to reach her. *Dear God, let him get there in time.*

If she died, he might as well die with her.

He surveyed the banks of the river between the two estates. It wasn't wide, but the river had a fast-moving current due to the recent rain. The banks were thick with mud.

It would make it too hard for the horse to cross. He grew desperate trying to find a way to save her. "Pull on the reins, Jules. Pull hard as you can!" he shouted.

God, let me get to her.

Tony urged his mount faster, but he knew he wasn't going to make it. Sophia was racing down the hill behind him as well.

Time seemed to stand still as he watched Juliet finally get her horse to stop, only to be slung off and into the mud at the edge of the river. She lay there, unmoving.

Tony's heart stopped.

Sophia stopped her own horse and dismounted as best she could from the sidesaddle. "Juliet, are you all right?" she asked.

There was so reply.

"Tony! Help me!" Sophia cried.

He forced his horse through the rapidly moving water and dismounted. "What the hell are you two doing?"

"Riding," Sophia said.

"Juliet doesn't ride." He knelt down and started checking her for broken bones.

"I . . . can't . . . breathe," Juliet whispered.

"Your breath was knocked out of you when you fell. Take it slow and easy. Let me see if anything is broken," he said as he tenderly ran his hands over her. She seemed none the worse for wear, as the mud had eased her fall.

Juliet sat up carefully, wincing in pain.

"You're going to be bruised pretty well tomorrow, I'm afraid." Tony wiped some mud from her cheek. "Now what the hell were you doing racing down the hill? And with child too! Do you even care about the baby?"

Sophia backed up toward her horse. "I'll just be going and let you two get on with it."

"Sophia! Don't you dare leave me!" Juliet shouted.

"Sorry, dear. I have other plans," Sophia called out as she galloped away.

"I'm not with child." Juliet's voice was small and filled with pain.

Tony plopped down beside her in the mud. "You aren't? But Grandmother said you were."

Juliet frowned. "Why would she do that?"

"Let's get you out of the mud and back home. You're not badly hurt, are you?"

"Not from the fall," she whispered. "I'm so sorry, Tony. I'm so sorry I didn't trust you, believe you."

He stilled at her words, afraid to feel hope, afraid to feel anything. "I've given up gambling. I had before I came home. I couldn't risk it anymore. I was becoming my father."

"I should have had faith in you." Juliet wiped at her tears, spreading more mud on her face. "I behaved childishly. I am so very sorry, Tony, that I hurt you so."

"I wanted to tell you so many times, but I was afraid."

"Ian told me you bought the house and made it right. You didn't have to do that."

"Yes, I did. I couldn't bring my bride to a house I'd won in a card game. What kind of husband would that make me? Besides, it was the right thing to do."

"It was the honorable thing to do." Tears coursed down Juliet's cheeks. "You are the most honorable man I've ever known. I only hope that I can make myself worthy of you."

Tony's eyes welled up. He thought he'd never hear those words from Juliet.

"Do you think I can get out of this mud now?" she asked.

"Let me take you home." He stood and pulled her up and into his arms. His mouth found hers, brushing her lips softly, easily, savoring the taste of her. He was afraid he was dreaming. "Come to Horneswood with me?"

"But what will everyone say?"

"They'll be glad I got that special license yesterday. I love you, Jules."

She removed her muddy gloves and caressed his face. "I love you."

The words fell so easily off her tongue. "Are you certain, Jules? I couldn't bear it if this were just an infatuation."

"I'm such an idiot. I let the fairy tale keep me from seeing the real you. I love you, Tony. I don't want the fairy tale. When I heard what you'd done, I thought you were a gambler, a man who really didn't care about anything except the next game."

"Like my father."

"Like my brother. When Mr. Bartleby told me about the bet, all my fears took over. I couldn't see beyond them."

"I should have told you myself. I won't keep anything from you ever again. I promise."

"Don't make a promise you can't keep, Tony." She looked out at the land across the river and at Horneswood. "It's a good house."

"It's not as grand as the Lodge," Tony said. He didn't think Juliet cared for such things, but he wanted to be sure.

"It's probably just as well. I don't know anything about running a house. You do realize that, don't you?"

He kissed her again. "Neither do I. I guess we'll figure it out together. Will you come home with me? Be with me?" His mouth found hers, tasting her hungrily. He needed her beyond comprehension, beyond the hard aching of his body. He needed to feel her skin against his. "Please, love."

She kissed him back hungrily. His hand searched for her breasts through the ill-fitting habit.

"What are you wearing?"

Juliet blushed. "Sophia's old habit."

"We need to get you one that fits," he said, his fingers on the buttons of the jacket.

She placed her hand over his. "Tony. Wait."

He paused, his hand already inside her jacket. "Must I?"

"You deserve a better wife than a hoyden, Tony. You deserve a wife who is honorable too."

"I want *you*, Juliet. I love you, just as you are." Tony punctuated his words with kisses. "You don't need to change."

She smiled. "I just meant that there's been so much gossip, perhaps we should do things properly for a change."

Tony groaned. "That means I have to wait until we're married to have you, doesn't it?" He leaned his forehead against hers. "If you insist, I suppose I can try—as long as we marry quickly. No reading of the banns. We marry tomorrow or sooner."

"But I don't have a dress!"

"I'll marry you in your oldest day dress, if it means I don't have to wait. Just don't make me wait weeks and months."

"I have it on good authority that the vicar would be happy to marry us as soon as humanly possible, especially if he gets a promise from you that I won't be running around the county in men's breeches."

His heart jumped a beat. "You'll be saving those breeches for me and only me," Tony growled against her mouth.

"Then let's get married, Tony," she whispered against his mouth. "Then we can try page twenty in the book."

"Page twenty?"

She grinned, looked down at his tented trousers, and licked her lips.

"You know, the page you marked, where the woman had her mouth on the man's—"

Tony interrupted her, capturing her mouth with his for a long, deep kiss. When he was done, he said, "We'll start with that and then work our way through the entire book."

Epilogue

Tony stood in front of St. Michael's Church and watched his love, his bride, walk down to the nave on his brother's arm.

Juliet glowed, probably because he'd snuck into the Lodge the last few nights to sleep with her.

Not that either of them got much sleep.

She now stood beside him in the blue gown she'd worn to their engagement ball a month earlier. The blue topaz necklace caught the sunlight streaming into the church. She was the most beautiful sight Tony had ever seen.

All those months ago, when he had sunk so low, he'd never thought things would end up like this. He'd never thought he'd end up happy, loved, and honored by the woman before him.

He might have a great deal of his father in him. He might be tempted to play a hand or two if they traveled to London, but he'd never risk losing what he had now.

The vicar gave them a disdainful look as he read through the wedding ceremony. He was probably relieved that the village hoyden was finally married. Tony couldn't look anywhere but into Juliet's eyes as she agreed to be his wife. She made a face while saying the word *obey* and he had to smile.

Tony had a feeling his life was going to be filled with many moments like this, of Juliet making faces at him. He placed the ring, his ring, on her finger, looked into her eyes, and made his pledge.

"You may kiss your bride, sir," Vicar Dellwood said.

As if Tony needed to be told. He took her mouth with his in a gentle, reverent kiss. "My honorable wife."

"I wouldn't hold your breath, Husband," Juliet whispered back.

They turned to greet the few friends and family who had gathered to celebrate. His tenants joined them outside the church, cheering as they climbed into the carriage that would take them to the wedding breakfast at the Lodge. "How long will this breakfast last? I find that I'm not really hungry. At least not for food."

Juliet elbowed him in the ribs. "You are incorrigible. We were just together last night."

"Yes, but that was different. Now you're my wife. I can have you any time I want."

"Are you going to want to do this often?"

"I have a great deal of catching up to do." His lips parted hers in a deep kiss while the crowds shouted outside the carriage. "There's a certain page in the book I've been saving for our wedding night."

She blushed deliciously. "There's one I've been meaning to show you as well, Husband."

Tony laughed, causing the crowd to cheer even louder.

Life was going to be good with this lady by his side.

See how the romantic trials and tribulations of
the Townsend sisters began in
Eileen Richards's

AN UNEXPECTED WISH

Keep reading for a special look.

A Lyrical e-book on sale now!

An Unexpected Wish

Sometimes a last resort
is pure magic...

A Lady's Wish

EILEEN RICHARDS

Chapter One

"I hereby decree the word *spinster* be stricken from all manner of speech." Anne Townsend waved her makeshift wand from her perch at the top of the Fairy Steps. She cleared her voice in her most royal manner. "Furthermore, the word shall be stricken from every document in my fair kingdom!" The small village of Beetham shimmered in the gold cast of the late autumn sun, completely unaffected by her pronouncement.

Typical. She threw the stick down the uneven stones she'd just climbed.

Plain, practical, boring Anne
Was too plain to catch a man.
If she caught the eye of one,
To her sister he would run.

The truth of the hurtful childhood taunt stared back at her every blasted day. She was plain. She'd never attracted any man she deemed suitable. It wasn't as if she was being picky. He just had to be reasonably wealthy, reasonably handsome, reasonably witty, and not stupid.

Therein lay the difficulty. No man had met all the requirements. If he was handsome, he was either poor or witless. If he wasn't handsome, he had funds and was as old as the Fairy Steps.

It was of little matter. A modern woman made the best of things. Modern women didn't settle for some old shriveled-up man. And she would be a modern woman if it killed her.

Five years ago, the lure of magic in the Fairy Steps had stirred her romantic heart. A wish could fix anything: poverty, loneliness, and love. God, what a ninny she'd been.

The only thing that fixed poverty and loneliness was money.

Daily her sisters, Sophia and Juliet, whined about their lack of funds. They argued over hair ribbons. They complained about their old, unfashionable dresses. Her sisters had no inkling of the trouble they were in.

They needed fuel for the approaching winter, food for larder, and coins to pay the two servants Anne couldn't do without. It took blunt. Blunt was what she needed more than anything.

If the confounded fairy showed up today, Anne wouldn't hesitate. She'd wish for the ready. Pots of it.

Anne closed her eyes and embraced the rare moment of peace. No arguing, whining, bickering, nagging, tormenting, or complaining. Just beautiful, glorious silence.

A cold gust of wind blew the tendrils of hair from her face and chased a shiver up her spine. Dried leaves rattled behind her as they skated across the rock. A twig snapped behind her.

Her eyes flew open. She wasn't alone.

Anne's heart pounded so hard she could hear it thumping in her ears. Hair lifted on the back of her neck. Anger warred with fear. Anger won.

She picked up a good-sized limb from the ground and gripped it with both hands. "Show yourself, coward."

"Speak your heart's desire, my lady." An odd, otherworldly voice filled the air. The breeze kicked up again.

Anne tightened her grip on the tree limb. She threw her shoulders back and stood taller. She wasn't going down without a fight.

"You climbed the steps properly and earned a wish, you have." The voice cackled.

She lowered her arm. Blast, this was nothing but a prank. Probably some child bribed by Sophia. She'd box the child's ears and send him on his way. She'd deal with her sister when she got home. "The joke is over. Come on out."

"'Tis a magical place you've found, as well you know for the many times you've climbed these steps." The crackling voice sounded old, not childlike.

"Enough!" Anne was sick to death of being the whipping boy.

A wizened, bent old woman with a twisted cane shuffled out of the trees at the foot of the stairs. "Always you must see to believe."

"You must think me dicked in the nob, madam. There are no fairies."

Anne threw the limb into the bushes behind her. "Be gone now, and tell my sister Sophia to try harder next time."

"How hasty and untrusting you young people are. Make your wish, child."

Anne studied the old lady. She looked like one of the Gypsies who came around at harvest time. How much coin had she bilked out of Sophia for this prank? "Fine. I wish you to be gone."

The old woman cackled. "I should take you up on that, but your heart speaks differently. It speaks of struggle and loneliness."

What did this woman know of her life? "I'm sick of this game. Good day, ma'am." Anne turned toward the path.

"Wish for anything, my lady. Wish grandly." A gleeful, wicked light gleamed in the old woman's eyes. She lifted her cane and jabbed it toward Anne. "Little wishes are for little souls. They are not for the likes of you. Now wish. You are wasting my time."

Well, rats, she might as well wish for something. It would shut the woman up, everyone would have their fun, and Anne could go home.

"Perhaps a prince? Grand properties? Great beauty?" the old woman teased.

Anne dropped her hands and glared at the old hag. "You are bamming me."

"Anything is possible, miss." The old lady cackled. "You'll never know, if you don't believe."

Anne had the old woman now. She'd make the wish so impossible, so farfetched, that it couldn't be fulfilled. No fairy magic could conjure love. Everyone knew that. The mad woman would look like a fool. "Very well. I wish for a handsome man so rich that he will be able to provide a Season in Town for my sisters. He must also be passionately in love with me."

"Done!" the old lady crowed.

"You cannot be serious!" Anne turned to glower down at the old lady who had just taken the fun out of the game, but found no one there. "Well, rats, where did she go?"

Dried leaves danced where the old bat had stood. Maniacal laughter echoed in the wind. The old witch probably knew the game was up.

"How foolish do they think I am?" Perfect. Now she was talking to herself. Her sisters were going to drive her crazy. "Wishes, indeed."

"Were you granted a wish? Or are you the fairy?" A deep male voice, filled with laughter, echoed up the stone steps.

So much for peace and tranquility. Suddenly the Fairy Steps were the most popular place in Beetham.

With a huff, Anne leaned over the edge of the steps. Her mouth fell open. At the foot of the steps, seated on a large black horse, was the most handsome man she'd ever seen. Gorgeous, dark wavy hair curled around his high collar. Blue eyes danced with laughter. A navy blue coat had been tailored just right to fit his broad shoulders. Tight-fitting buckskin breeches outlined muscular legs. *Thank you, Providence, for buckskins*, thought Anne.

She swallowed to ease the dryness in her throat. "Excuse me, sir, did you pass an old lady on your way up the path?"

He smiled and those crinkles appeared around his blue-blue eyes. Anne fought the urge to swoon. Seriously? No man made her swoon. She looked down at his face again and fought the urge to gape.

"Depends. Are you the wisher or the fairy?" The elegant tone of his voice echoed a bit against all that stone.

Anne was done with being the ball for the bat. It was outside of enough. She crossed her arms over her chest. "Sir, if you didn't pass her, then just say so."

His smile fell and he shook his head. "An unbeliever."

"There is nothing wrong with being sensible."

"You are right, of course. Perhaps the fairy will grant you a wish for some fun in your life."

Good Lord, Anne hoped the fairy didn't hear that statement. She'd probably take it on as a challenge. Sophia was forever accusing Anne of extracting all the fun out of life. "Who are you?"

She cursed her propensity to speak before thinking. His face grew hard at her rudeness. Anne pulled her shawl tighter around her shoulders. Her embarrassment aside, no one came to Beetham without a reason for being here. It was ten days from London and so far off the main road, it rarely showed up on a map of the area.

"Nathaniel Matthews, at your service, ma'am." He touched his hat.

Oh no, he definitely had a reason. Anne's heart tripped in her chest. Her stomach clenched. He wasn't here for pleasure. He was here to stop the engagement.

"You're Lady Danford's grandson."

"Yes, ma'am. She is my maternal grandmother."

His tone hit her like the cold November wind blowing off the steps. She shivered and wrapped her shawl a bit tighter around her.

"Why are you at the Fairy Steps?" She narrowed her eyes at him. "You're lost."

He had the grace to blush. "It's been a while since I've been here."

What man couldn't find his way home? Men were supposed to be good at directions. It was probably more likely he was too busy to call on his grandmother. Did he not know how lucky he was to have her? "Take the path back to the lane. The Lodge is down farther, to the right."

His dark eyes flashed. "Thank you, Miss—You didn't tell me your name." His tone, saber sharp, cut through her skin to the fear she buried deep. This was not a man to cross.

"Anne Townsend." She dipped a curtsy.

"Thank you, Miss Townsend." He tipped his hat again. "Perhaps we shall see each other again?"

"I'm sure we will, sir." He reined in his horse and turned toward the lane. Anne watched him disappear into the woods. *Blast.* As if things couldn't get any worse, she'd just angered the one man who could make or break the match that would save her family. She just couldn't keep her mouth shut.

Nathaniel followed Miss Townsend's directions and arrived at the Lodge in short order. His brain had a natural aversion to coming here. Too many bad memories.

The dark gray stone house looked like the set of a bad play filled with ghosts and tragedy. He could vouch for the tragedy. It was tragedy that brought him here the first time.

Too many images filled his head. The sound of a gun being fired. Pity on the face of the man who'd ruined his father so completely that a gunshot wound to the head was the only answer. The fear and uncertainty of what would happen to him and his brother. There was nothing he could have done to stop those events. He hated that he couldn't avoid the memories, couldn't move past them.

Lady Danford, his grandmother on his mother's side, had brought Nathaniel and Tony to the Lodge. Yet even her kindness couldn't remove the pain of those awful years. Her husband had been knighted and had left her a comfortable sum when he passed. With no other heir, the house would one day be Nathaniel's.

As much as he loved his grandmother, he hated what the house represented: his father's weak mind and foolish decisions. Decisions that would have left Nathaniel and his brother to fend for themselves if not for their grandmother. Decisions made trying to keep up with the *ton*. Decisions that left Nathaniel no choice but to sell the house in Sussex to pay his father's debts.

Nathaniel wouldn't be staying long.

"Sir, we were about to send a search party for you!" the footman said as he approached.

"Has the carriage arrived with my trunks?" Nathaniel dismounted and handed over the reins to the worried footman.

"Yes, sir," the footman said as he led the horse away.

Damn, his ability to get lost was well known and once again affirmed by the servants. Nathaniel pulled down on his jacket and girded himself to enter the house. Though much of it had been completely redone, it hadn't wiped away the images in his head. Like a hammer to his skull, they hit him hard as he entered.

He shoved the bad memories deep as he found his grandmother in her overdone, floral drawing room. Dust motes danced in the late afternoon sunlight that was streaming into the room. "I see you are holding court as usual, Grandmother."

"There you are. I thought I was going to have to send someone after you." Lady Danford's tone was sharp, but her smile was warm. She reached out a hand to him.

Nathaniel clasped it and raised it to his lips. Her skin was cool and papery. "I thought you at death's door from the sound of your letter."

"You're gone for nearly a year and treat me to impudence." She sat back in her chair and pulled her coverlet about her legs. "Come kiss me and tell me why you have stayed away so long."

He pressed a kiss to her papery cheek. "Beetham doesn't have a port."

Lady Danford laughed. "I've missed you, Son."

He studied her for a long moment. The years had taken their toll. He'd lost his parents, but she'd gained two grandsons to care for. He took a seat near her and crossed his legs. It was time to get to the point of his visit; the only reason he'd come back to Beetham.

"I take it I was summoned because my brother, Tony, is in some sort of trouble." Nathaniel leaned back in his chair, his hands folding and unfolding. "I've paid his gambling debts from Cambridge."

"He's a young man. You remember what that's like, don't you?" She smoothed the coverlet over her legs.

Nathaniel winced. "I'm not that old."

"Good heavens, your own father had more of a life than you do." Her voice was sharp.

"Don't compare me to him," Nathaniel said rather sharply. *Damn.* Lady Danford watched him closely. "Forgive me, ma'am," he muttered.

"Still haven't let that go?" She shook her head. "Nathaniel, Son—"

He stood and paced to the window, staring out. "We aren't discussing this." The last thing he wanted was a discussion of his cowardly father.

"Our past always comes back to haunt us in one way or another." Lady Danford's voice was soft but firm. "At least until we deal with it and move on."

Nathaniel let the comment pass. It was a reoccurring argument. "Has Tony been giving you any trouble during his visit?"

"No more than usual." Lady Danford picked up her embroidery. "He's infatuated with one of the local young ladies."

"Next week it will be some other girl." Tony changed women like most changed stockings. Nathaniel could hardly keep up. "You brought me this far from London because he's involved with a local girl?"

"He's driving me to distraction," Lady Danford huffed. "He's spouting that god-awful poetry he writes. All that education to write bad poetry."

"A quality education," Nathaniel quipped.

"You had the same, and you didn't turn out that way," she grumbled.

Thanks to his father's propensity for gambling away every shilling they possessed, Nathaniel had been head of the family at sixteen. He had been forced to grow up fast and figure out how to rebuild the family fortunes. It left little time for poetry. "Who is the young lady?"

"Sophia Townsend. She is the prettiest girl in the county, until she opens her mouth."

Nathaniel's bark of laughter filled the room. "So I take it you don't approve."

"The girl is a twit."

He fought the urge to chuckle further. "Townsend? Would she be related to Miss Anne Townsend?"

"Anne is her older sister." Lady Danford eyed him speculatively. "How do you know Anne?"

"I happened upon her on my way here," he said casually. He didn't need another person making note of his inability to get from one place to another without getting lost.

"She gave you directions to get home, didn't she?" Lady Danford cackled.

Nathaniel felt the heat rise in his face again. Hell, this was worse than when he was a child. "I did *not* get lost."

His grandmother rolled her eyes. "Where did you find her, then?"

"At the Fairy Steps." He flicked a string off his sleeve. Truth be told, he'd wanted to find the steps first, hoping for a moment of peace before going to the Lodge and facing his demons.

"She must be hiding from her sisters again."

Good to know he wasn't the only one who hid from his family. "What's wrong with this chit that Tony is interested in, if her own sister hides from her?"

"I'll let you decide when you meet her." Lady Danford motioned for a footman. "Bring tea and wake Tony. A good dousing of cold water should do the trick."

"He's still abed?" Tony had obviously been spending too much time with gentlemen. "Things will be different when I get him to Town."

"And you call Tony a dreamer." Lady Danford's tone was acerbic. "He'll be out every night with the rest of the young bucks."

Nathaniel sighed heavily. Tony's spending habits were eating into the cushion Nathaniel had worked hard to build with his investments in the textile business. If Tony wasn't going to contribute, he'd have to marry well. "What are this girl's connections?"

"Her half brother inherited the title, but doesn't support his sisters." Lady Danford had a white-knuckled grip on her cane. "I have no patience for such a lack of responsibility."

Nathaniel had no doubt she would use her cane on this missing brother if she could. "Who is he?" He'd been so distracted by his meeting with Miss Townsend that he hadn't connected her to *that* Townsend family. Surely she wasn't related to—

"He's a baronet. Sir John Townsend. The family is very old."

Nathaniel set down his teacup with a rattle. Hell, it couldn't be. All the way up here?

"Mind the china, Son. I have no desire to replace it."

What did he do to deserve the continuing irritation that was Sir John Townsend? Or his relations? Sir Walter, the elder Townsend, might as well have put the gun in his father's hand after winning everything Nathaniel's family had. Sir Walter had died before Nathaniel could confront him with what he'd done. Now Sir John was bent on continuing down the same path as his father. Nathaniel couldn't allow that to happen. He couldn't let another man suffer what he'd seen his father suffer at the hands of Sir Walter, not that Sir John seemed to be experiencing the same success his father had.

And Tony's marriage would join the Townsend family to their own. Over his dead body.

"Are you sure he's not providing for his sisters?" Nathaniel didn't know why he felt the need to try to salvage something of Townsend's reputation. The man couldn't be so bad as to not take care of his own family. But perhaps Townsend was following in his father's ruthless footsteps.

"I'm unsure of the particulars, but Anne brought her sisters to Beetham five years ago with nothing but the clothes on their backs," Lady Danford said. "God knows what would have happened if I'd turned them away. They lease the old gamekeeper's cottage on the estate."

His jaw tightened and hatred chewed at his stomach. "I only hope that it's not too late to stop the engagement."

"Had she a dowry, it would be a good match." Lady Danford sipped her tea thoughtfully.

"Not to that family." Nathaniel stood and paced the room. He flexed his hands, itching to punch something.

Lady Danford carefully set her teacup down. "I thought you let that go, Son." She watched him closely, her face soft with understanding.

"Justice must be served." His voice was hard.

"What justice? Your father took the cowardly way out. He killed himself." Lady Danford's tone was cold, emotionless.

"Townsend forced him to when he lost everything. For that there must be justice."

"Oh, Nathaniel, what have you done?"

Nathaniel winced at the disappointment in her tone. The past ate at him like acid on skin. "I've given Sir John a taste of his own medicine. He is determined to repeat his father's mistakes" He stared out through the window at the garden. Devoid of leaves, it was as desolate as he.

A wrinkled hand tugged at his arm. "This is beneath you, Son."

"I had to stop Sir John before he ruined another man." Before he caused a good friend to shoot himself to escape his problems and left his family destitute. Nathaniel's hands tightened into fists. "I'll take Tony back to Town with me. Distance will cure any emotion he feels for this young lady."

Lady Danford sighed. "You can't stay longer?"

He winced. "I only came because you implied an emergency. Besides, you'll be in Town in a few months for the Season."

"I've not decided yet." Lady Danford shot him a meaningful look.

He looked back at her, startled by this sudden revelation. The London Season was Lady Danford's favorite time. He always looked forward to having his grandmother at the town house in London. "You won't miss a Season in London. You thrive on the gossip."

"I'm getting too old and stiff for the long carriage ride, dear."

Nathaniel watched his grandmother. She moved slowly. Her face was etched with deepening lines. Her shoulders had a slight stoop. He'd never thought of his grandmother as old until today. Panic clogged his throat and he had to clear it before he could speak. "Are you sick?"

Lady Danford laughed. "I'm just old, not sick."

At that moment, Tony burst into the room. "Nathaniel! You're here? Why?"

"Good to see you, as well. I'd say you look a bit worse for wear." Nathaniel took in his brother's wrinkled linen and lack of a coat. His hair was a mop of uncombed curls. At least he had shaved. "Didn't bring your valet?"

"Still the stick, I see. I'm sorry I'm not up to your usual standards." Tony slumped into a nearby chair and grinned. "Still, I make this look good."

"I was hoping university was going to make you realize your place in the world," he said dryly. "What have you been doing here at Beetham?"

"He didn't get in until almost dawn," Lady Danford grumbled. "Woke the staff trying to get into the house."

"What is there to do at that hour in Beetham?" Nathaniel said.

"Shared a pint with the locals." Tony ran his fingers through the tangle of his hair. "I repeat, what brings you here, dear brother? I know you didn't come all this way just to see me."

There was a bitterness in his tone that Nathaniel didn't understand. "I'm not allowed to visit our grandmother?" Nathaniel raised an eyebrow.

"You never leave London." Tony glared at his grandmother. "I suspect you told him about Sophia."

"Yes, she did."

Tony slouched lower in the chair. "I think I may have found my future wife. I've a mind to paint a picture of her."

"Paint? You?"

"It has to be better than the poetry," said Lady Danford.

Tony frowned. "It's not that bad."

Nathaniel laughed. "Why did you stop writing?" Tony had a tendency to flit from interest to interest, never staying too long. Currently he was supposed to be studying law.

"I couldn't get anyone to publish it. But Sophia inspires me. Such a beauty."

"Let's be honest here. Tony, your poetry is awful." Lady Danford waved the maid over with the tea tray. "You need a focus for your life."

Tony raised his chin defiantly. "I have a focus. Sophia and my art."

Nathaniel sighed. Once again it was up to him to be the responsible one, the voice of reason. "And do you propose to support this woman with your art? Have you given any thought to her connections or fortune?"

"I don't care what her connections are, nor that she lacks a fortune," Tony said. "It's not as if we need the money."

"The lack of fortune is a material issue," Nathaniel pointed out. "With your spending habits, we'll be in the workhouse in no time."

"I take it back. You're a bigger snob than you are a stick," Tony said. "You'll have to increase my allowance after we marry. And provide the younger sister with a Season. I suppose the eldest is firmly on the shelf. You'll probably have to provide for her as well."

Nathaniel cocked an eyebrow at his brother. The man had it all planned. Except it was the vision of a boy, not a man. "Why would I do that?"

Tony looked puzzled that he should ask. "It would only be right given they have no other protection."

"While it's honorable that you wish to take care of these young women, do you think it wise to marry someone of such reduced circumstances?" Nathaniel fought to keep the edge of impatience out of his voice. His brother was acting like a child. "We were left nothing by our father. He had no entailed property. You must consider what income a bride will bring to the marriage."

"You speak of dynastic marriage," Tony said. "I would rather marry for love than live such a cold existence."

"Poverty is a cold existence. Your young lady may not be suited for it. Unless you marry a fortune, there are few choices."

"We aren't poor."

"Nor are we wealthy, though your brother's investments and careful management have improved our circumstances," Lady Danford said. "It's time you did your part as well."

"And doing my part is marrying someone for her fortune? Someone I don't love?" Tony slammed his fist into the side of his chair. "That never made anyone in this family very happy."

"Enough!" Lady Danford pulled herself up slowly from her chair with the aid of her cane. "Don't assume that my marriage or that of your parents was less than it was. I loved my husband."

Nathaniel studied the stubborn look on his brother's face. "Tony, if you are serious about marrying this girl, then you have some decisions of your own to make. As of your birthday, your allowance will cease. Find a way to support your new family. Take your place with me in London. Practice law as you were trained to do."

"Gentlemen do not work." Tony jumped to his feet. "Nathaniel, be reasonable. Four months' notice is not enough time."

"All of us must attain adulthood at some point, Brother. Even you." Nathaniel sipped his tea, ignoring the growing color in his brother's face. "I suggest you think long and hard as to whether you can afford this young woman."

"Grandmother—" Tony whined.

Lady Danford paused at the door. "Tony, I must agree with Nathaniel on this. The next move is yours." The door closed behind her with a sharp bang.

Tony stared at the closed door. "She's in a fine temper."

Nathaniel shrugged. "With good reason, I think." He had to know where they stood. "Have you proposed to Miss Sophia?"

"Not yet," Tony mumbled.

Good. It would be a bit easier to extricate Tony if he hadn't proposed. "But her family is expecting you to?"

"Of course." Tony looked up. "This is madness. Why can't I marry for love?"

"You can—just make sure she brings money to the marriage."

Tony groaned and collapsed back in his chair. "I hate this."

Anger bloomed as Nathaniel witnessed his brother's petulant behavior. "You do realize who her father was, don't you?"

Tony raised his head, his eyes cold. "I'm not an idiot. I don't hold the children accountable for their parents' mistakes."

"Unlike me?" Nathaniel held his brother's gaze for a long time, waiting for confirmation. While Nathaniel had borne the brunt of the stigma and cleanup after his father's suicide, Tony had been protected from it all. He'd only been nine at the time, too young to remember the worst of it.

"I didn't mean that." Tony stood and started pacing in front of the fireplace. "I thought you'd be more supportive, especially given the nightmare that was our parents' marriage."

Nathaniel sighed. "If her relations were anyone else, I might consider, but not this family."

"It was a long time ago, Nathaniel." Tony sat across from him. "Do you really blame Sophia and her sisters for their father's sins?"

Nathaniel studied his brother for a moment. How much should he tell him? He fought the urge to protect him, but decided against it. It was time for Tony to deal with the consequences of his choices. "Have you met Sir John, the brother?"

Tony shook his head.

At least he wasn't moving in those circles–yet. "I caught him cheating at cards at White's."

"Does Grandmother know?"

"No one does." Nor would they, if he had anything to do with it. "You certainly can pick them, Tony."

"I had no idea!" Tony plopped back into his chair and draped one leg over the arm. "I still think you should meet the family. It will at least prove that the sins of the father have nothing to do with the children."

Nathaniel sighed. "If you insist." He had no doubt that the girls would be charming. He already liked Anne Townsend. Hell, even Sir John was charming when he wanted to be, but good manners did not imply scrupulous behavior. In his experience, good manners served more as a veneer for the unscrupulous to hide behind.

Anne walked briskly toward home as the wind picked up. She pulled her shawl around her and quickened her pace. The old lady she'd spotted at the steps must be from Beetham. Or perhaps the Gypsies were back in the village, though they usually went south before now. It'd be easy enough to find out. Beetham was a thriving community of gossips. Someone would know who the old lady was.

She should be focusing on Nathaniel Matthews. Not because he was handsome as sin, but because of why he was here.

To keep his brother from marrying Sophia.

Instead, she was worrying about some old lady and fairies. But there were no fairies.

The air came alive with sound, causing Anne to jump. She looked around her to see Cecil Worth, the vicar, leaning against a tree, watching the path back to the cottage. She quickly stepped back out of his line of sight. Maybe he wouldn't see her. Please God, don't let him see her.

"Miss Townsend!"

Lovely. Could this day get any worse? "Mr. Worth." She dipped a curtsy. "What brings you out this far?"

"I was hoping to find you, Miss Townsend. Miss Sophia said you walk this way most days." He doffed his hat and bowed prettily. He was dressed in a blue coat that stretched across his girth.

"You came to see me? For what reason?" In the three years he had been the vicar of St. Michael's, he'd never even noticed her before.

"Do I need a reason to visit a young lady?" He chuckled as he replaced his hat with a flourish. "My dear Miss Townsend, I have shocked you."

"Sir, I—uh." Shock was an understatement. While the man never missed a chance to speak with the lovely Sophia, he wasted no time on plain Anne Townsend. Being plain and poor had a dampening effect on most men's ardor.

He moved closer to her and smiled. "I imagine you have come to expect only sermons from me."

She took a step back, not liking the strange heat in his pale gray eyes or his scent. The man had apparently bathed in perfume. "You are the vicar, sir. Why would I expect anything else?"

He clutched dramatically at his chest. "Ah, you wound me, Miss Townsend."

Anne forced a laugh at his comical expression. "Then I offer my apologies."

"Apology accepted." He offered her his arm.

Anne took it and fell into step beside him. "How is your mother, Mr. Worth?"

"She is quite well. I will tell her you asked after her."

Mrs. Worth would probably give him a severe tongue-lashing for walking with Anne. Anne and her sisters were not rich enough for her precious son, despite having a baronet as a father.

"I wanted to speak with you privately before I spoke to my mother." He paused, looking down at her hand on his arm. "Such a small hand for the burdens you carry."

"Burdens?" Anne desperately needed him to get to the point. She had the beginning of a headache brought on by his cologne.

"You've taken care of your sisters for years, all on your own. Such a strength of character." He stroked his hand over hers, caressing her skin.

Anne snatched her hand away and put some distance between them. She suddenly didn't like that she was in these woods alone with Cecil Worth. She glanced around, hoping that perhaps someone else would also be walking in the woods this afternoon. But they were quite alone. Too alone. A frisson of fear coursed down her spine.

A twitter sounded in the trees around her. Was it the old lady? Please let it be the old lady. Anyone to keep her from being alone with the creepy vicar.

Mr. Worth shot her a pitying look that caused her temper to heat. "Have you heard from your brother?"

"My brother? No. I suppose he is still in London."

"Being so connected to a baronet, I can't imagine why you would abandon the position it offers you and your sisters. I imagine he worries about you all. Three young women quite unprotected."

John, worry about them? As if that would happen. Anger bubbled up and out of Anne's mouth before she could stop it. "Thank you for your concern, but this is none of your business."

"I only meant that it would be better for you if you had stayed with your brother."

"You've no idea what you're talking about." Anne started down the path toward the cottage.

"And to settle for being the companion of an elderly lady." Cecil Worth's voice echoed through the empty woods.

Anne turned and glared at him. "Lady Danford has been very generous. I feel privileged to be of assistance to her."

"Still, your brother . . ." He let the thought trail off.

Enough was enough. "Mr. Worth, my half brother's title doesn't put food on the table or provide heat for winter, and, for that matter, neither does he."

"I can see you still harbor anger toward him. As the vicar, I must urge you to forgive. He is your brother. Perhaps you may yet reconcile."

"I harbor no hope of our brother seeking reconciliation." It would be a cold day before she let John enter their life again. She glared at Mr. Worth and noted the odd expression on his face. He looked like a fish. She stepped farther away from him as Mr. Worth beamed at her, his gray eyes half-lidded and a crooked smile on his over-full lips.

She fought the urge to grimace. "I beg you to not discuss the matter further. Thank you for accompanying me. It looks to rain soon. I'd best hurry home. Good day, sir."

"But Miss Townsend—"

She ignored his cry and kept moving. Presumptuous man. How dare he cast judgment upon her and her sisters? They had no say in the decision. Leaning against a tree, she closed her eyes and still she could see his cloying, besotted face. "Fairy wishes indeed. Absurd."

Anne entered the cottage from the back. She hung up her pelisse and removed her bonnet. If, by some bizarre chance, she had been granted the wish she hadn't spoken, she needed to find a way to undo it before something even more horrid and humiliating happened. Lady Danford's grandson and Mr. Worth were quite enough.

"Anne, you will never guess!" Sophia rushed into the kitchen, but stopped short at the sight of her sister. "What's wrong with you? You're as pale as a corpse! An unkempt corpse."

"You've never seen a corpse, Sophia, unkempt or otherwise. Why do you ask?" She closed her eyes and tried to relax the scowl from her face.

"Your hair is tumbled, you are out of breath, and your expression is twisted more than usual." Sophia glided farther into the room, looking perfect, as usual.

"Thank you, Sophia, for reminding me." The comment flew out of her mouth before she could stop it. "If you have something to tell me, please do so."

"We are invited to Lady Danford's for supper and cards. But that isn't the best news. The best news is that Tony's brother is here!"

Anne bustled to the cabinet and placed cups out for tea. Just what she needed—another evening of men fawning over her sister. "Must we go?" She scooped tea into the pot.

"Of course we must go." Sophia plopped down into one of the kitchen chairs. "I will need a new gown."

Juliet huffed as she walked into the kitchen. "You had the last two new gowns, Sophia. I think it's Anne's turn." Seeing Anne laboring alone to set the table for tea, while Sophia sat like a princess, Juliet tsked and plated the cake.

"Anne doesn't need anything new. It's not like she'll attract notice." Sophia toyed with one of her dark, glossy curls.

Anne paused, the lid of the teapot suspended in her hand, and tossed aloft a prayer for patience. On the best days, Sophia was trying. Having Mr. Matthews in the village would only make her even more intolerable.

"Really, Sophia. You don't need to be cruel." Juliet plunked the cake on the table and glared at her sister.

"Thank you, Juliet." Anne poured hot water over the tea leaves and then returned the kettle to the stove. Sophia was working herself up into a fine temper.

"Well, I hope there will be some new people at the party." Sophia waved her hand dismissively. "I want to consider my options before accepting Tony. Did you see the invitations, Anne?"

"I thought you already had an understanding with Mr. Matthews," Anne said carefully. Her plans depended on Mr. Matthews coming up to scratch. If he didn't, she was going to have to come up with another way to buy the fuel they needed for winter. That meant borrowing money from Lady Danford. There was no other way.

"Not yet," Sophia said. "I do wish we could go to London for a Season. Then I could have the chance to marry a titled gentleman."

"Don't reach beyond your grasp. We have little to offer such a man," Anne said sharply.

"We? You do not, but I have had no end of offers, even without a fortune. Why wouldn't a titled gentleman want a pure, beautiful bride? Besides, the further I reach, the better I shall be able to take care of my sisters," Sophia said confidently.

Too confidently, in Anne's opinion. She rolled her eyes. This plan to marry off Sophia was getting more complex as the day went on.

"You have had no end of offers from the local gentry, Sophia," Juliet snapped. "I thought you liked Tony."

"I *do* like Tony," Sophia said. "I just want to make sure he's the right one. Anne, if you would only contact our brother, I'm sure he would invite us to London. I don't know why you hate him so. What has he ever done to you?"

Anne clenched her teeth to keep the bitter truth behind them. Her sisters would never know the extent of their half-brother's perfidy, if she had anything to do with it. "We've not heard from him in five years," she reminded them. She took a seat at the table across from Juliet and poured the tea. "We must go on without him."

"But we can't be seen by Lady Danford's guests in these old rags," Sophia whined.

"Since we will be meeting some of them for the first time, they won't know these are our old dresses." Anne passed a cup of tea to Juliet.

Sophia huffed. "Why must we be so poor? Our father was a baronet!"

"Be thankful that our mother left us a little to live on," said Anne. That was something John couldn't take from them no matter how he tried.

"Sophia, some things we must accept," Juliet said, and pushed her old spectacles back on her face. "Besides, no one notices your dress."

"Well, it isn't fair." Sophia pushed away her cup. "I think I'll go see if I can make over a dress. I'll take the lace off of your dress, Anne. And the flounce."

"As you wish." Anne waited until she heard Sophia's steps on the wooden stairs. "You don't have to defend me, Juliet."

"She can be so hateful," Juliet said. "As if her beauty entitles her to act like that."

"Sophia will save this family if she marries well. She can be a bit overbearing, but she knows her duty."

Juliet crossed her arms. "I don't have to like it."

Anne laughed. "Perhaps marriage will soften her up a bit."

"That's doubtful, isn't it? I don't want her to marry Tony. She's not good enough for him."

"I see." Anne laughed at the blush that rose on her sister's cheeks. "I'd wondered if you admired him."

"Don't be ridiculous."

So that was how it was. Juliet was suffering through her first infatuation. Better that she learn now that Sophia would capture everyone's attention. No matter what.

"Take care, Juliet. He has eyes for Sophia." Anne patted Juliet's hand.

"It doesn't matter. He sees me as a child, not a grown woman of eighteen," Juliet complained as she stood to clear the dishes.

"There will be other men like Mr. Matthews. I'm sure you'll have your pick of gentlemen in the coming years. You're every bit as pretty as Sophia, though I doubt she agrees."

Photo by Richard Pfaff

Eileen Richards's stories are filled with what she loves: snarky humor, love, laughter, and lots of village gossip. She lives in North Carolina with her husband, a greyhound named Honey, and a bunch of exotic fish. Eileen has two grown sons, a fabulous daughter-in-law, and the most beautiful granddaughter. Of course she is a bit biased.

Visit her on the web at eileenrichardsauthor.com